Cover art by: Arlin W Wright
Printed in the United States of America

Contents

Fortnight

Jealous C

Odin's Night

Landing

Five post adolescent students were easy to handle in a classroom but getting them through a crowded airport, especially Heathrow airport, was a whole other subject. However, now that they had found their seats, which was easily enough since they were the only passengers on the private plane, and had their carry-ons stowed, in just a few moments longer, they would be in the air and at cruising altitude. That's when Elise Thornson let out a sigh of relief. She was their chaperone for this trip through Europe before their graduation next month. They had just spent the last three days in London seeing the sights as she enlightened them of the history and they were now on their way to Stockholm, Sweden. She was a little excited to see Sweden and couldn't help but smile as her eyes drifted over at a girl just one seat up and across the aisle from her. The Viking era was her favorite age of study, and she had a trip to Birka planned for them. She knew Sara Tyr, would be the most interested as she listened and stared wide-eyed at all the different previous sights, but the others, not so much. Nice, quiet, peaceful, Sara was easiest for her to get along with and they had the most in common. They both had a love for history and could talk for hours on the subject. Sara usually had her light-red hair up in a ponytail, but not today. Today it hung in graceful waves down her back over the flannel shirt she elected to wear for traveling. Also were her ever-present vintage style cat-eye glasses that framed her brilliant green eyes beautifully, which she constantly kept pushing back into place.

Elise looked over at Bryndan Ornirdreki, Bo for short, seeing he held tight to his laptop and smiled. He was always sending a 'newsfeed' back to his friends and family telling them where he was and all that he had seen, even uploaded pictures for them. Bo was another of her favorites. He may not be so much into history, but he was well mannered and so intelligent, it was a wonder he hadn't excelled into university before now. Science was his cup of tea, but if it was a logic problem, he was all over it. Bo wasn't exactly built for athletics. He had the height, but not nearly the weight behind him. Not to mention he had no love for sports at all and found them to be a waste of his energy.

As for the other three... She wasn't certain why they even came on the trip at all. She could still hear Kristin and Tristan Firestone complaining about having to carry their own luggage and Jesse Peterson laughing loudly at them as he breezed by with his extra-large duffle bag slung over his shoulder. The girls had been best friends since birth as they were twins. Both natural blonds, blue-eyed, and spoiled beyond belief. She was certain if they wanted it, their parents got it for them. They didn't dress alike, but Elise had her suspicions that they had never heard of Walmart... unless they owned stock in it. They were always dressed immaculate, perfect hair, nails, and make-up, in essence, they were the perfect Barbie dolls, at least outwardly. They exuded the entitled, shop 'til you drop, snobbish, my family has more money than yours, aura. And, she had noticed that they pretty much shunned Sara. And then there's Jesse, the all-around sports athlete and built to perform. It's just too bad his mannerisms were completely barbaric. He was tall, at least six-two, with a muscular build, short dark hair, and adorable dimples, which she was certain gave him a pretty large female fan club. However, he walked with a bit of a swagger, reminding Elise of the arrogance his sports-pro father had instilled in him since the day he caught his first football at the age of six.

Bo was sitting across the aisle from her and seemed to have a semblance of a frown on his fine porcelain chiseled features.

"What's the matter, Bo?" she asked softly. He turned the laptop toward her. It showed a video of a volcano erupting. She looked up at him confused, "Why does that worry you?"

"It's in Iceland. The ash could travel our way. If that happens, we could be grounded for the duration." He spoke quietly so he wouldn't panic the others, but she could see with the bite of his lip that he knew it *would* happen, not *could* happen.

"Oh..., well, let's pray we land first, huh?" she smiled nervously at him then glanced back at the others.

Just then the seatbelt sign lit, and the flight attendant made Bo put away his laptop and buckle in and made sure the others had too before she seated herself and fastened the strap across her own lap. Elise heard the girls gasp when they hit the turbulence and she closed her eyes. This was going to be a very long two-hour ride, and an hour of it had already passed. She thought she heard the captain say something right before being hit on the back of the head by a very hard object and then the world suddenly went mute and dark.

"Miss Thornson," Bo shook her shoulder gently as he spoke. "Miss Thornson... Elise!" he shouted the last.

Elise scrunched up her face as the pain hit her once again in the back of the head and she opened her eyes with a groan. "What is it, Bo? Have we landed? And why is it so dark?" She evidently wasn't thinking clearly yet as she was lying on the cold ground with Bo leaning over her.

Bo swiveled his head around a bit, "You could say that. Can you get up? We should probably head for cover. I found as many of your things as I could, but I'm afraid some might've been lost." He hooked his hand under her arm to help her to her feet.

"What do you mean, 'found my things'?" Then Elise peered around through squinting eyes. Nothing, absolutely nothing looked familiar to her, and it certainly wasn't the Stockholm airport. What she did see was the others picking up their things that were scattered across the rocky windswept landscape similar to blowing leaves in the fall. Kristin and Tristan were carrying a suitcase between them stuffing what they found inside and pulling another one behind them as tears streaked their faces and small whimpers escaped their mouths. Jesse had his duffle bag slung over his shoulder as he mumbled quietly to himself while he too tried to rescue the rest of the items. However, as she watched them scavenge their belongings together in the moonlight, she noticed there was no plane parts from the wreckage, just their things scattered to the winds. She turned her head around then looked back at Bo, who still held her upright and cradled into him.

"Where's Sara? What happened? Did we crash?" she asked Bo, in a panic as she held on to the back of her head.

He pointed up the hill, "She went to see if that building would be a good shelter for the night to get us out of this chilling wind. In the morning we can find help." He gave her a weak smile and urged her up the hill before he turned a bit toward the others and whistled sharply then directed them to follow.

Elise stumbled along as she wondered in awe at Bo. "Who's the adult here?" she whispered and then chuckled briefly as she looked up at him. His lips curved into a smile, but that's as far as it went. There was something he wasn't telling her.

"That would be you, Miss Thornson," he said quietly. His voice was somewhat deep, but he was always soft-spoken.

"I was teasing, Bo. You're a lot more responsible than some others your age. I meant it as a compliment, really," she said trying to cheer him up. She knew that when morning came, they would find help. If there was a... She tilted her head slightly to look up at the building before her and saw a spire at the very top. A church! If there was a church here people had to be close by. Who would build a church in the middle of nowhere? As they walked toward the only building that they could see of civilization, she began to suspect they were stranded on a deserted island, and all that was left was a primitive wooden church silhouetted against the horizon.

"I started a fire in the fireplace with what I could find," Sara said as she came out of the narrow doors pushing her glasses up her nose then followed them in. "There weren't any matches, but I actually found a flint and tender. Can you believe that?" she said incredulously and almost excited.

Bo gave the church a glancing look and nodded as he helped Elise onto a low bench near the fire. "Yeah, I can. Look around, Sara. Can you see if there's any drinkable water? We can go without food for the night, but water would do us some good."

"Sure, did you see below?" she asked him quietly.

"Yeah, but we'll wait till morning. We have no idea where we are, and it'd be best to meet strangers in the daylight."

Sara nodded at him and picked up a pail that hung on a peg by the doors then stepped out. She could see what must be a village near the southern coast, by the twinkling lights, and a few small lights dotting the landscape in the northern direction. From where she was standing, it appeared she could see the whole valley past the tree line, but... she was after water. She circled back around the building to a rain barrel and dipped the bucket in.

When she returned, she saw Kristin and Tristan on either side of Miss Thornson as she tried to comfort them. Rolling her eyes, she took the water to Bo.

"Honest, it'll be all right girls. In the morning we'll find help. There's nothing to worry about. Why don't you two just try to get some sleep?" Elise said softly as she patted each on the shoulder in comfort. The girls sniffled as they looked around.

"Where are we supposed to sleep?" Kristin asked with a whine to her voice.

"You can sleep right there on the floor," she replied as she gestured to a space between the bench and the hearth.

"I'm not sleeping there. It's dirty and gross. Forget it," Tristan said and plopped down on another bench toward the front of the church.

"Why don't you just sleep on a bench?" Jesse suggested as he leaned back against his duffle on his own bench.

Bo shook his head at them and then dipped his hand in the water to taste it. It seemed all right to him, but Sara had said it came from a rain barrel and he just couldn't trust it with that volcano spewing its ash like it was. Better they just use it to wash tonight until he could find them some clean water in the morning. He took it first to Miss Thornson.

"You can wet your lips with it, but I'm not sure it'd be good to drink. Sara got it from a rain barrel," he said as he squatted in front of her.

"Thanks, but I could really use my purse. I have a pounding headache and I have some Ibuprofen in it," she smiled slightly and winced at the same time.

"How bad is it, your head injury, I mean?" he asked as he pulled her bag from beneath the bench she was sitting on and handed it to her.

"I have a pretty good goose egg. Did you see what hit me?" She rummaged through her bag until she found the bottle and opened it. She slipped two pills out and popped them into her mouth then dipped her hand in the water to wash them down.

"Not too much, the bacteria may not agree with us here and I haven't the chance to look yet, but I haven't seen a bathroom," he said as he quirked a brow, emphasizing his meaning.

"Got it," she chuckled and dried her hand off on the leg of her jeans. "Did anyone else get hurt?"

"I don't think so. None of them are complaining of any injury anyway, just our situation." He smiled wryly and nodded toward the two girls. "But they'll feel it in the morning. Best we get some sleep now."

"Good idea. Do you think we're safe for the night?" she asked as she glanced back at the two tall wooden doors of the church.

"Yeah, safe enough. There's no lock for the doors, but it's pretty late and we *are* in a church," he grinned up at her.

She returned his smile as she moved a soft case in front of the hearth to use as a pillow and then maneuvered into place. She looked around at the others and saw they all had elected to sleep on benches but her and were fast asleep. She laid down and pulled her denim jacket tightly around her then closed her eyes as Bo stretched out on the bench beside her.

Eirik was coming back from the tarn with two buckets of water when he noticed the smoke hazing the sky above the kirke on the ridge. His tall, broad-shouldered frame was shrouded in darkness as he stared up at the building. He thoughtfully rubbed a hand over nearly six months' worth of beard covering his face before he lifted the buckets again and headed back toward his house.

"Leif, what happens at the kirke at this hour?" he asked as he spotted his younger brother, younger by several years, and very similar in appearance except he had flaxen hair as bright as the sun in contrast to his own midnight shade, but the same sapphire eyes trimmed in thick dark lashes and beard growth.

"Naught, that I'm aware, seems you know more than I," Leif turned and gave his brother a grin. "Shall we go see?" he asked as he rose from where he'd been stirring the fire.

"Yea, let me take these to the kitchen before Ingrid arrives and then we'll see." He walked through the longhouse then exited through the door in the hindmost of the building. He poured the two buckets in a large thick black pot that hung over the fire then headed back to his brother.

As they walked up the rise, Eirik gave a glance to the southern harbor, but didn't see any additional ships. With his brows furrowed they circled the building quietly before they met at the front once again.

Quiet as thieves, they entered the old building and scanned the room. Eirik counted six figures and with his hand to his hilt, he silently looked through their items, very odd items, to find out more about them. Cases made of the most bizarre fabrics stumped him as how to open them, although some they identified as leather, and of the ones he could open, contained more fabrics uncommon to them and cut in odd ways, as well as other strange objects that neither had ever seen before.

Eirik took note that they were all a bit younger than even his brother, except one. The one he crouched by now lying close to the flickering fire. Something strong stirred from deep within him and made his eyes alight with a silvery sheen. She had the features of a goddess to his mind; long blond hair, defined nose and chin, high cheek bones, and her lips were full and plump as a ripe fruit. However, she was dressed in the oddest garments. He reached out and gently touched the fabric then withdrew his hand quickly for fear of waking her. He didn't want to do that just yet. Her small hands were fisted as they crossed over her chest drawing the outer garment around her tighter. She must be cold, he thought. Perhaps she is a princess, and the others are her thralls or maids, and the two males for protection. He snorted softly to himself at his fanciful thoughts, especially at the two males. The one nary look to him to be much of a threat at all, and the other nary could possibly be able to protect the four females alone.

Among all that they carried, there were nil bedfurs, nil food or water, nary even a weapon for defense, nothing that would indicate they had planned to be there. He then thought perhaps that the stout northerly winds had wrecked their ship. They would look when day broke, but for now he'd let them sleep as he and his brother would bring up food and water, just in case they were of some import. He felt a hand on his shoulder and turned as he was pulled from his daydreaming. He stood and headed back out where they could talk freely.

"So, what do you think?" Leif asked excitedly, his mouth drawn back into a grin framing the gleam of his teeth. Perhaps they had the same thought?

"Outlanders, methinks we should wake them and take them back with us. They look cold and hungry," Eirik said quietly, changing his mind from his earlier thoughts.

"Ah, good, then you think we should keep them as I do." He rubbed his hands together in anticipation.

Eirik furrowed his brows. "I ne'er said as such. I said we should offer them hospitality," he grumbled at his brother.

"But we should claim them before any others do," Leif bemoaned. He knew they were entitled to the outlanders.

"If we offer them our home, none other will lay claim,

especially if we nary tell them otherwise." He nary wanted to brand them without consent. "Besides, if we keep them from straying, then none other will know."

"But 'tis nearly spring, Eirik," he lamented again. He seemed to do that the closer it got to spring.

"Then we'll have ta occupy their time ta keep them from wandering," he said matter-of-factly. He hid his smile from his younger brother, seeing his grin fade into disappointment.

With the decision made, Eirik brushed his hands down the front of his tunic and opened the door. Just as he did so, the wind whipped in behind him and blew through the church causing a few of them to stir in the chilly draft.

Bo sat up and looked in the direction of the doors. He blinked a couple of times to clear his vision then very slowly reached down and tugged on Elise's sleeve. "Miss Thornson," he whispered, never taking his eyes from the two massive men that were now moving toward him, one gesturing to the other with a wave of his hand. "Miss Thornson, you need to wake up." He shook her shoulder gently.

Eirik pressed a finger to his lips as he moved closer to the young male. "Hush," he hissed quietly, locking eyes. Bo froze in place as he watched the dark-haired man squat in front of him. "Nary a need ta wake your mistress just yet. You appear ta need some assistance and we offer ours. Our home is just down the rise to the south. We offer food and drink and warmth and perhaps a bit more comfort," Eirik spoke softly as his gaze remained fastened onto the boys' russet brown eyes.

Bo nodded his head slowly then blinked when he felt a hand grip his. Elise woke at the sound of the voice and grasped Bo's hand as she sat up quickly.

Eirik stretched his right hand out toward the woman. "Greetings, Milady. 'Twas telling our young friend here that you are more than welcome to accompany us to our home. This building wastes the heat of the fire's effort," he said with a rich voice, no longer whispering, and smiled.

"Oh...," she shivered. "That would be wonderful. I would hate for any of the kids to catch a chill." She gave him an uneasy smile and grasped his fingertips. Eirik brought her to her feet as he rose to his full height and Bo stumbled to her side, since she never released his hand. "Oh my," she chuckled as she craned her head back to look up at him. Elise wasn't a short woman by anyone's standards, but he made her feel as such as she stared up at his blue eyes and dark hair, of which the sides were braided back over his ears and disappeared behind his head. "I'll just wake the... others." She looked around and saw they were already gathering their things under the supervision of another tall man with blond hair also braided intricately behind him. "Um... all right, come Bo, let's get our stuff together and follow these nice men to their home."

"Yes, Miss Thornson," Bo said warily as he made sure the cases on his cart were secured.

Eirik peered down at her feet and then lifted an eyebrow at her. "Hath you nil shoes, Milady?"

"Oh," she grimaced and slipped her feet into her heels raising her height another two inches, almost bringing her to his height, shy of about five inches or so.

He cocked his head to the side to see her footwear and snorted softly at the unpractical slippers. She must be a princess, he thought. Nary a woman could toil in such a shoe with an unstable heel as those.

Elise saw the others heading out the door and as much as she wanted to believe that these men were good to the core, she had to be cautious still. After all, even though she could understand them, they weren't exactly speaking English and she had no idea where they were. She slung her purse over her shoulder and started forward.

Eirik wrapped her arm around his elbow and placed his hand on hers, as one would escort a lady, as they followed the others out. He was a bit rusty in his courtly manners around ladies, but he thought he was doing it right.

The brothers brought them to their longhouse near the

southern coast set just to the west, beyond the rise separating them from the other dwellings, near a spring fed freshwater pond. As they entered, Elise could hear the complaints from the girls already. The building was roughhewn wood on the inside and possibly grass on the out, it was quite long with trestle tables along the left wall with a lit fire pit in the center of the room. At the far end there was a raised area with another table that looked stationary and more ornate. There were four doors on the right wall and one at the back, behind the main table. She tilted her head up and could see the smoke vented through a hole in the ceiling. Elise was in awe at what she saw, a perfect reproduction of a Viking longhouse. She had only seen pictures of them up until now, except those didn't have planking floors as this one did.

"How many live here?" she asked in whispered tones and then looked and saw not one of the bed closets were taken. She knew bed closets were filled with straw then covered by animal furs for warmth at night, but during the day they were used for seats to eat breakfast and dinner, in essence resembling modern daybeds. It was too early for breakfast, by her reckoning, and no one was sleeping.

"Just my brother and I reside here. Ingrid will come soon to start on our meal, but she lives down in the thorp at the south bay harbor, with her life-mate, Oslo," Eirik said softly as he guided her to a fur lined bed closet nearest the fire and sat beside her, adjusting the axe he wore at his waist as he did so. He could see her soft green eyes were filled with wonder as she gazed around their home. He knew the house was too large for just the two of them, but they were hoping to fill it... someday. His lips curved at that.

"Will you be all right, Miss Thornson?" Bo asked giving the older male a quick glance.

Elise looked up at him and smiled. He had brought her suitcase and was going to follow the others into a room just off the main hall. "Yes, I believe I will, Bo, thank you. Why don't you get some rest with the others, and I'll come get you for breakfast?"

Bo nodded and his lips rose in a semblance of a smile, then gave the large man a warning look before he headed off with the others, seeing Sara waving him to her. She watched him walk away pulling his heavy cart behind him.

"He worries," Eirik said thoughtfully almost to himself as he absently rubbed at his left palm.

"Yeah, he's a good kid, very kind and soft hearted," she said smiling after them.

"He has an ill heart?" Eirik's brows raised in surprise at her knowledge of the insides of the lad.

"No, he just cares about people and he's thoughtful. I know some people find that to be a weakness, but not me," she said smiling, then as she turned back to him, was taken aback by his startling blue eyes and lowered her head quickly.

"I see," his fanciful thoughts riddling his brain again and he shook his head to clear it. "Tell me, how may we be of service, Milady? What brings you to our island?"

"A plane crash, I guess. I'm not real sure what happened. I was hit on the back of the head and when I woke up, Bo suggested we take refuge against the wind in the church for the night. Seemed like a good idea at the time. We didn't break any laws or anything, did we?" she suddenly looked worried.

Eirik chuckled deeply, "Nay, Milady, 'tis good the old building came ta some worthy use."

"Oh, my goodness, forgive my manners. I am Elise Thornson. I was so taken in by your 'milady's' that I forgot to introduce myself," she smiled up at him and extended her hand in greeting.

"And I, as well. I am Eirik of Dragerhjem. My brother, Leif," he took the hand that she offered and gestured his other toward the other man now walking toward them. As his lips brushed against her fingertips when she looked away, he noticed she bore two silver rings upon her thumb. One, he could clearly see Odin's horns and the other had the Vegvisir in its center with the Skuld's net wrapping its band.

"Sowing seeds, brother?" Leif grinned as he came closer to

them.

"Raven sigh, Leif," Eirik mumbled as he straightened and furrowed his brows, emanating a low rumble in warning.

"I've settled the others in the guest chamber and started their fire. Seems the conditions nary be up to some's standards, but they will rest better here than where they were," Leif continued, ignoring his brother.

"You must be talking about Kristin and Tristan. I'm so sorry if they've offended you. They're more used to the Hilton than this kind of place," she grimaced slightly.

"Nay, Milady, nary offence was taken, but the wee lad be a might brooding," his grin was ever present although often obscured by his blonde facial hair.

"Sorry again, he gets like that when he's worried. He'll be all right come morning," she gave him another apologetic smile.

Leif grabbed a three-legged stool and sat to her other side. "If I may ask, why were you at the old kirke?"

"Like I was telling Eirik, we were traveling from England to Sweden when we wrecked. When I came to, the kids were trying to rescue our belongings from blowing away and the church was the first building we found." She looked from one to the other, both were nodding their heads in understanding.

"And what do you propose to do now?" Eirik asked gently. "Nary will a ship sail to the mainland for at least another fortnight. 'Twas treacherous of you ta be traveling this time of year, Milady."

Leif smiled as he stood, recognizing his brother's attempt to persuade her into staying, he thought some mead was in order... mead was always in order. "Would Milady care for a respite of beer or mead?"

"No, thank you, but coffee would be nice," she smiled imploringly up at him. Leif lost his grin as he looked at Eirik in confusion. "How about hot tea then? No? Mead will be fine," she chuckled seeing they didn't have any of her preferred morning beverages. Then Leif nodded his head and swaggered off toward the back of the building. "You truly don't have any coffee here?"

she asked Eirik as she turned back to him.

"Mayhap, if I knew what it was," his lips curved, she could tell by the rise in his beard.

"Hmm, it's a bitter bean that's roasted, ground, and steeped in water until it turns a dark chocolate brown. Ring any bells?"

"Nay, Milady," he shook his head.

"Elise, please," she sighed out being disappointed by the news of both having no coffee and no ships for at least two weeks. "What *are* we going to do now?"

"Stay here, please," Eirik said quickly then puffed out his breath. "'Twould please us if you would honor us with your presences for the duration of your inconvenient holiday." He moistened his lips hoping he worded it correctly and nary offended by what he blurted out.

"Are you sure? Is there not an inn we could stay in at the village? We don't want to be a bother." She could see how he was trying to polish his words for her and wasn't sure what to think.

"I assure you, Milady, nothing would pleasure us more..." He stared wide-eyed at her for a moment then dropped his head in his hands. "Bragi wept," he mumbled. "Nothing would be more delightful than to have you stay with us." He raised his head and smiled at her. She looked like she was about to either cry or laugh, he wasn't certain.

Elise tried very hard not to laugh at his misspoken words. "I have terms... You must allow us to help with your chores and you have to stop calling me 'milady'. I'm Elise or Miss Thornson, unless you want me calling you milord or Sir Eirik," she smiled broadly at him.

"Haven't heard those titles in a while, eh, Eirik? Leastways, from other than Ingrid." Leif came back into the room carrying a tray with a pitcher and three cups on it. "Ingrid said she would bring you some tea when she returns, but for now, this is what we have." He scooted the tray onto the table then filled the three cups.

"Oh, thank you so much for asking her." Elise's face lit up as Eirik's darkened.

"'Twas my pleasure, Miss Thornson, is it? Or should I call you Lady Elise?" He smiled as he took his seat.

"For the love of all that is good and kind, just call me Elise, but stop with all this 'Lady' business. Do I look like a 'Lady' to you, I'm wearing blue jeans for Pete's sake?" She laughed as she timidly brought the cup to her lips to taste the sweet honey mead then drank deeply from it, liking the flavor.

"Yea," they both said as one with a smirk.

"But I'm hesitant ta ask...," Eirik started then glanced at his brother. "Where might you be a lady from? Your attire is most foreign and even the lowest caste women wear dresses here and all where I've roamed." He finished and then drank deeply from his cup, glad that Leif thought to bring a pitcher. He was getting much too warm sitting this close to the fire and that was unusual for him.

"I thought you would have guessed that we're American by now. And I'm guessing that you are...," she looked around the longhouse for other identifying clues, missing the shrug the two gave to each other, not knowing where American was. "Norway? That's where we are... Am I right?"

"We are Norsemen, yea, but where is American?" Leif asked completely confused by her.

"North America... about thirty-three hundred miles west from here. We've been traveling a while," she snickered and sipped at the cup again. "Oh, wait, you might call it Vinland, if I remember right. I did hit my head."

"Ah," they both said together.

"Perhaps you may have need of a healer?" Leif said as he laughed from behind his mug.

"No, I don't need a doctor. I'm fine. I was only playing. But I may need one soon. What is in this stuff?" she looked down in the cup then Eirik caught her before she fell forward and laid her back on the bed. She had passed out.

He looked at Leif with a scowl, "Ravens feast, what did you do? Nil one gets this besodden with just one cup of mead."

"'Tis a strong brew," he grinned back at him. "I was just trying ta help. Now brand her and get it done with." Leif dropped his grin quickly. "If nary ye do, then I will," he lowered his tone as he reached for the woman.

"Nay! You'll nary brand her or any of them and neither will I without their permission. You know that is the only way it holds true, and I want it to hold," he reprimanded Leif as he stretched his arm over the top of her protectively.

"Ah, so that's how it is. All right, brother, you have the fortnight to entice her. If she nary be branded by then, then she's fair game, as are her brattles." His brow arched to emphasize his words.

"Nary threaten me. You would do well ta remember who the elder is here," Eirik's face darkened as he met Leif's gaze head on, and a quiet rumble vibrated from his chest. "For the thralling ta hold true ta us, consent must be given, or else they could be swayed by any other thereafter, as you well know."

Leif lowered his eyes knowing Eirik was the stronger. "But 'tis spring and you know what we must do. We only have until then to enthrall them or...," he flipped his hand over and showed him. The crescent scar on the palm of his left hand was just starting to become enflamed and soon the rest of the brand would fill in too.

"I know, Leif. Just be tolerant and patient. We have plenty of time. They have nowhere ta go. All we have ta do is keep them here... and be *nice*. No more drugging them." When he was sure his younger brother understood, he turned his attention back to the woman. He adjusted her body to lie comfortably in the small bed and then covered her with a fur. As he finished and stood, Leif then helped him dismantle the trestle and attach it to the side wall of the sleeping closet, enclosing Elise with privacy.

They walked to the head table and sat to finish their mead. Eirik's mind filled with worry that Leif would nary hold to working them in carefully. He knew their time was short and the six of them would have to be enthralled before the turning, but he wanted to make sure this woman stayed. They nary had many on their island and having four more will make them valuable, furthermore this one was exceptional. Any one of the other three would make a good mate for his brother as well, and then they could use the others for labor, maybe even put the large male to work at the harbor. He be nary sure what to do with the small protective one. He snorted to himself as he dragged his hand over his bearded face.

Eirik downed his drink then stood and headed to his chamber as he felt his brother's eyes on him. He closed the door behind him then quickly searched for his razor as he swung a small pot of water over his fire. He wanted to shave. Winter was over and he nil longer needed the beard to hide his face from the chilling winds.

His room was quite large and contained an ornate bed with a mattress stuffed with down instead of straw. There were several chests that lined the walls and a table near the hearth, in which was always a fire, with a pottery bowl setting on it to use for washing. Unfastening the button at his collar, he pulled off his old work tunic from over his head along with his serk and started cutting his beard.

As he finished removing the hair from his face, he washed it clean along with his long dark mane and chest then cleaned out his ears and used a frayed twig to scrape his teeth. If he was going to court this woman, he had to look the part. He carefully combed through his hair and banded the top in the back, allowing the rest to flow freely along with the two braids on each side. When he was finished fussing with his hair, he took out a fresh serk and an overtunic, one of his finer ones with silken embroidery, although not his finest, and donned them. He felt much more presentable now as he smoothed it into place.

Thor's day

The Longhouse

Eirik quietly opened the door to the main hall of the longhouse from his chamber. He figured he'd catch some taunting from Leif for his grooming, but he thought it'd be worth it if it would make him more attractive to Elise. He be nary a bad looking fellow, by any means, and he has had an abundance of women in the past, but he nary knew what would appeal to such a woman and he had higher plans for this one besides the casual slaking of needs. The calling was quite strong with her.

Leif was sitting alone at the high table with a mug of mead and Eirik let out a sigh at seeing him then shrugged as he moved forward. Leif too had thought to present himself in a more civilized manner, with a clean-shaven face, fresh tunic, and even had re-braided his hair.

"They have yet ta arise?" Eirik asked as he gave a glance toward the only closed sleeping closet.

"Nay," Leif sighed out with boredom. "And you preen longer than most females," he laughed as he gave him a onceover. "But I have ta admit, you be a handsome drake."

"Yea, and you be as well, brother," he grinned in return as he joined him. "Ingrid's taking longer than usual."

"Yea, she said it would ta fix for eight, rather than two, when I inquired a bit ago. Methinks we should wake the woman and allow her to prepare herself. After all, she'll have ta rise before now in the days ta come, best get her used ta it now, eh?" Leif smiled behind his mug at his older brother, who was nodding absently and staring at the closet with great interest.

"Leif, does she not cause the calling ta stir within you?" Eirik asked distractedly, still watching the only occupied bed closet.

"Nary especially, but nary would I decline should she offer," Leif grinned at his brother, intentionally goading him. "She does have a beauty unlike any other on the island with her lengths of gold stretching to her..."

"I think she's waking now," he tossed Leif a grin as he watched the board shift slightly.

Elise woke with a pounding headache and felt as though she was going to sneeze. The furs that surrounded her were delightful, but not the straw. As she sat up, she found herself boxed in. She looked the board over and found a latch, unhooking it. When she pushed the door open, she exploded with a resounding sneeze, "Ahhhhchooo!"

"Oh, my goodness, excuse me," she snickered when she spotted the two men sitting at the high table staring wide-eyed at the thunderous noise she made. "I think I'm allergic to the straw." She sniffled then looked for her suitcase and purse. "Is there some place I can clean up?" she asked as she looked at them again. It just dawned on her these were the same two men, and they were incredibly handsome without all that face-fluff hiding their features.

"Eirik and Leif? I hardly recognized you two," she smiled as Eirik came toward her.

"Yea, we appear human without the winter bear fur," his lips turn up at the corners as he winked. "You can refresh in my chamber, if it pleases you," he offered as he reached for her case and then walked off without her answering.

She ran after him, "That will be great, thank you." She glanced back at Leif, who had lounged back in his chair watching them thoughtfully.

Eirik opened his door and allowed her first entry then followed. He set her case on one of his chests and poured fresh water into the bowl on the table. He then found her a clean cloth and soft scented soap.

"Thank you again, but I don't suppose you have a bathroom in here?" she smiled timidly at him.

"A room for bathing? Nay, the bathhouse is up by the tarn." He wondered why she would want a bath. When he was sitting near her earlier, she smelled alluring and a bit flowery. She certainly nary needed ta bathe and it was only Thor's day, two days away from washing day.

"No, I mean to... um...," she shifted her weight from foot to foot. "I have to urinate," she blurted out, unable to think of a nicer way to put it.

"Ah, you have to piss. I have a chamber pot, but nil a special room to provide for you." He shrugged slightly as he thanked the gods that he had emptied it earlier and washed it out. He gestured toward the corner where a privacy screen was set up next to the bed and across from the fire.

"That'll work," she said quickly and ran behind it with her purse still slung over her shoulder.

Eirik eyed her feet beneath the screen and saw her bag hit the floor then heard the rustling of cloth then finally the trickle of liquid into the pot along with a soft sigh, bringing a smile to his face. "If ye have a need of anything else, I'll be out in the main hall," he said loud enough for her to hear.

"I suppose toilet paper is out of the question," she chuckled and started looking in her purse for the small packet of tissues she carried.

"We have very little parchment here and none that would be wasted on... um... waste," he snorted to himself as he left. He heard her say thank you before he closed the door.

Elise finished her business and came out from behind the screen to find she was thankfully alone. She dropped her purse on the table as she headed to her suitcase and opened it, pulled out her toiletries then returned to the table to wash up and brush her teeth. Tossing her jacket on the bed along with her clothing, she then washed herself down. After which, she twisted her hair up on her head and clipped it in place, adorned her ears with diamond studs, then applied a bit of lip gloss and smiled at her reflection in her small mirror. She had decided to dress in an ankle-length gray wool skirt and a blue snug sweater, hose and her heels, since she had seen that they had dressed to impress, so would she.

There was something definitely different about this place. The building was authentic, and it seemed the two men were too. That meant that they were stuck in the past, a thousand years in the past, but at least they were alive. She wasn't going to tell the kids until she had to, maybe in two weeks, when the ships sail. They can get a ship to the mainland and find a way back to their own time, if it was possible. Until then, she would make the best of it, after all, this was her favorite era and now she would get to experience it for herself.

She came out of the room hesitantly, smoothing her sweater down and taking a deep breath, she started toward the high table.

Eirik saw her coming toward them and nary would his eyes wander away as they drifted over her appreciatively. "Freya hath mercy," he whispered below his breath. These new clothes were different than before, though she wore a dress, it outlined her figure much as the breeches did and the bodice hugged her curves tightly, leaving very little to imagine of what lay beneath. He was speechless as he rose to his feet.

"Greetings, Milady," Leif smiled broadly at her approach and stood to greet her.

"Now, what did I tell you about that, *Milord* Leif?" she smiled up at him.

"Well, you certainly appear ta be a 'Lady' now," he grinned, taking her hand and leading her to the high table.

"I should probably get the kids up," she said as she hesitated to sit.

"Nay, I'll rouse the brattles from their beds. You just sit here, Milady," he gestured toward his chair.

"That word would work for most of them," she laughed softly

then glanced up at Eirik, who had said nothing since she entered the room. The stunned expression on his face was easy to read, but why was the question that made her wonder.

Leif moved off after giving Eirik a stern look and headed to the guest chamber. He knocked softly and after receiving no answer, he continued on. He woke the small male first.

"'Tis nigh time ta break your fast. You should wake and dress. Ingrid would take great offense should her hard work be wasted." He spoke softly, but it was enough to wake Bo from his light slumber.

"I'll get the others and we'll be out shortly," Bo replied as he sat up.

"Be sure that you do," Leif said quietly with a nod.

This room was similar to the main room. It had sleeping closets lining both walls with a fire pit in the center to heat it, which Leif was now stirring and bringing back to life. Just as in the great hall, it too had a planking floor except stone surrounded the pit. The only light was from the central fire.

Bo watched Leif swing a large pot, which reminded him of a witch's cauldron, over the fire before he turned back to him. "The water will be hot soon for your morning washing."

"Thank you, sir," Bo said politely and curved his lips into a slight smile.

"'Tis just Leif and my brother 'tis just Eirik," he grinned at Bo as he moved toward the door.

"I'm Bryndan, but everyone calls me Bo. Thank you again for your hospitality," he added the last as politeness dictated. His instincts told him to be wary.

As the man left, Bo got to his feet and pulled his jeans on then his sneakers. He looked around the room and sighed heavily, reluctant to wake his companions and listen to their complaints. He knew Sara was in the next bower, so he went to her first. She would be less likely to have any complaints, considering where they were. He had tried to use his laptop last night, but it had no power, none of his electronics did. He figured they were either drained in transport or they just didn't work here, either way, he knew they were no longer in their own world.

"Sara," he whispered softly as he knelt by her head.

"Good morning, Bo," she replied cheerfully, but remained quiet.

"You're already awake?" His form was almost a silhouette against the fire behind him, giving his mussed russet brown hair flaming highlights. If his eyes glowed, he'd appear to look like a demon. She snorted softly to herself at such an impossible thought.

"Yeah, I heard you and Leif talking, but didn't want to get up while he was still here. It wouldn't be proper for a man to see a lady before she was completely dressed in this age."

"So, you suspect the same. Do you think we're stuck here?" he whispered then stood back as she rose out of bed. She had changed into a long t-shirt and shorts to sleep in.

"I don't know, but I think we should learn all we can while we're here. It's a great opportunity to study the Viking age firsthand," she spoke excitedly as she searched in her suitcase for something appropriate to wear.

"I hope Miss Thornson's all right. She never came in and the dark one, Eirik, seemed too friendly, if you get my meaning." He shoved his hands in his pockets as he watched her select a red wool sweater and jeans from her case at the foot of her bed inside the small closet.

Sara turned up to him and gave him a knowing look. "I'm sure she's fine. She's a thirty-year-old modern woman from 2010. I'm sure she can handle these primitive men just fine... as long as she came to the same conclusion we did." She grimaced slightly thinking that if she didn't, they might think she's either too outspoken or wanton, if she didn't watch what she said. "No, I'm sure she's fine," Sara concluded and then hurriedly found some socks and hiking boots.

"I'm going to wake the others," Bo said as he suddenly became aware of her actions when she shifted out of her shorts to put her jeans on.

He went to Jesse's bed closet next and then to the twins.

Rolling his eyes at hearing them whine about not having enough sleep as he went to the center fire and dipped his hand in the water, he brought it over his face and then through his hair, smoothing it back before he retrieved his toothbrush and a shirt. The warm water felt good to him.

When Sara was ready, the two of them came out of the room after issuing the warning Leif had given him about Ingrid. They weren't about to wait on the other three. It could take the girls hours before they'd be ready and neither of them wanted to listen to them whine anymore.

They could hear Miss Thornson laughing and both relaxed with the sound. She was sitting at the high table with Eirik beside her and Leif was leaning against it talking to them. Bo took note of the way Eirik was somewhat turned toward her with his hand resting on the back of her chair as he smiled up at his brother. He had also noticed that both men had shaved and groomed themselves. It didn't sit well with him. Sara urged him forward.

"Good morning!" Sara greeted them with a sunny smile as Bo's had darkened. She elbowed him.

"Good morning," he mumbled.

"Greetings!" Eirik beamed. "I trust you slept well?"

"Yes, thank you. May I help with anything?" Sara asked as her gaze looked over the empty table.

"Nay, today you are guests," he answered and gestured to the tables that were set up but were also empty. "Ingrid assures us it will be only moments," he smiled encouragingly at their young faces. He noticed Sara wore the same bodice type as Elise wore but had similar snug-fitting blue breeches as the scant fellow and her footwear was most practical for outdoor use, made of strong leather as they were. That drew his attention to the lad's feet. His brows rose at the odd white footwear. Sara bowed slightly then went to the first table and sat in the bed closet dragging Bo with her.

"That is Sara and Bo. They are the easiest to get along with, the other three, not so much, but they're all good kids," Elise said fondly.

"Are they betrothed?" Eirik asked quietly as he watched the small girl take command of the lad.

Both Elise and Leif peered toward them. "No, I think they're only friends. When you get to know the others, you'll see why these two hang together," she laughed softly.

"So, she is available for courting?" Leif asked as he craned his neck around to see her better.

Elise looked up at him a bit surprised by his interest, although he didn't seem much older than Sara. "Um... I suppose so," she said with uncertainty. She then looked back at Sara and smiled as she put her glasses on.

"What is that?" Leif exclaimed, although quietly.

"What?"

"That apparatus she put on her face. It gives her the appearance of an owl or mayhap a cat," he said lowly and slightly in awe.

"Those are her glasses. They help her to see better," Elise said amused by his wonder.

"Do you think she'd mind...?" he asked as he wandered toward the two never finishing his sentence.

Ingrid just then came out carrying a heavy platter laden with meat and set it on the high table. This was the first look Elise had gotten of the woman. She was heavy built, not fat, but strong, for hardy work. Her hair was reddish and braided up into a coronet, but she could see the under layers were darker, almost as if she dyed it. She was dressed in a long gown with an apron over the top and short leather shoes that came to her ankles. She appeared to be older, but she couldn't determine just how old.

Ingrid returned with another tray filled with bread, cheese, and other things that Elise wasn't sure what they were. The last to come out was a dish of porridge of some sort and pitchers of water and mead.

"Milord," Ingrid said quietly to get Eirik's attention. "I've put on chicken stew fer yer supper t'night and made fresh bread, but I must away fer my li'l Astrid has taken wit' chill." She stood with her head bowed not meeting his eyes as she wrung her hands nervously.

"'Tis all right, Ingrid, away with you. We can fend for ourselves for a while. Worry naught, just care for your wee one and see she gets well. I'll come around to look in on her ta see how she fares." Eirik had reached out to her and lifted her chin, so their eyes met when he spoke. She visibly relaxed and slowly nodded her head.

"Thank ye so vera much, Milord, an' I'll send Oslo up wit' the tea fer Milady." She glanced quickly at Elise, dipped in a slight curtsey then hurried away.

Elise wasn't quite clear about the arrangement between them and the woman, but it looked like fear to her. "Is everything all right?" she asked Eirik quietly.

"Yea, 'tis that we may have ta accept your offer of chores. We had thought naught before, but without Ingrid here 'tis much ta be done," he gave her an apologetic smile.

"Oh no, that's fine, but I meant with the little girl. Is there anything I can do to help her?" The concern on Elise's face softened him a might.

"Nay, Ingrid will get her right," he said dismissively then stood to fill the trencher they shared and her cup with water.

Elise looked toward Sara and Bo and chuckled at seeing Leif with Sara's glasses on, but then saw the look on Bo's face, he wasn't pleased at all. "Come, kids. Get your plates before Jesse gets in here or you won't have any," she called out to them and recognized Bo's relief. Maybe they did have something going.

"Did I hear my name?" Jesse came sauntering from the guest chamber in blue jeans and a bright yellow sweatshirt.

She looked at him and held back her laughter. "It's time to eat. Where are the girls?"

"The 'Princesses' are still getting ready," he laughed loudly displaying his dimples.

"Well, go ahead and grab a plate. I guess they'll eat what's left and maybe next time they'll be faster, huh?" She rubbed at her temples. This was going to be a long day.

"Are they truly princesses?" Eirik asked as he reseated himself beside her.

"They only think they are," Jesse said as he stabbed a slab of meat with a short-bladed knife and tore off a hunk of bread.

Eirik looked to Elise, and she nodded, "Unfortunately it's true." She then took notice of what he sat in front of her and intended for her to eat. "Would you look at all that cholesterol?" she snorted while shaking her head.

"What? Trolls to break our fast?" Leif exclaimed as he approached the table, overhearing Elise. "What kind of trolls be Kholes? Black trolls? I wonder how Ingrid found those." He peered down at the trencher in front of Elise and narrowed his eyes, only seeing fish and pork.

She looked up at him to see if he was serious, especially when she heard the others burst out laughing. Not even a semblance of a smile was on his face.

"Not trolls, cholesterol. She means all the fat," Sara pointed out to him the oily residue floating among the meat.

Leif looked at it then to Eirik and shrugged slightly. "There's nary wrong with eating a little fat. It helps make the other food go down easier," he grinned as he pointed to the porridge, "Like that horse fodder."

"Whose father?" Jesse shot him a dimpled grin then turned away to find a seat when all he got were soft chuckles.

When the others had gotten their plates and were seated at the same trestle Sara had chosen, Eirik watched Elise delicately pick at the food. She ate like a princess. Then again, perhaps she nary cared for the taste. Nary everyone likes salted fish, especially in the morning, but the pork 'twas nary bad.

"'Twould care for something different, Milady?" he said quietly, hoping nary ta attract the attention of the others.

"No, please, this is fine. I just have a headache. But I was wondering what you needed us to do for you. This is all new to us and I'm afraid we won't know how to do much." She then turned to peer up at him.

"The hearth duties are done, save for the cleaning, with

Ingrid's forethought. But we'll have ta bring in some peat for the fires, tend ta the stock, and such beyond the threshold. You and the females can tend ta the chores within. Leif and I will take the two males out with us." He eyed Bo thoughtfully as he gathered a bit of meat with his fingers and brought it to his mouth.

"What's the matter?" she asked as she followed his gaze.

"Will he be able ta keep up?" he nodded toward Bo's lanky form.

"Um… you have to allow him to try, Eirik. He may not be as muscular as you are, but he's smart and he'll figure out a way."

"If he be nary betrothed ta Sara, is he *argr*?" he whispered the last word near her ear. He nary wanted to bring insult to the lad, for a holmgang would surely disrupt his plans.

She looked at him as she was trying to decipher the meaning of the word then looked at Bo's delicate features and frowned before she turned back to Eirik. "No," she said decisively. "If that word means what I think it does." Then she lowered her voice, so he had to lean closer to hear her, "He does not prefer the company of men over women. For Pete's sake, just because he's not overly muscular doesn't mean he's…"

He put his hand on hers. "I meant nary offense, Milady. One likes ta know things as such ta know better how ta treat him. If he prefers a woman's work over the harder man's…" he stopped mid-sentence when he seen her brows draw together once more in anger and scanned the rest of her face thoughtfully. "'Twill take him with me," he said finally and looked back to his meal.

"Good, just make sure he doesn't get hurt," she said and also went back to eating, but glanced over at him and saw his lips curve. "What?"

"Treat him like a man but protect him like a woman?" he murmured from behind his cup.

"No!" she whispered vehemently. "Yes, sort of. Let him work with you, but don't goad him into getting hurt."

"Ah… Milady, I have reared my brother since he was a brattling. I believe I know how ta judge one's strength. Trust in me with your scant lad, he'll nary be scathed. I'll have him haul water up from the tarn while we tend ta the animals." Which was still considered women's work if it was brought to the house, but nary would he say as such ta her.

She nodded her head with satisfaction as she drank deeply from her cup. The thought occurred to her that she was drinking pond water just then and she lowered the cup feeling her gag reflex activate. She would have to make sure their water was boiled before she drank anymore of it. They couldn't chance getting dysentery from it.

When they finished eating, Eirik took them to the kitchen. The room was made of stone, resembling Eirik's room somewhat, except with a door leading outside. There were two large hearths for baking and cooking, one with a huge pot simmering over it, and a strong sturdy table in the center of the room for what she assumed was where the food was prepared. There were different herbs hanging from the rafters and crates of vegetables kept to the coolest part of the room. She eyed rings of bread hanging from pegs as she looked for the cold storage for milk and meat supplies. She wasn't too pleased in finding how unclean it was and knew what they would be doing today.

She had Sara start carrying in the dishes and sent Bo and Jesse after water as she drew Eirik to the side out in the great hall. "Are you freeborn?" she asked quietly.

With a surprised look he nodded his head, "We are," he stated slowly.

"Are you a Chieftain or Jarl?"

"Why do you ask such questions?" he deflected as his brows creased.

"Because Ingrid seemed subservient, almost fearful of you and I thought you would have more servants if you were. I don't wish to disrespect you. I was just curious," she said as she lowered her eyes.

"We pay Ingrid for her services. There be nary many people on this island, Milady. The ones that be here be mostly men with very few women. Which brings me to another issue...," his eyes lit as they grazed over her gently and his lips curved before he recaptured her gaze. "I nary wish any of you wandering about or going ta the village."

"Are we prisoners?" she asked as her eyes widened with the thought. She knew the Vikings would capture people as slaves and either sell them off or use them for their own benefit.

"Nay, but 'tis been a long rough winter and as I said, the village 'tis mostly comprised of men and with but one slake-whore. Please know I wish nary harm ta come ta you or yours, Milady."

"Oh… Then we'll do as you ask," her cheeks tinted a light shade of pink with the understanding of his meaning. She was a little relieved that they weren't prisoners, but she now worried about how they were to get off the island without incident.

Eirik gave her a nod before his attention was drawn to the two females standing across the room from them curling their noses up at the longhouse hall. One was dressed in white breeches and a matching soft-looking bodice, while the other one elected a pink shift that showed entirely too much of her legs to be considered proper, even more than the afore mentioned slake-whore, and both were in the high-heeled slippers that were not a good choice to do chores in.

"I believe your princesses have graced us with their presence," he said quietly then returned his gaze to her. "Although, the one seems ta be wearing naught but a night shift. I'd have her dress before Leif returns with the lads."

Elise turned to look at the girls, "I see what you mean. Those clothes will never do to clean in."

"Yea, 'twere my thoughts," he mumbled quietly as his head turned once more toward the two and his lips curved.

"Yeah, you just keep those thoughts out of your head. They're only twenty," she said as she started off toward the girls rather stiffly.

Eirik understood her to mean that a man his age shouldn't or perhaps *couldn't* attract women years younger than himself and took offense. With a low growl, he caught her arm before she got out of reach feeling as if he needed to defend himself. "They are perfectly acceptable for a man my age…"

She jerked free of his grip before he finished and hurried off to the girls to get them changed into jeans. As she ushered them back into the room, she glanced back at him. His brows were drawn into a scowl as he stared at her and crossed his arms over his chest. She knew it was because she had disrespected him by not letting him speak, but she didn't want to hear how a twenty-year-old girl was prime marrying age for a man thirty and older. Where would that leave her in this age? She *was* thirty and if they were stuck here with no way home… She sighed out her breath as she closed the door behind her.

"… But I prefer my woman ta have a bit more wit," he finished under his breath watching her close the door.

"You've got that right. I'm pretty sure their family's money gets them through school," Sara said as she picked up the two pitchers from the table.

He turned to look at her, not realizing she was even in the room, being as quiet as she was, and blinked at her. He knew only families with wealth even received an education, but nary many women do at all. "Sara…," he moved toward her with a slow and easy swagger and smiled. "Tell me more about your mistress, please."

She eyed him suspiciously, "Like what?" she asked and turned to go back into the kitchen.

He followed after her hesitating in the doorway to keep watch for any eavesdroppers. "Why have you traveled so far from home?"

"We were on a trip to see some of the places we were learning about. Little did we know…" she chuckled dryly. "Miss Thornson is our teacher." She sat the pitchers down on the large table, pushed her glasses up and started scraping all the scraps into one dish, with the exception of the porridge, it remained untouched. She was saving it for the twins to eat.

"She is educated? She must be well sought after or betrothed, eh? Mayhap ta one called Pete?" he came closer and leaned on the table bringing their heads level and watched her.

Sara stopped her work to scan his face for a moment before she spoke. "I don't think she even has a boyfriend, at least I haven't ever heard her talk about anyone of interest. Why?" her lips curved up slightly as she wondered if he would tell her the truth or lie.

Eirik didn't answer at first but met her gaze fully. "I'm of interest," he said simply, then, "Hath she any quirks that make her ill-acceptable to suitors where you're from? There must be reason for her not to be wedded by her age, perhaps widowed?"

Sara snorted softly. "No, the only quirks she has are her love for knowledge of the V..." she bit her lips together realizing where she was and who she was talking to. It was something the two of them had in common. They both loved learning about the Viking age and were always amazed at how they're making more discoveries every day.

"Knowledge of what, lass?" His brows were arched in suspension of her answer.

She pushed her glasses up and then, "Vitticeps dragons," she hedged quickly... okay she lied ...a lot, but she couldn't tell him the truth and was pretty sure he didn't know what a bearded dragon was seeing as how the lizards are indigenous to Australia.

He looked at her wide-eyed then composed himself quickly and nodded thoughtfully. "What more can you tell me?"

"You mean like taking long walks on the beach? That sort of thing?" He nodded and drew closer. "Her favorite color is blue. She loves the smell of lavender, but she likes heather as flowers go. She's not afraid of hard physical work, but likes to relax with a hot bath, candlelight, and aromatherapy. Oh, and her swordsmanship isn't bad either. Anything else you want to know?" she giggled as she went back to cleaning.

"Nary for now, mayhap later. You have given me much ta think on. Thank you. But if I may ask, what is a roman there-pee? 'Tis a chamber pot, aye?"

"No, silly, Aroma, as in smell and Therapy, as in healing treatment. It's a scent you put in your bath or candles that induce relaxation." She let out a laugh, "Chamber pot. Ha!"

"Thank you again, you have been most helpful, lass," he grinned at her and turned away mumbling to himself. He deduced that Lady Elise liked dragons, blue heather, hot baths, and the scent of lavender. He would have to use this information to his benefit to sway her toward him, especially after he somehow angered her earlier. He completely dismissed the remark about swordsmanship, not understanding it entirely. What a sword, a man, and a ship had ta do with a woman, he nary knew. And after she found amusement from his last assumption, 'twas nary going to ask.

He passed the lads and Leif as he walked out the door smiling. "I have an errand ta run, but get Jesse started on the other chores. I believe Bo will be hauling water for quite some time," he chuckled as he turned away and hurried on.

Leif supposed he was off to attend to Astrid, but nary questioned him; instead, he delivered the water and then took Jesse out to the byre and got him started on mucking the stalls. It nary'd been done since fall and figured what better way to get him accustomed to the work. And it meant he'd nary have to do it.

Within the threshold, Elise heated the water and had the twins working on the dishes as she and Sara started on the room itself. There was a lot of cleaning to do. She thought that when they were done in the kitchen they would start on the hall and then the chambers. Little did she know just how long the kitchen would take even with the other three girls' help. She also had to put up with the twins complaining about all the water ruining their manicures. They quieted down when she threatened to send them out to clean the barn.

Sara and Elise were working in the dry goods storage pantry when Sara cleared her throat to speak. "So, what do you think about where we are?" she wanted to know if Elise had come to the same conclusion that Bo and she did.

"I think we crashed on a little primitive island in Norway, and we won't be able to leave for at least two weeks," Elise said without looking at her. She was removing the dry goods from the shelves so Sara could wash them down. She was also taking inventory of what they had so she could think of what to cook for them. It was definitely going to take some ingenuity on her part.

"Did you see any wreckage, the pilots, or the flight attendant, because I didn't?" Sara stopped and looked down at her from where she was cleaning the top shelf of the pantry while standing on the larger lower one, that most likely served as a table for grinding herbs and grains.

"So, what are you saying, Sara, that we suddenly appeared on this island just out of the plane?" Elise was staring up at her now.

"I don't know how we got where we are, but I suspect when we are. And I'm sure you know that too, you're just reluctant to say it."

"Say what, that we're stuck in the Viking age without a longboat to get us home?" she snorted then realized Sara wasn't laughing. "Okay, suppose you're right, and this isn't some reenactment village; how are we to get home?"

"I'm not sure I want to go back, I kind of like it here," she smiled happily down at her.

"Bite your tongue, Sara!" she scolded her. "*Here* we are commoners, without land or titles, you *know* what that means. We'd be little more than slaves, that is if we don't get sold off as slaves."

"But you know I have nothing back home either, at least here I have knowledge of what's to come. And maybe Eirik and Leif will let me stay here. I have a reasonable knowledge of what they eat. I can learn to cook, and I think I have proven I can clean." She spread her hands out gesturing to include the room they were standing in. "And maybe I can make pottery for them to sell, if they have the right clay around here."

Sara was right about that. She could make pottery. Elise had seen her doing it at the Renaissance fairs that they both attended. And she didn't have anything back home. The state had been paying her tuition since she had earned a scholarship when she was fourteen. She was an excellent student. Elise thought she'd be at least in the top ten when she graduated next month. She had no real home to speak of, her parents had died when she was thirteen and actually, she would probably fair quite well here.

Elise sighed out her breath and looked away. "Sara, we don't know them. We've only been here for a day," she said lowly and began moving more stuff.

"Yeah, and after just a day, I already love it. I can be myself here without ridicule. I'm sure in time, I'll learn how to sew and weave, all the stuff that we take for granted because we can buy it pre-made." She was still defending her decision.

"What if they're bad men, Sara?"

"Is that the feeling you get from them? I sure don't. They've opened their home to us and have made us feel welcome. They could have left us to freeze in the church or locked us in chains the moment they found us, but they didn't. They brought us to their home and fed us. Besides, I think Eirik likes you," she smiled down at her as she pushed her glasses up.

"What on earth would make you think that?"

"Oh, I don't know," she giggled and busied herself with the cleaning.

"No, I think I'm too old for him," Elise mumbled to herself, earning a doubtful look from Sara.

"OMG, OMG, OMG!" they heard the cry from the kitchen and Elise ran out to see what was wrong followed directly by Sara.

"What's wrong?" Elise asked wide-eyed with worry. She scanned both girls for blood and injury, but she saw none.

"Oh, Miss Thornson," Kristin cried, "I broke a nail and there's no one here qualified to fix it. What am I going to do?"

"Maybe we can go down to the village and see if they have a manicurist there?" Tristan suggested soothing her sister then they both looked to Elise with hope filled eyes.

"For Pete's sake, Kristin, you scared me half to death. I thought something dreadful had happened." Her brows creased as she stared at the two girls.

"Oh, but it is dreadful, Miss Thornson," she said as she coddled her hand as if she was truly injured.

"Please, may we go check the village?" Tristan begged.

"Absolutely not! None of us are to leave this house unchaperoned. Do you understand me? That goes for Bo and Jesse too. And under no circumstances are any of you to go to the village. Now, have you two finished the dishes *yet*?" She stood with her hands on her hips furious that they caused all this ruckus over a broken nail.

"No, Miss Thornson," they mumbled together.

"Then I suggest you get them finished instead of whining over a broken nail," she huffed out and spun around headed back to finish the pantry. Sara turned quickly to hide her smile and followed her.

After several more hours of cleaning, they had the kitchen sparkling... well maybe not sparkling, it's a bit difficult to make wood and stone gleam, but not one area of the kitchen had been left untouched by soap and water or a dusting cloth. Elise had made Kristin and Tristan wash every dish, soup pot, wooden spoon, and utensil she could find, not to mention the large cauldron that was used for heating the water. She wanted to make sure it was extra clean to boil drinking water for them and then she had to find something to store it in.

Elise hadn't seen the boys or either of the brothers all day, being as busy as she was, except when Bo would bring them pails of water. She had wanted to ask them about storage containers for water and leftovers. The enormous pot of chicken stew Ingrid had made would last them for days. What she wouldn't give for some plasticware!

Now that the kitchen was clean, she was going to start on the main hall to the dismay of both Kristin and Tristan. Sara had politely reminded her that it was near dinner time and that maybe they could save some work to do tomorrow. So instead, they found some pitchers to chill the water in and prepared the rest of the meal, consisting mostly of bread, butter, and cheese.

She thought that perhaps tomorrow she would figure out

something they could have for a dessert, a sweet bread of some sort. But since the cleaning took up so much of their time today, she hadn't even thought of their evening meal. In fact, she had tried to keep herself busy all day or her thoughts would dwell on being lost in the past with no way home and no prospects for them surviving this century without money or name.

They were just bringing the food out to the main hall when the others were coming in. Eirik and Bo had come first, smiling and laughing, followed by Leif, who was joking with them. Jesse brought up the rear, shuffling along behind them.

"I'm telling you, if we build a windmill on that rise, it will pull the water from the pond, or tarn as you call it, right up to the house. Then put a spigot by the barn to water the animals, then no one will have to carry water that far again," Bo said as they entered, energized by the idea.

"'Tis an interesting notion, Bo, but then what would we have you do all day?" Leif said from behind them, bringing laughter from the first two.

"He can muck the stalls," Jesse mumbled dryly.

"Nay, lad, 'tis your duty," Leif chuckled. "'Tis a noble duty at that, but you get ta sit at the far end of the hall," he said as he waved a hand in front of his face. They all laughed at that, everyone but Jesse that is.

"And sleep at the far end of the room," Bo added, bringing another bout of laughter.

"All right, lads, get washed up," Eirik said as he stopped by his chamber door to do the same.

At that, they each entered their respective doors. Eirik went into his chamber and peered around. It was just as Elise had left it that morning. Her clothes were left on his bed and her case was where he had put it. In fact, it appeared she had nary been in the room at all since that morning, even the bowl of water she used remained. He picked the bowl up and dumped it in a bucket by the door, but noticed it still carried her scent. He squatted down in front of the hearth and reignited the fire with a single breath then stood and swung the kettle over the flame, checking first that it still contained water.

Eirik went to the table where her items were strewn across and looked them over closely. He picked up a small shimmering object that about startled the breath right out of him when a face appeared in it. It was so real and life-like he thought it was another person until he recognized it was his own reflection. Realizing it was a mirror of the finest quality, he gave a snort as he put it down carefully, thinking it must be precious to her. Next, he found a brush on the end of an odd feeling stick. 'Twas nary bone, antler, wood, or stone, nor even metal. He discovered soft mushy tubes and other brushes made of strange material. He shook his head at all of it. It was all so outlandish.

He poured the water into the bowl and stripped off his tunic and serk to wash before evening meal. He certainly nary wished to smell like a heap of shite, if she was going to sit beside him again. If he had thought of it, he would have bathed before coming up to the house, washing up would have to do for tonight, but he made for certain that he used scented soap.

After running a comb through his hair, Eirik left his chamber feeling quite good and in high spirits. He paused at the sight of Elise directing the others where to sit and furrowed his brows. Leif and Jesse had removed the two throne-like chairs setting them near the central fire and carried a couple of the long benches up to the high table so that everyone could sit together at Elise's suggestion. It was more like insistence with the convincing notion that should there be any visitors then they would retake their seats at the trestle tables. But for now, she thought they should eat at the same table for convenience, and it would help them all get to know one another better. Privately, she thought she wouldn't let the two men lord over them like they were less than human.

He gazed at her as she rubbed at her temples. He stepped back into his chamber and retrieved the small rattling bottle from the washing table he had seen her use much earlier that day. He had noticed that she would take something from the bottle following the rubbing of her temples. Nary was he sure what it was, but assumed it stopped the pain.

Eirik stepped up to the high table and took the only seat remaining, between Kristin and Tristan with creased brows. He was displeased as he stretched his arm across the table and set the bottle in front of Elise with a nod. She looked tired to him.

Elise peered up at him with surprise and smiled slightly as she opened the bottle and took one of the pills. As she began to spoon her soup into her mouth, she realized she was hungrier than what she had thought and the longer she sat idle the more tired she felt. She had been on the move since early morning and hadn't even stopped to eat any lunch when the girls had. She sat there and held her head up with her hand as she sipped at the soup, not even listening to the conversations droning on around her.

Eirik sent the others to bed after Leif had rekindled their fire and they cleared the table. They obeyed quietly and with their lack of energy, they had no will to argue. He then picked Elise up off the table where she had fallen to sleep and took her into his chamber. It was warmer in his room than it was in the main hall and his bed was much more comfortable.

He laid her on his bed and pulled off her shoes. He was about to remove her clothing when he heard a knock on his door. When he opened it, he was surprised to see it was Sara.

"I know it's none of my business, but if you plan on her sleeping in here... with you, you might want to take a bit of advice from me. Allow me to dress her in her nightclothes. She will feel less compromised in the morning," she smiled up at him.

He acquiesced, opened the door wider to allow her entrance, and then busied himself with emptying the chamber pot and getting fresh water from the tarn for in the morning while she redressed Elise. He had nil notion of what they had done to make her so tired, but he figured she was nary used to it. And then it struck him. She had said she had been injured. He had heard tale of people with head injuries falling asleep and ne'er waking again. He ran back into the house to his chamber.

Sara was just covering her with the bedfurs. He beckoned her to him by the door and away from Elise. "How bad was her head wound? Should she be sleeping?" he whispered quietly.

"She can sleep now. If she had had a major concussion, it would have been in the first twenty-four hours that we should have been waking her every couple of hours. She's just tired now and she still might be feeling the pain from the lump on her head. If there's nothing else...?" her lips curled up as she reached for the door.

"Thank you again, Sara. I want you ta know, I have nil ill intentions this night. I just wish her to sleep well." He spoke quietly so he'd nary wake the woman as he tried to reassure the lass.

"Oh, I'm sure, Eirik," she chuckled. "I trust your intentions, but I'm not sure she does just yet. You may have to step up your game, but if she spends all her time cleaning, like she did today, she'll be like this every evening and not have the energy to even talk to you."

He nodded his understanding, "I had wished to discuss with her this eve about taking her ta the village on the morrow ta see Ingrid's Astrid. She had expressed concern about the lass."

"I think she'll like that. But she said something today that I thought was odd. For some reason she thinks she's too old for you. Know where she might get such a notion?" she arched a brow up at him as she headed out the door. Sara was hoping that Elise would like Eirik enough to not even think about going back home. She wanted to stay in this time but would prefer to have a friend here too.

Eirik looked toward the sleeping figure in his bed and pursed his lips, knowing exactly where she got that notion, but 'twas nary true at all. Sara nary had only dressed her but had taken her hair down and it was splayed out in curling waves reminding him of a gentle rolling sea. Who was this woman that commanded his attention and stirred the calling within him so strongly that 'twas difficult ta keep his mind on his chores? She was so strange to him with all of her odd bobbles, including the long silky robe that hung from the screen, which he grazed his hand over and found it delightfully soft as he caressed it. However, he deduced that 'twould nary warm a mouse lest it shredded it for a nest, even then, he had his doubts. And her words and actions were certainly puzzling, but somehow, she seemed the perfect one to choose for a life-mate, as if his heart yearned and reached for her, especially so when she was near.

He sat on the side of the bed as he unlaced his boots and after he pulled his feet out, he unstrapped the dagger from his thigh and the axe from his hip, placing them carefully on a nearby chest, all the while in thought. Some words she used were beyond him as was with the others, specifically Bo and his talk of windmills. He snorted softly and drew his overtunic off directly followed by his serk, tossing them onto the same chest. 'How will the wind draw water from the tarn?' he snorted softly as he begun to remove his breeches and then pulled them back into place as he remembered what Sara said about Elise feeling compromised. He wanted her to feel safe with him, but also knew he would get too hot with them on, so he removed them and slipped beneath the top fur before blowing out the candle Sara had lit. The only other light source was that of the hearth and it gleamed off her soft tendrils in russet highlights.

He took in the woman at his side and listened to her restful breathing. His lips curved peacefully as his thoughts flowed to her permanence here beside him and he drifted off to sleep, only to be awakened after what had merely seemed seconds by the feel of her minor tremors. He then worried she had taken chill, turning onto his side, he glided his hand around her waist. The fabric that she wore to sleep in was as soft as lamb's wool and felt warm, but he pulled her up against him to share his warmth until he felt her shivering subside. Only then did his worries rest allowing him to fall back to sleep.

Freya's Day

The Thorp

Elise woke the next morning and stretched out her sore muscles. The bed she was in was so very comfortable and warm she didn't want to get out of it. She had never known a hotel bed to feel so luxuriously soft. Her eyes popped open when she remembered where she was, the bed closets weren't this comfortable either.

She sat up and glanced around and then she knew she was in Eirik's chamber, furthermore someone had changed her clothes. The last thing she remembered was falling asleep at the table. She blew out her breath hoping he wasn't the one that did it... she shook her head. No, he wouldn't have known what to dress her in. It had to have been Sara. Thank God!

She rose from the bed and slipped into her robe that was hanging thoughtfully from the screen next to the bed and got ready for the day. Someone had put the water over the fire already, so she went to her suitcase to pull out her clothes. If she was going to do more cleaning today, she was going to wear jeans, but then she noticed that there were clothes already laying out for her. These clothes were of Norse design. A soft gown of dark blue and a white apron with identical golden broaches with some kind of stylized animal, perhaps a dragon, she thought, to pin the straps into place, even short leather slippers. Someone wanted her to dress in period clothes and she wondered why as she traced her fingers over the many strands of glass beads as well as the golden torc that usually denoted marriage for the ones that could afford such luxuries.

After she washed, she braided her hair so it would hang down her back and donned the clothing intended for her, without the jewelry. She started for the door and noticed the bucket sitting there. She went back to the table to get the bowl, dumped it in the pail and then washed it out before she went out to the main hall.

The table was already set with trenchers and cups, so she went on into the kitchen. "I'm sorry I overslept...," she said then noticed it was Eirik and Leif preparing the breakfast.

Leif grinned broadly at her, "'Tis all right, Milady, you must have exhausted yourself." There was a gleam in his eyes that she couldn't quite figure out as if he was making some innuendo of which she was unaware. "The hearth room is so clean you could eat off the floor."

She smiled appreciatively at him, "Although I wouldn't recommend it, thank you." Then she looked to Eirik, "Do I have you to thank for my attire today?"

He turned toward her giving her a gentle perusal, noting the missing objects with a slightest of frowns, before he nodded, "Yea, I thought you would like ta go see Astrid this morn. You seemed concerned over her well-being."

"And so, the clothing would help me blend in, huh?" she asked, and he nodded. "I would like that a lot actually, but why didn't you wake me to start breakfast? I thought it was part of our deal?"

Leif looked from one to the other seeing he wasn't really part of this conversation, then, "I'll go wake the brattles," he said excusing himself from the room.

"You did so much a day ago that you deserved ta sleep in this morn," he spoke as he kept his attention on breaking the hard cheese into small blocks for easier handling.

"Speaking of which... I noticed I woke in your bed. Not that I'm ungrateful at having to not sleep where I fell, but how'd I get there and why?" She looked up at him with tight lips. Her next question would depend on his answer.

"You said you had an aversion ta the straw. I just thought the down would appease you. If I've mistaken...," he met her gaze and scanned her face for telling signs of displeasure.

"Oh... That was generous of you to be so thoughtful. But if I may ask, where did *you* sleep?" she asked as she watched him.

"I abed with you, Milady. You were cold, your teeth nigh shook from your mouth and 'twas an easy task ta share my warmth," his lips curved at the corners as his stunning blue eyes came even with hers.

Elise's eyes widened and her brows skyrocketed. "Then I suppose I should thank you," she said graciously, but had different thoughts in her head that she would address later when she had time to think it through.

"Nary liberties were taken with you, for a certain, Milady." He felt as if he needed to defend himself again to her at seeing the expression on her face.

"No, I wouldn't think you would," she said lowly and began taking the food to the table.

Eirik furrowed his brows thoughtfully as he picked up the trays of cheese and meat then followed her. 'Twas nary certain what she meant by her comment, but felt it was somehow irksome. She seemed displeased to abed with him but also displeased he took nil pleasures of her.

When all was carried in, he was sure to take the seat beside her instead of between the two sniveling lasses. He could nary bare another sup wedged between them. Last eve, he thought his ears would bleed, to be certain.

Leif had already seated himself beside Sara with Bo on her other side, leaving Elise and Eirik across from them. When Jesse finally dragged his body to the table, he wasn't as gleeful this morn as he was the last. He complained of sore muscle aches and pains as he sat beside Eirik.

"You sound as if you've been keeping company with Tristan and Kristin," Leif teased. "'Tis a good answer to the work. Does a man's body good ta work the muscles, eh?" he chuckled as the lad sat beside him.

"Yeah," was all Jesse could say in reply. He thought he worked out enough at home, but this work was nothing like that.

"I was wondering if I could start on engineering that windmill today... after I do the watering," Bo asked looking over at Eirik then to Leif.

"'Tis up ta Leif, I will be on errand as will your mistress. Leif will guide you but explain ta me how you will manage ta bring the water from the tarn if your wind catcher 'tis on the ridge," Eirik lifted a doubtful brow at him.

Bo looked to Elise and smiled slightly then back to Eirik. "If the windmill is on the ridge, it will catch the wind and power the pump that in turn will siphon the water from the tarn up to the house. I just need to figure out what to use for piping." He furrowed his brows in thought.

"Ah, I see and how much of this piping will you need?" Leif asked as he leaned around Sara to see him.

"Enough if you set them in a straight line they'll go from the pond to the mill and then to the house. But what do you have around here to make them out of?" Bo looked at him skeptically.

"I'll see what I can find," Leif smiled and gave Eirik a wink.

"So, you're going to the village today?" Sara leaned forward asking Elise the question as she smiled and glanced at Eirik.

"Yes, to see Ingrid's daughter. I think that maybe if she still had a fever, I may have something that could help her." Elise gave Sara a pointed look.

"Well, you look pretty in the local costume. I'll have to see if I can find some for myself," she grinned at Elise.

"If you don't mind, could you take over the supervision of the cleaning while I'm gone? I'll be sure to instruct the twins to do as you say. Someone's got to keep them moving or they'll do nothing all day then complain about being bored." She snorted and the other's laughed, then she immediately regretted saying it. She shouldn't say things like that about her students, true or not.

"Surely, they have some compensatory qualities, eh?" Leif asked looking around at the others. They were all silent.

"They're pretty," Jesse spoke up and glanced at Sara with a

slight shrug, to which he received quiet nods to his comment, but Eirik was sure not to respond at all and continued to eat.

Elise rose from her seat and took her dish to the kitchen. She had noticed Eirik's purposeful ignorance of the statement Jesse made, and it ruffled her feathers for some reason. But as she was passing through the hall to the guest chamber to rouse the girls, she heard him say something that caught her attention just before she entered.

"Beauty in one's youth has its purpose, but as one ages, knowledge and knowhow are more desirable. Alas, should you retain your beauty as you gain your wisdom then you'll be well sought after. 'Tis a delicate balance," he smiled and winked at Sara as he got up and turned to go into the kitchen just in time to see Elise go through the door.

"Come on girls. You better hurry or it'll be oatmeal again for your breakfast," Elise said as she seen they were just now brushing their teeth. "And wear something practical again today. You'll be cleaning the hall under Sara's supervision."

"What? Why her?" Kristin groaned.

"Because I'm going with Eirik this morning and the hall still needs cleaned. Sara is responsible enough to make sure it gets done. If I left it up to you two, you'd have her doing all the work. So, after you eat, clean up the kitchen then start helping Sara in the hall."

"Do we have to dress like that?" Tristan asked with a disgusted look on her face.

"No, certainly not to clean in. Wear your jeans, like yesterday," Elise said as her chin rose, and she smoothed down the front of her apron. She loved the dress. "And I'd suggest getting a move on it." She spun around and headed back out the door.

As she closed the door behind her, she let out her breath in a sigh then went to get her purse and find out what happened to her pill bottle. When she went into Eirik's chamber, she found the bottle setting right on the table. She picked it up and started to take one, but then thought she had better save them just in case Astrid or someone else needed it more. She dropped the bottle in her purse as she heard the door open behind her.

Eirik came in silently and incased her in a warm cloak with a thick fur mantle and a deep hood that she could draw over her head. He attached the brooch at her collar without turning her around.

"Mayhap this will keep you warm on our ride ta the thorp, eh?" he said quietly and allowed his hands to linger on her shoulders.

She turned and smiled up at him softly, gliding through his hands, "Thank you. I'm ready if you are." Maybe if she could prove she was wise, then maybe... Who was she kidding? There was no way she could compete with the likes of the twins, besides why did she even care? In two weeks, they were going to be gone, it was best to just focus on... what? Trying to find a way home? Cleaning? Maybe while she's visiting Ingrid, she could ask her about some recipes or how to weave. She needed something to keep the twins busy and if Sara planned on staying, she could use all the information she could get.

Eirik lifted his hand to her cheek caressing it gently. She was staring at him but nary a word did she speak. He wondered at what she was thinking, but instead of asking he brushed his lips to hers unable to stop himself in time. That brought her out of her reverie, and she lowered her head as the heat flooded her cheeks and she shouldered her bag.

"Let's away," he said lowly and brought her arm around his to usher her out. He led her out of the longhouse to a large horse that was saddled and waiting near the door. "'Tis Farfame," he said as he closed the door. It was all shiny black with a long glossy mane and tail and little tuffs of silky hair around each hoof like fuzzy socks. She thought perhaps it was a Friesian but wasn't that familiar with horses. He helped her on it then hesitated before he swung up behind her. Most women sit sideways on a horse because their skirts don't allow for them to sit astride it. But she hiked up her dress and sat like a man exposing her hose clad leg nearly to the thigh.

As he took the reins, he engulfed her within his arms and booted the horse into action. She fit quite neatly between them and after a while she relaxed against him causing his lips to curl at the corners. Having her back against his chest summoned a much baser desire than the calling and just as strongly felt and tempted him to fold his arm around her to increase the feeling. But it 'twas nary quite the right time. Therefore, he prolonged the ride by taking them in a roundabout way down to the village, through a small forest, across a stream and field, and over several rises.

It seemed to her that it would have taken only half as long if he had taken a more direct route, but she didn't question him. In fact, neither of them talked the entire way until they neared the village.

"Keep your hood up and speak ta nil one, aye?" he spoke near her ear causing her to shiver. She nodded and pulled the hood up over her head as he tightened his arm around her at feeling her tremble once again and to prepare for their descent. She stiffened slightly. "Hold tight, Milady. We're nigh there then you can warm yourself at the hearth," he mumbled and directed the horse down a steep slope at the back of a building.

They came to a stop, and he dropped from the horse. He turned around after scanning the area for others and offered his hands up to her to help her down. Leaning into his awaiting hands, she gave a soft gasp when he pulled her free and set her on her feet.

Eirik gently took her hand and guided her around to the entrance. Ingrid was there and opened the door to them.

"Milord, 'twas nary expectin' ye," she said nervously and bowed her head.

"We've come ta see about Astrid. Milady was quite worried," he said in low tones.

"Oh, goodness me, she be over here, but we've managed. Nay a need ta bother ye with, Milord... Milady," she glanced up at Elise ever so briefly.

Elise went to where Ingrid had gestured, a small cot near the fire, and squatted at her side. She smiled down at the small dark headed girl and felt her forehead. She was feverish.

"We should bathe her," Elise looked up at Ingrid and Eirik as she released the clasp of the cloak and pulled it from her shoulders handing it off to Eirik as he reached for it. "It will help bring her fever down," she clarified for them. She then rummaged in her bag for the pill bottle. She took one out and broke it in half before giving it to her with a sip of water.

Eirik stood back and watched Elise and Ingrid bathe the girl gently and dress her in a clean night shift then cover her again. Before they were finished tucking her in, she was sleeping restfully and sweat was starting to dot her forehead.

"Just keep swabbing her with cool water and keep the fire high. The fever should break by morning," Elise said gently to Ingrid and smiled.

"Oh, thank ye, Milady. Milord said ye wished fer some tea. I've been saving it, but 'tis well worth the visit," Ingrid said as her face lit up with joy, happy she could pay the woman for her healing.

"I couldn't take something so precious to you…," Elise started then seen the woman deflate with disappointment. "Perhaps we can share it, if there's enough, huh?"

Ingrid nodded enthusiastically grinning and hurried off to get the tea. Elise was happy she could help as she gazed at the child with a quiet smile on her lips then glanced at Eirik. He had been silent the whole time and appeared to be studying her. She had just noticed he wore the same cloak that she had, except his left his right arm uncovered and she could see an axe hanging from his belt as well as a dagger strapped to his thigh. She would bet that a sword hung from his back. She opened her mouth to ask him about it when Ingrid came back with a small tin in her hand and aglow with joyfulness, drawing her attention away from Eirik.

"Here be what I have, Milady. I meant ta have Oslo take it ta ye last eve, but with Astrid feeling as such, the thought raced from me mind. Please forgive me?" She glanced up at Elise then to Eirik before lowering her gaze, making Elise wonder to just whom she was apologizing.

"Don't give it another thought," Elise said as she accepted the tin of loose tea. "Perhaps when Astrid is feeling better you could come and share this with me? I have some questions I'd like to ask," she smiled softly to put the woman at ease, but it seemed to make her more uncomfortable as her eyes darted toward Eirik as if to ask his permission.

"Perhaps in a day or two," Eirik suggested, "giving Astrid time ta heal, aye?" He leaned toward Ingrid with his hand outstretched toward hers and pushed two coins in her palm. Ingrid started to protest, but then he said, "Have Oslo purchase more tea."

"Aye, Milord," Ingrid whispered with her eyes downcast. "Thank ye," she glanced up at Elise with a slight nod of her head.

"We should away, Milady," he then said quietly to Elise as he held the cloak open to her back and drew it around her, clasping the brooch once again, jarring her from her thoughts. She would be sure to question him on the ride home about the relationship he had with Ingrid. Something wasn't quite right with the way she wouldn't make eye contact with either of them. She would also ask him about the small tattoo she had noticed on the little girl's hip when she was bathing her. She seemed much too young to have made that decision for herself, perhaps it was a clan marking.

"Thank you for the tea and I hope to see you soon," she smiled again then turned toward the door. Eirik pulled her hood over her head before he opened the door to ensure her face was covered. He gripped her hand and hurried them around the building before they were seen to where Farfame remarkably still stood waiting untethered.

However, before they could mount, a masculine voice sounded from behind them, "Good day, Milord."

Elise kept her face toward the horse as Eirik turned then casually came forward to greet the man and stood between him and Elise. "Greetings, Nidpigger."

"'Tis nigh spring. Do you require my services this season?" the man said as he leaned ever so slightly to peer around Eirik.

"Aye, mayhap. I await word," Eirik replied and tightened his lips.

"Very well. Do keep me apprised if needs must," Nidpigger gave him a short nod and turned to leave.

Eirik scowled as he turned back toward Elise and helped her astride the mount. Without speaking, he distractedly pulled her skirt down from where it had come more than halfway up her thigh and drew her cloak around it before he alighted behind her then bent to do the same on the other side. As he embraced her between his arms to take the reins, he felt her back stiffen against him. Shaking his head, he backed the horse up a bit. "Hold tight, Milady, and lean forward," he said quietly just before the beast's powerful legs jarred them into motion.

Elise quickly grasped a good tight handful of Farfame's mane as she bent completely forward against the beast's neck, feeling the weight of Eirik's torso against her back sufficiently securing her in place as they swiftly climbed the sharp slope. Cresting the rise, he gently coaxed her upright and back into him as they raced out of view of the village.

When they slowed to a casual walk, she started to ask him again about Ingrid, but he spoke first, although softly as if he was unsure of the consequences of his question. "Are you a völva?" Any number of strange items she carried in her large bag may be her wand. Though none resembled a distaff, she did have the totems, he just nary knew. He nary felt any Heill around her, but perhaps she had found a way to hide it from others. That too also raised questions.

Elise turned slightly to look at him, but his arms tightened and restricted her movement. "You think that I'm a witch?" she asked in disbelief, wondering what had given him such an idea. She then considered her own actions and how outlandish all her things and clothes must seem to him and understood.

"'Tis acceptable if you are," he said to put her at ease, but he was uncertain how he felt. 'Twould make her unattainable for a life-mate traditionally, which disheartened him a bit. All know völva live a solitary life, without a mate, but not necessarily celibate. His lips curved slightly at that, and then scowled with her next words.

"Are you? Ingrid seems incredibly frightened of you," she said as she straightened in the saddle, facing forward and taking notice that they weren't taking the same route back as they had come. She thought she heard him growl.

"Nay, 'tis nary so," he said indignantly, obviously she had insulted him. She then remembered it was considered unmanly for men to be witches among the Vikings. "Ingrid hath nil reason ta be frightened of me, nor my brother. 'Tis respect for our … station."

"I'm not either," was all she said with the same indignation he had, but he 'twas nary sure if she was responding to her being a witch or being frightened of him.

"I meant nil disrespect, Milady." He sighed out his breath thinking he had gone about this all wrong. His brother would take great joy at this. "And you have nary a reason ta be frightened either. Nil harm will befall you as long as you are under my shield. Leif and I will protect you and yours." He hoped that would smooth things over between them.

"For the next fortnight," she said on a heavy sigh, wondering what would happen to them after that. Having no idea what the future would hold for them, or even if there would be a future.

"Or longer, if needs must," he mumbled as they crested another rise and heard her sharp intake of breath as the field of heather came into view. He brought the horse to a stop midway into the field and sat there for a while enjoying the scenery as well as her company, her nearness. He nary cared if she was a witch or not, he still felt a pull toward her as a life-mate. Perhaps she was an enchantress, or mayhap he was just lonely. He laughed at himself this time for he knew 'twas more than that; 'twas the calling.

"Does it please you?" he asked. "Do you wish ta dismount for a bit and walk afield?" He swung from the horse and stepped up to face her after receiving her nod.

"Oh, it is lovely here, Eirik." Elise scanned the field of blue heather that was wedged between two minor rises sufficiently blocking the wind for the shallow valley of flowers. She glanced down at him with a small smile. "Thank you so much," she said as she reached for him to help her down.

Eirik placed his hands on her waist and easily lifted her off the horse bringing her right down in front of him. "As long as it pleases you, Milady," he said quietly, hesitant to move away.

She turned slightly and hung the long straps of her purse over a peg on the saddle then walked on ahead of the steed with Eirik at her side. Farfame just seemed to follow after them. "May I ask you a question?" she paused as she glanced up at him, seeing the serene look on his face she changed what she was going to ask, and then continued. "How long have you lived here?"

"'Tis nigh four and ten years since we claimed the island," he stated then his brows drew together with the falsehood not liking the taste of it on his tongue. Shaking it away, "We encouraged these others ta settle here ta help work it into a prosperous village. Albeit few women wish ta be stranded here for the winter, but the men see the potential for wealth. Mayhap, once they build up their coffers, more women will come." He gave her a slight shrug, telling her it made no difference to him.

"But don't you want...," she stalled in her thoughts in how to ask what she was thinking then changed her question completely. "And how does Leif feel about the lack of choices for woman companionship?" So, the question wasn't exactly changed, just the person she referred to.

He arched a brow at her question then drew them together in thought before he answered... or rather questioned as he stopped to face her. "Are you of interest in Leif? I be certain he would be honored to have your hand." Then he moved back by the Friesian. "We should head back. 'Tis chores ta do yet."

Elise advanced on him as she studied his countenance; he looked everywhere but at her eyes. When he had her lifted into place and was seated behind her, she mumbled just loud enough for him to hear, "I have no interest in Leif." His arms tightened around her just before he booted the beast into action. He could nary quite keep from smiling as they rode off.

It wasn't too long before she could see the church on top of the hill, but instead of turning toward home, he veered them off in the direction of the sea and to where they had ...landed -for lack of a better word to describe their odd arrival. She stayed quiet as he took them to the cliff's edge and rode along it for some time as he looked up and down the coastline searching for debris, she assumed. Giving up, he turned them towards home. What could she say? That they arose out of thin air? He would truly believe she was a witch then.

He halted the animal at the door of the lodge and slid off from behind her before he came around to face her once again and lifted her down afore him. With his hands still resting on her waist he said, "Thank you, Milady, for riding with me. 'Twas quite pleasurable."

"It was lovely, Eirik. Thank you for taking me," she smiled up at him with shining eyes of emerald and then turned toward the door. He followed as the horse moseyed off to the barn on its own.

She went directly to Eirik's chamber to change her clothes and when she had unclasped the broach on the cloak, she felt it lifted away, just then noticing he had followed her in causing her to jump. "You scared me," she chuckled. "I didn't hear you come in."

"My apologies," he smiled and then saw the jewelry still lying where he'd left them out for her. Tossing the cloak over his arm, he went to gather them and put them away.

"I was meaning to ask you about those," she said quietly.

He turned to look at her. "I meant for you to wear them on our journey today," he said without explaining further. He then laid the cloak over a chest and left the beads and torc where they laid.

"Eirik, I may be an outlander, but I know what they mean. What was your intention for them?"

"I meant nil ill by them. If we had been approached by any on our journey, they would have announced that you were wed and nary ta be bothered with. Otherwise, you would have been up for any ta have, nil matter that I was with you. Without them, they would feel you were free for the taking."

"Because I didn't wear them, you took the long way there to avoid anyone else from seeing me. Is that right?" He nodded. "And also, why you didn't introduce me to that man today?" His brows furrowed at the mention of Nidpigger, and his lips tightened. "I'm sorry that I caused you trouble, if you only had said something," she said then sighed.

"Nil a need, Milady. The day went without incident, and as you said, 'twas lovely," his lips curved into a smile as he winked.

"I better get changed and see about the girls," she said as she pulled her jeans from her suitcase as well as a sweater then ducked behind the screen to change, but it was more to hide from him. He was definitely throwing her signals, although sometimes mixed, and she wasn't certain how she felt about that. He was some kind of hot, that's for sure. If she had to be stuck in the past, he would certainly be a good choice, but if they were to find a way home…

Eirik wanted to speak with her about her ship, or the lack thereof, but felt they had a good day and nary wished to ruin it. He thought he had made some headway with her as well, therefore, he would ask her later, for now he had work to do and left to go do just that.

Elise heard the door close and let out her breath as she unfastened the shell broaches and caught the apron before it fell. She slung it up over the screen and wriggled out of the shift and hose then quickly donned her jeans and sweater. When she came out, she found the room empty, thankfully, and went to get her socks and tennis shoes.

Once appropriately dressed for cleaning, she left the chamber and glanced about the hall. It was clean and smelled of fresh threshes, which gave it an aroma of newly mowed grass. Not bad. She made her way into the kitchen to see if she could make some kind of dessert for dinner.

The girls, all of them, were kneading dough on the large center table and arranging them in rings to bake. She smiled at seeing even the twins seemed to enjoy this task. "Hey, girls," she greeted them.

"Hey, Miss Thornson," Sara replied with a smile. "I thought we could use more bread. It seems like we go through quite a bit of it."

"Good idea, Sara. Save me some dough. I was thinking of making some sweet bread for dessert tonight. I thought I saw some cinnamon in the pantry and perhaps I could use honey for the sugar,"

"Cinnamon rolls?" Kristin asked and grinned. She loved sweets even though she restricted herself on them. But here, she didn't feel the need to.

"Yeah," Elise nodded and went into the pantry.

"Gosh, I haven't had a cinnamon roll in years," Tristan said and smiled at her sister.

"I know, right?" Kristin said and continued kneading the dough in front of her.

Elise returned with the cask of cinnamon and a jar of honey then went to get butter from the dairy larder. While she was in there, she found something that resembled cream cheese and sniffed at it. It smelled like it too! She would have to do something with that, maybe try her hand at a cheesecake. But for now, she had cinnamon rolls on her mind, which would hopefully keep other thoughts away.

She took the rather large dough ball that Sara had set aside for her and flattened it out then looked about for a rolling pin, or at least something to be used as a rolling pin. Seeing the handle of the grinding stones for grains, she pulled it free and returned to the dough. It wasn't perfect, but it'd due for now. As she rolled the dough out to about a half inch thick, her mind drifted towards their predicament, and she bit at her lip. Then she smeared the butter lightly over the entire surface, knowing it wouldn't need as much with the honey as it would with sugar but would keep the dough soft. Following the butter, she sprinkled the cinnamon on and then carefully drizzled the honey over it all. How was she going to tell them that there may not be a way home, sure Sara knew, but Tristan and Kristin didn't? As she rolled the dough into a log, she glanced at the two girls and tightened her lips. Maybe she should wait until she had a better idea of what was going to happen. Taking a sharp knife, she sliced the log into thick sections and sighed out heavily. She was going to have to tell Eirik the truth although she didn't want to. They were safe here, for the time being, and she needed them.

"What's wrong?" Sara whispered near her.

Elise looked at her and smiled slightly, shaking her head, "Nothing, honey. Nothing that we have to deal with right now. Kristin and Tristan seem to be enjoying this." She nodded her head toward the girls as she separated the rolls.

"Yeah, they said it was better than cleaning," she chuckled. "And I told them I would clean up tonight if they'd help me, so...," she indicated toward them.

"Smart cookie, but don't let them get away with not doing some kind of chore, they need to be useful in some way, to Eirik and Leif," she said as she gave her a meaningful look.

Sara nodded her understanding and said, "For something other than a bedwarmer, you mean,"

Elise nodded solemnly and then smiled, "Maybe they have some other hidden talent, eh?" she winked then turned to the girls. "Girls, what do you like to do as a hobby?"

"Besides shopping?" Kristin said.

Tristan giggled, "The only shopping we do is of the window variety, except of course for accessories. Purses, handbags, shoes, scarves and such."

Elise glanced over their clothing and jewelry and raised a brow. "What do you mean?"

"Kristin designs and makes our clothes, except for jeans, but she tailors them to our liking," Tristan said with a smile at her sister.

"And Tristan makes all our jewelry. Everything we own are one-of-a-kind originals," she grinned.

"Oh," Elise said unable to keep the surprise out of her voice or off her face. "Well, that should be handy," she chuckled and glanced at Sara.

"Yeah, you probably thought what everyone else thinks, that all we do is shop and get mani-pedi's, right?" Kristin said a bit disheartened.

"Not at all," she lied, "I just wasn't aware of your fashion design passions," she smiled, hoping to cover her thoughts. "Is that what you two planned to do after school?" Elise bit her lip; she hadn't intended to bring up that particular subject.

"Yes," they said in unison, both smiling.

"Good for you," she returned their smile. Two problems down, if they had to stay, and only one more to go: Jesse. He would be stuck doing all the physical labor, just like a slave, she thought as she found a flat heavy baking pan to put the rolls in. Craftsmen would do better than slave labor here, although they would still need to do the farmstead chores, as with any household.

After buttering the pan, she placed the rolls in and set them near the hearth to rise a bit then had Sara start on the side dishes to go with the remainder of the chicken stew as the girls finished up the bread while she began the cheesecake.

Eirik helped Jesse finish up the stalls while Leif and Bo tended the animals. They had a menagerie of horses, cows, sheep, goats, pigs, and chickens, all of which needed fed, watered, and their pens cleaned, except for what Jesse had done the day before. Although it was an extravagance, they heated the barn with a central firepit, much like in the longhouse, to keep the animals warm in the winter. Eirik nary cared much to smell them throughout the winter, or smell like them. Once the animals were taken care of, they would get the fields planted before the turning. However, he'd rather not go this spring at all and leave Elise here to fend on her own. Perhaps he would send a message to the king and dissolve their pact. He thought he had helped him enough; the kingdoms were nigh aligned. He surely could do the rest on his own. Maybe he should teach them to defend themselves in case of raiders, nary that many would raid their farmstead, save one mayhap; Nidpigger. He had an uncontrollable urge to spit, his name soured on his tongue. He nary trusted the man, especially with his new charges, but he was the one who normally looked after their farmstead while they were away. Mayhap he should ask Oslo instead. He should certainly teach Elise bedplay... um...bladeplay. He shook his head and concentrated on his work even as his lips curved.

When they had the stalls mucked, all but the sty and coop, he stoked the fire for the night and followed the others into the hall. The aroma of fresh baked bread filled the room along with cinnamon and something sweet; it made his stomach growl with hunger. Instead of washing up in his chambers like the others, he grabbed a clean serk, a pot of soap, and headed off to the tarn to bathe. He was nary going ta sup with the others while he smelled like the shite that he'd been pitching all day. Arriving at the tarn he swiftly undressed and dove in letting the cold water assuage his thoughts as well as cleanse his body. He had hoped the work he had done today would have kept his mind from Elise, but it seemed to just allow him that much more time to think about her. Quickly scrubbing his body with the soap, he then ran it through his hair. He dunked under the surface again before he swam to where he left his clothes and walked out of the tarn. He used his old serk to dry off with before he put on the clean one and pulled on his breeches. After he was dressed, he slowly walked back to the house and back into his chamber to comb out his hair and get a clean tunic.

He approached the table quietly and took his seat across from Leif, and as he waited for the food to be set, he poured his cup full of mead. Mayhap a meadhead will help, he chuckled at himself.

"What be amiss, brother?" Leif said as he leaned across the table and refilled his cup.

Eirik shook his head at him as he eyed the women parading

out with bowls of chicken stew and trays of bread, butter, and cheese, then returned for more. "'Tis naught ta be helped, ta be certain," he creased his lips into a smile.

Leif lifted a brow at him then sat back in his seat as a bowl was set in front of him and others placed around the table.

Elise then came in with the pan of rolls and set it on the end of the table and smiled, obviously pleased by how they turned out. "Where's the boys?" she asked looking from one man to the other.

"'Tis likely they're scrubbing the stink of shite off, 'twould be my guess," Leif chuckled and eyed his brother.

"Aye, methinks I should have had them wash at the tarn afore coming ta the house, Milady. My apologies," Eirik said and winked at her.

"No need, they'll eat when they're finished, I guess," she smiled down at them then took her seat and began breaking the bread.

As they ate, they all chatted about their day and seemed in high spirits. No one was talking about going home as if they were all resigned to being here. They joked and laughed and carried on as if it was an ordinary day. It was good to hear, to Eirik. Then perhaps that was one worry off his mind, however his biggest was sitting right beside him.

"I hope you enjoyed the rolls," Elise said as she started to rise and clear the table, but Eirik's hand swung down and grasped her wrist to halt her.

"Aye," Leif said as he stuffed the last one into his mouth and rose to go to his chamber. Bo and Jesse had already left the table along with the twins.

"Let Sara do it," he said lowly causing her to look at him. "I wish ta speak with you in private." He then rose from the table and nudged her into motion.

Washing Day

Washing Day

When they entered Eirik's chamber, it was nearly dark except for the low embers in the fireplace. He quietly locked the door behind him before he said, "Ready for bed while I breathe life into the fire for you."

"All right," she looked at him quizzically as she went behind the screen, wondering what he wanted to talk to her about.

"Miss Thornson…," he said but it didn't sound right crossing his tongue. "Elise, I nary saw any wreckage along the shore from your ship," he said from somewhere on the other side of the screen, but she did notice the room flared with a bit more amber light.

"Um… Yeah, I noticed that too," she said as she removed her sweater and quickly drew her flannel nightgown over her head before removing her bra, flinging both discarded items upon the top of the screen.

"Elise…, how did you come to be on the island?" His voice was closer than it had been before.

She pulled off her jeans slowly as she thought about her answer then tossed them over the screen top. "I told you," she said as she came out barefooted and paused at seeing him lounged back on the bed wearing nothing but his pants.

"You told me you wrecked, but there is no wreckage," he said casually from the head of the bed as he absently rubbed his thumb on his left palm.

She quickly started across the room to her case to retrieve

socks. "I can't explain that," she said matter-of-factly.

He lunged out and halted her progress with one strong hand around her wrist. "I need ta know," he said lowly and then brought his eyes up to meet hers. "You have objects of which I have ne'er seen the likes, nor can I fathom the uses of, and I have traveled far, Milady, to be certain."

"I... I... don't know how to answer you," she stuttered out, unsure of his intentions.

"With the truth, preferably," he pulled her closer to sit next to him, indicating that neither of them was going anywhere until he had his answers.

"The truth?" she chuckled wryly, "You wouldn't believe me if I told you the truth." She sat at the foot of the bed and pulled her feet up off the cold floor.

"'Tis much I'll believe," he smirked then released the grip he had on her wrist.

Exasperated by him asking the same questions repeatedly, she broke, "I told you the truth, several times now, except I can't explain why there's no wreckage. I don't know why or how we ended up here, just that we are. I don't even know if we can get back. Even if we get to the mainland, where are we to go to from there? We're about a thousand years from...," she stopped her tirade before she really told him all of the truth and bit her lips together.

His brow lifted. "You were saying?" Thus far, she'd nary given any answers, just raised more questions.

"Fine, Eirik, we're from the future and we don't know how to return. Is that better? Is that the truth you want? How about that I'm responsible for these five kids and I need to find a way to get them back to their parents. Except Sara. No, she's ecstatic to stay here and live out her days as a slave, if you wish it." She twisted toward him, "But you better not want her as a slave. If that's your intentions for her then she must go back too. I'll not have any of them end up as..."

He came forward swiftly and pressed his lips against hers just to stop them from moving. She was either going mad or perhaps telling the truth but nary could reconcile it. Whatever the reason, he wanted her to stop. 'Twas nary how he wanted this to go. He eased back from her and said calmly, "Breathe." As she slowly opened her eyes, he was certain to capture them and then repeated, "Breathe." After she had taken several slow breaths, he then said, "Tell me the truth of how you came to this island," all the while keeping his silvery blue gaze fastened on hers.

"We were flying from England to Sweden when we ran into some turbulence. I was hit on the back of the head and when I woke, we were here. I don't know how we got here," she said quietly and shivered slightly, although she could feel the heat radiate from him. "I don't know what else to say that will satisfy you, Eirik."

She was flying? And has a love for dragons, but she wore the totems on her fingers of a witch as well as that of Odin. Eirik furrowed his brows at her momentarily and then sighed out his breath. "What if you nary be able ta return, would it be such a hardship ta stay here?" he asked gently.

"I suppose not so much for me or Sara, we don't have any family, but the others do. Bo and Jesse could adapt well enough, but the twins would find it difficult, although even they have talents that I wasn't aware of. I just don't want them ending up as slaves," she said a bit downhearted and yet determined.

"'Twould nary allow it. As I said before, they be under my protection and I can make it permanent, nary for just the fortnight, and only if they concede."

"What does that mean?" she looked at him in confusion as she drew her arms around herself.

He tightened his lips as he thought of the words. He could nary tell her the truth yet, but he would soon. "I'm reluctant ta say for now, perhaps soon... when you trust me. Just know they will be protected... I'll protect you."

"When I trust you or you trust me?" she asked hugging her knees into her.

"'Tis a bit of both, I'll admit," his lips curved at the corners. "'Tis time enough ta happen." He sat back and lounged once again against the head of the bed.

"So, you won't kick us out after two weeks?" she asked tentatively.

"Nay," he chuckled, "'Tis for certain."

"And we won't be slaves?" she clarified.

"I swear upon my sword, Milady, nil harm will befall you under my shield," he reassured her once again.

"And what do you want in return for your protection?" she lifted a brow at him.

"Little more than what you have done, hearth duties and such... Just until Ingrid can return, two days hence," he smiled to set her at ease, "After which, you may do what you will."

"Astrid should be better by tomorrow," she said.

"Nay, 'twill take three days for the fever ta loosen its hold on the lass, but after she'll be able ta return."

"Then maybe I should go back to see her tomorrow?" she questioned.

"Nay, we chanced the outing this day, we ought nary go again for a few more... unless you consent to wear the wife beads and torc?" he lifted his brow and his lips twitched at the corners.

She tightened her lips as she studied his face but said nothing. She still wasn't certain of his intentions with the beads. What he had said was logical, but lies, really good ones, usually were, and he looked like he could take care of any unwanted attention. And he did seem to be the Chieftain or Jarl here, so she didn't understand why anyone would challenge him.

"Let us abed," he said as he reached for her, seeing her tremble from the cold. "We'll discuss it more on the morrow."

Elise just realized he intended for them to sleep together again. "Um...," she glanced around the room. "Is there not another bed for me to sleep in?"

"Nary with down, 'tis only straw," he tugged on her arm to encourage her as he scooted over to allow her room, albeit not much room. "I'll take nil privileges, to be certain," his lips curled as he winked.

Elise sighed out her breath as she slowly unfolded her form

and rose from the bed. That wink always made her unsure if he was just teasing her or if he meant it as an enticement. She slipped under the furs, turned with her back to him, and reveled in its warmth, he had warmed it nicely for her. However, it wasn't long before it cooled without his body heat and she tugged up on the top fur, but it stopped short. He was lying on it. She then yanked harder, and as she felt the bed shift, it came free, and her hand hit her square in the face with a quiet grunt. After she rubbed her eye, silently consoling it, she pulled the fur around her just before she heard the rustle of cloth and felt the cool breeze when he lifted the furs up to get beneath them.

Thankful that he hadn't noticed her mishap. "Eirik?" she said quietly. "I do trust you."

"Sleep well, Milady," he said on a sigh as he laid on his back with his arm tucked under his weighted head. She had said the words, but nary did he feel her heart in them. If needs must, he'll tell her the truth, at least about the thralling. She will be displeased by the branding, but 'tis better than the vanishing, to him. He sighed out once again as he tried to push his thoughts away so he may rest.

Elise woke in the darkness of the room with sweat dotting her lip and a tremendous amount of heat all along the back side of her, where Eirik was pressed up tight with his arm hooked over her waist holding her there. Her first thought was that she may have caught something from Astrid, but then again, she didn't feel sick. She did have to pee though. And she was hot! She lifted the covers, immediately feeling the cold air strike her, and eased out of bed to empty her bladder. Well, she tried to.

Eirik's arm constricted around her, pulling her even tighter into him, but just briefly before he woke enough to ask, "What be amiss?"

"I have to urinate... um...piss," she whispered finding the term he used. He released his hold and lifted the furs.

Elise hurried to the chamber pot and relieved herself with a sigh then dug through her purse for a tissue as she continued. By the time she finished, she had to clench her jaws together to keep her teeth from chattering and shivers violently shook her body. As hot as she was before, she was equally cold now and rushed back to the bed and climbed in. She didn't turn her back to him though, no, she needed the heat that radiated from his body like an inferno. It was all she could do to keep from throwing her arms around him and pulling him into her now. Instead, she crossed her arms over her chest, to keep from doing so, and scooched as close as she could without touching him except for laying her head on his now outstretched arm. Eirik woke again, feeling her body tremble, and pulled her into his chest, tucking her head under his chin and held her there before he fell back to sleep, if he had even woken to begin with. Whatever the case, Elise was thankful for his warmth as she tried not to think too much about their intimate position. Hypothermia 101, she reminded herself and then relaxed enough to go back to sleep.

Elise woke early the next morning to a soft growling purr near her ear and still cradled within Eirik's arm, except now he was lying on his back and her head was on his shoulder with her arm across his chest. She must have gotten hot again during the night because the upper portion of their bodies were exposed, but she wasn't cold. With the furs ending at their waists, she could clearly see the full expanse of his chest right down to his...

"Pisswick and the raven sighed," Eirik mumbled to himself as he carefully grasped her hand to move it from his chest so he could get up.

"What's wrong?" Elise said as she jumped from him startling her.

"My apologies, I nary meant ta wake you. 'Twould seem I've slept in a might," he said as he now delayed his departure. He had intended on rising before she woke so that he could dress without offending her but seems that raven has flown.

"It's all right. I should probably get up too, to start breakfast," she said as she started to move.

His arm tightened around her, "Nay, you have time yet," he

said thoughtfully as he brought her hand to his lips and gently kissed it before he laid it on her hip then slid his arm out from under her as he sat up. He sat there for a moment gathering his thoughts, then rose and opened a chest to find clean breeches and pulled them into place before getting out a serk and tunic. As he turned to rekindle the fire, he glanced Elise's way to see if she had fallen back to sleep, nary had she done so.

Elise had stared at Eirik's back when he sat up and was amazed by the full tattoo in the design of a dragon, she presumed, by the scales and wings it depicted along with the gaping sharp tooth grin it wore on its thorny face. It was so lifelike that she had reached out to touch it, but he had stood and moved away. Her eyes had followed him across the room with his movements right up until he faced her.

"Absolutely beautiful," she said as she brought her eyes up to meet his and smiled, bringing the furs up around her.

Smiling, he squatted and cocked his head as he blew across the embers while he tossed on small sticks and peat then swung the water over it to heat. He was grinning so big he could hardly purse his lips to blow, when she said that, but now he realized it must have been his back that she referred to, not him. He looked at her as he straightened, just her head peeked out of the furs, and he chuckled before he strode her way and sat beside her as he waited for the water to get hot.

"I thought mayhap you'd go back ta sleep, but seems I was mistaken," his lips curled as he glanced over her only feature that remained unhidden; her eyes, because the fur now covered her nose as well. He placed his hand on her torso, his heat penetrating the furs, as he said, "As I was mistaken by your words just now. My pride and vanity emblazed thus 'twould sear the raven's wing with your words, ta think you thought such of me. Only ta diminish ta ember when I grasped that they were for something that was not altogether me, but merely displayed upon me. Within this moment, it occurred ta me how much I greatly desired the other to be true." He sighed and then mumbled, "Oh, Bragi wept," as he rose from the bed to continue getting ready for the day.

"Wait," she said quickly and fought with the covers to get out from under them. He reseated himself. "I'm speechless," she said as she sat up and grabbed his hand. "The dragon on your back is indeed beautiful, but pales in comparison. Trust me," she licked her dry lips, "You are... hot," she chuckled out. "I'm sorry, I'm not a poet, but there it is," she grinned up at him.

He blinked as only the left half of his mouth curled into a smile. It nigh sounded like a compliment. "My apologies for the heat I exude, but I thought of all, that is what pleased you most," he said as he gestured toward their hands.

She laughed and shook her head. "Yes, you're that kind of hot too, but I mean," she opened her eyes wide and said, "HOT! Sexy, provocative, gorgeous, magnificent, stunning, lovely, and beautiful," she rambled trying to find a word that he understood.

That brought the full smile to his lips as he grasped her meaning through only some of the words she spoke, having his ego sufficiently stoked once again. Then he tilted his head and said, "Why have you nary said as much until now, nor showed much interest? I have been trying ta bring about such emotion within you since... well always."

She shook her head as she lowered it. "You know why," she mumbled.

"Nay, I do not," he raised her head by two fingers poised under her chin. "'Tis why I asked."

"Home," she said quietly.

He sighed deeply as he searched her eyes before lowering his hand. "I need must tell you of something I have been loath ta say, but you have removed my choice." He tightened his lips as he gazed at her. "This island, my home, is extraordinary. As I exude heat, it exudes Heill," he pulled her hand up to rest on his chest to feel the heat within him. "I am enthralled by it and bound to it, like this," he intertwined their fingers together.

Elise nodded slowly but also furrowed her brows. "What is Heill?" she asked.

He shook his head, "Nary do I have the words, but I feel it

all around me even as it flows through me." He sighed, "What I'm trying to say is that it can happen to you too, if you're here long enough. Nay." He shook his head and prayed the right words would flow from his lips. "Others have come here before, mainlanders and seafarers, both. Those that consent ta the bond, stay and those that decline, within a fortnight and a half they vanish."

"You mean leave?"

"Nay, I mean vanish. I know naught where they go, they're just nary here any longer nor do we see them again. Although, we've ne'er had a visit from one such as you and your kith, from another time. 'Twas always within my time or nigh enough there was nil ta distinguish."

"Are you telling me that if we choose not to stay then we'll just disappear?"

"Vanish, aye," he said at the same time he nodded his head. "'Tis nary the fate I wish for you."

"But if we stay, we can't ever leave, right? No going home ever?"

"Methinks there be nary going home ever now. 'Tis hard ta fathom how ta do so," he said as he looked at her. "I wish for you ta stay."

"Eirik, even if I decided to stay, I have to at least try to find a way for the others to go home, especially Jesse, the twins, and Bo. I can't imagine any of them choosing to stay here if they had the choice. Can you understand that?"

He smiled softly as he nodded, all he heard was, 'I decided to stay' and stopped listening after that. 'Twas going ta be a good day. Between those words and waking with her in his arms, 'twas for certain a good day.

"Eirik?" she said as she considered his face.

"Aye, for certain," his lips curved. "But for the now, perhaps we should ready ourselves for the day for it has gotten away from us."

"That's true," she said as she noticed the brightness of the room and moved to get up.

Eirik stood with her and went immediately to get the water. They each readied themselves in their own way, but shared the bowl of water, to which he had to add cold water to cool it for her. However, he did pause in his grooming to watch in amazement as she brushed her teeth. Deciding right then and there that he must also have one of those tiny brushes in which to scrub his teeth clean. It seemed much more capable than the frayed sticks that he would use. When he was completely dressed, he then sat on the bed and watched her finish. She had braided her hair once again and dressed in the tight-fitting breeches and a bright blue snug bodice but was now applying lacquer to her lips which he eyed with skepticism.

He stood when she turned toward him and smiled as he drew closer. "What be that?" he asked as he scrutinized her lips.

"What?"

"That which make your lips as glass," he sniffed the air between them, and it had a fruity aroma, nary akin ta the mint with which she scrubbed her teeth. 'Twas more like strawberries, but sweeter. He licked his lips and slanted toward her just for a taste as his hands came to her shoulders and nudged her to him. He pressed his lips gently against hers, finding them slippery yet sticky, much like honey. But as he did so, she moved hers across his, igniting his heart, causing it to throb within, and he pulled her closer deepening the kiss and compelling him to linger longer than he first intended, then he eased back and licked his lips. "Strawberries," he breathed out.

"Lip gloss," she breathed out, completely overwhelmed by him then shook her head. "Breakfast," she said louder. "We need to get moving."

Eirik cleared his throat. "Aye, 'tis work ta be done," but he couldn't keep the smile from his glossy lips.

As he started to turn toward the door, she snagged his arm turning him back to her and slid a wet cloth across his mouth as she smiled up at him and said, "The silent kiss and tell." Then did the same to her own.

"Nary would I mind so much," he winked, but thought that

he'd never hear the end of it from his brother, although he would happily endure.

"I'm sure you wouldn't," she chuckled and followed him to the door.

As they entered the hall, she saw the table had been set and cringed, but then smiled as she noticed Eirik seemed to swagger as she followed him toward the table. Instead of sitting with him she went into the kitchen to help whoever was up preparing food. She could smell pancakes but could hardly believe who was doing the cooking.

Jesse was just pulling one off the pan with a large wide bladed knife and carefully added it to the stack as Sara was frying bacon closer to the fire. "Jesse, I didn't know you could cook," Elise said astonished.

"Shush, not so loud," he feigned a frowned before he smiled. "I needed a bit more carbs with my protein," he said as he poured more batter on the pan.

Sara smiled over to him then up at Elise and said, "He had had the pork sliced up even before I got in here. I don't think it'll taste like bacon, but it's as close as we can get right now. But those pancakes smell like the real thing."

"Can I help with anything?" Elise asked as she glanced over the kitchen seeing that it had been cleaned last night and felt a bit guilty for it. "Maybe make some syrup?"

"Nah, we got this," Jesse said as he turned the pancake and then smiled at her.

"Okay, but if you need me, I'll be right out here," she indicated to the hall as she turned and went through the door. She paused briefly when she saw that Leif and Eirik were speaking in rather hushed tones, but then continued when Eirik gestured for her to come. "I didn't want to intrude," she said as she approached.

"Nay, Milady, nil intrusion," Leif grinned up at her.

"We were just speaking of the plans for the day," Eirik said. Elise eyed him then raised a brow. "I had asked you about Bo on our first meeting, but ne'er thought ta ask about Jesse," he elaborated then bit his lips together as he met her eyes.

After a moment's thought, a long moment, she grasped his meaning and chuckled. "No," she shook her head, "No, he isn't. Please understand that our culture differs greatly from yours. Women work alongside men beyond the threshold just as men enjoy culinary work," she smiled.

Leif grinned as Eirik said, also with a broad grin, "Culinary work? Methinks 'tis nary mean what it sounds."

"No, it does not, I'm sure. Cooking, he enjoys cooking," she chuckled down at them. "Although, he probably enjoys the other as well, but I'd rather not go there."

"Aye, I wish you nary ta go there either," Eirik said and winked.

"What more did you have planned for today besides discussing sexual preferences?" she asked as she took her place at the table.

"Again, I can only guess your meaning," Eirik smiled at her.

"Well, I'm not going to explain that one," she laughed. "For it's a vast subject."

"Speaking of which, 'twas thinking on starting the fields, but I had another thought ta replace. Leif wishes ta help Bo with the windcatcher after the animals are cared for, so I thought of teaching you some bladeplay, ta ensure your safety should we not be about."

Elise arched a brow at him then looked to Leif's smiling face before returning her gaze back to Eirik and said, "What kind of blade?" then smiled.

"'Tis but a small one ta hide within your clothing," he glanced over her apparel. "Mayhap, nary hide so much."

"A fibula? I was hoping for at least a saex," she said and sighed out her breath.

Sara came through the door carrying a tray of 'bacon' and cheese followed by Jesse with a huge tray overflowing with pancakes and set them near the middle of the table. "Is Bo not up yet?" she asked seeing just the two men as Jesse returned to the kitchen to get the syrup.

"Oh gosh, we've been talking, and time just got away from

me. I'll go check on them," Elise said and started to rise.

"The girls will be out soon," Bo said as he came toward the table. "I've been up, just working out the schematics in my head for the pump." He smiled as he took a seat beside Leif.

Once everyone was seated, they began filling their plates with the delightful foods. It truly was a taste of home, Elise thought as she cut into her second dinner plate sized pancake. "I must say it, Jesse, these are absolutely wonderful," she grinned at him. "Oh, sorry, I forgot. You have a rep to protect," she giggled. He simply grinned back at her exposing those dimples as he ate.

"Aye, 'tis sweet cakes," Leif said and smiled.

As they ate their fill, Bo and Leif discussed the windmill and Sara talked with Tristan and Kristin about making something different than chicken stew for their dinner, even Jesse chimed in a few ideas as Elise and Eirik stayed quiet and listened.

When she pushed her plate away but continued to listen, Eirik slid his hand to her knee causing her to glance up at him. He smiled gently and inclined his head towards the others, but she shook her head and rose from her seat to take her dish to the kitchen. He followed her with his own.

"Not yet, Eirik, not today. I can't tell them today," she looked up at him and tightened her lips.

He set his trencher on the table as he drew closer, and said, "Mayhap nary this day, but soon. I feel they are settling in and may nary be as upset as you think."

"They'll be upset. They'll miss their families, Eirik. They may be coping now, but three of them are clueless, I'm sure. I just would rather not tell them today, please?"

"Aye," he said and sighed as he drew her into him. "But soon," he whispered and pressed his lips to her head.

"Soon, I promise," she said and stepped back then smiled up at him. Having him that close nearly overheated her, he emitted so much heat. "Are you sure that you aren't sick, you feel like you're on fire?" she said as she raised a hand to his forehead.

He caught it and chuckled, "Nay, I'm nary ill. 'Tis normal for me, nigh enough, but I seem ta emit more around you. That 'tis nary so normal but worries me naught. I be certain of the cause," he winked at her.

"Are you saying that I'm the cause?" she said softly so as not to be overheard.

"Aye, 'tis for certain," he chuckled and laid her hand upon his chest. "See, it emanates from here outward."

Elise could definitely feel the heat radiate from his chest, but it didn't quell her fears, if anything, it made her worry more. "If you're sure, I'll try not to worry."

He moved her hand up to his lips before he released it and smiled. "I have a task ta do after caring for the stock, but I'll be back shortly thereafter for our bedplay…," he closed his eyes and slowly said the word, "Bladeplay," before he opened them again and smiled. "My apologies, truly so. Bragi has abandoned my tongue."

Elise smiled as she bit her lips together before she said, "It sounds more like Freya has hijacked your head."

"Hijacked?" he furrowed his brows.

"Um… stolen? Captured? Raided and taken over or sacked," she arched a brow to see if that made more sense to him.

"Ah, aye, I grasp the notion and mayhap so. 'Twill return by the time the washing is finished," he winked and kissed her brow then turned away and headed out the door as Sara came in with a stack of trenchers.

She smiled quietly at Elise as she set them on the table and paused before she said, "You two are getting along better."

Elise rolled her eyes then smiled as she leaned against the table. "And you don't look one bit surprised. If I didn't know any better, I'd say you choreographed it in some way."

Sara giggled, "Well you deserve to be happy and he's hot!"

Elise turned away to get the water boiling to do dishes as she saw Tristan and Kristin come in with the rest of the dishes and leftover pancakes. "Who's hot?" Tristan asked as she set the pancake platter down beside the load Kristin carried.

"Eirik," Sara said and wiggled her brows at them.

"I prefer blonds, like Leif," Kristin said and giggled. "Now, his hotness factor is to die for."

"You don't think they're too," Tristan shrugged as she thought of a word, "big?"

"Not at all," Kristin giggled, "I like them strong and athletic with lots of muscles."

"I don't know," Tristan shrugged, "Big men scare me, especially the alpha types," she scrunched up her nose a bit.

"Oh, not me," Kristin said wistfully and smiled.

"I don't know," Sara said, "There's something about a man that is strong enough to offer you protection, but at the same time be gentle or tender with you."

"Yeah, but in my experience, those alpha types are savage," Tristan said then turned away to finish cleaning off the high table.

"She just thinks that way because a certain member on the football team crushed her with his aggressive behavior," Kristin divulged in whispered tones.

"Not Jesse, I hope," Sara said, "Because that would be awkward."

"No, not Jesse," she giggled, "He's more of the defender type, even if he doesn't show it most of the time. I think his tough arrogance is mostly an act. I've seen him with kids at the hospital that we used to volunteer at."

Elise couldn't keep the smile from her face as she listened quietly to the 'girl talk' going on around her. She had never heard them all talk in such a way, at least not around her and they seemed so relaxed she didn't want to ruin it, so she let them talk as she busied herself with cleaning up.

After the kitchen was cleaned and they prepared a roast for their dinner, Elise said, "Guess what today is?" She paused to look at each of their faces. "Washing day, which means we have to lug all the dirty clothes up to the tarn to wash," she waited for their groans to die down before she continued. "However, it also means we actually get to take a bath today and wash our hair," she grinned.

"I think I'm going to like Saturdays," Kristin laughed.

"Yeah, it'll be nice to have everyone smelling good, rather than the foul odors of late," Sara giggled. "I'll be glad when they're finished with the barn."

They each nodded in agreement then separated to gather everyone's dirty clothes. Elise entered Eirik's chamber and glanced around in wonder what she was going to carry all the clothes in. She supposed she could use her suitcase and then began taking out her clean clothes and shoving in the dirty ones, she even put Eirik's in with hers.

Once it was all gathered, they made their way up to the tarn. Elise set the case down and stood there looking over the small lake, smiling. It was a beautiful setting, even spring flowers were in an abundance surrounding it. She could even hear splashing water from somewhere, and after a bit of investigating she found that just below the tarn, around a rocky outcropping, water skimmed off the top of the lake and poured down into a stone room then trickled out once it reached a certain height. "This must be the bathroom," she said to herself as she inspected it. "I bet we can wash the clothes in here too." Having that resolved, she turned to get the clothing.

The girls made quick work of the washing; two washed and rinsed while the other two took them back to the house instead of laying them on the stones to dry. They spread them about the great hall. Elise thought they would dry faster this way and then they wouldn't have to return to the tarn to retrieve them after they were dry.

On one of the trips back to the tarn, Elise saw a mounted figure on the rise above the tarn and quickened her steps toward the girls, hoping he didn't come down, as she kept her gaze on him. When she arrived, she stood outside the washroom to keep watch as she hurried them. Luckily, they were nearly finished, and she sent them back as she gathered up what was left.

As she exited the washhouse, she saw the man was nearly to her and there was no way she could get back to the house in time. Whatever happens, she was glad the girls weren't there now. She held the dripping clothing in front of her as she watched him draw closer.

"Greetings, Milady," the man said as he pushed his hood back revealing light red hair that hung freely and straight around his head but seemed to be shaved above his ears and a short, trimmed to a point, beard and mustache of the same color, and she recognized him to be the same man they came across in the village. She hadn't seen his face then, but the voice was the same. What was his name again?

"Good day," she smiled up at him politely, but then noticed the bow and two dead cats dangling from his horse and unintentionally scowled.

"Fine day for washing," his slim mouth creased into a mischievous grin as his narrow blue eyes looked from beneath a heavy brow and down his sharp nose as they wandered over her appearance.

"Aye, 'tis so," she said adopting a bit more of their language so as not to completely give away her foreign origin.

"Sir Eirik about?" he asked as he scanned the landscape for any others before he dismounted and tossed half his cloak over his shoulder to expose his thickened sword arm as he moved toward her. She could see now that he wasn't as tall as the brothers but broad and formidable just the same.

"Nay, the now. 'Twill be returning shortly," she said as she wanted to retreat from this man, but held her ground. She really wished she had brought a knife or sword with her but had thought they'd be safe on this land.

He lifted a sleek brow. "How shortly?" his grin widened.

"Any time now," she said eyeing him suspiciously.

He drew closer as his icy blue eyes scanned her form and his grin never faded. "He ought not leave such a fair lady on her own. He may return ta find her... ruined," he flicked a brow with his last word as he closed in on her with his arms stretched a bit to corral her.

Elise raised her chin a bit to display her defiance and fixed her jaw, but still hugged the clothing to her. "'Twould one dare such a feat on his own lands?" she arched a brow and held his gaze.

"Who would tell?" he asked as he quickly glanced at the area to his left and right while still advancing on her. "What could he do, once done?"

Elise shifted her weight to one foot as she held tighter to the clothes with her left arm and loosened her grip with her right. She just needed to be able to grab his knife, but with a quick glance she saw he wasn't carrying one. "He won't be pleased," she warned as she slowly turned her right foot toward the house. She was going to make a run for it.

"Nay, I expect not, but 'tis naught ta be done once done," he grinned shifting slightly to his right and taking small steps the closer he got to her, ready to lunge or give chase.

Elise tossed the clothes at him as she shot out toward the homestead as fast as she could run, but she didn't get four strides before she was brought to the ground by his weight, landing hard on her chest. As she struggled to free herself from beneath him, she felt him grasping at her hands and flipped her over onto her back. That was his mistake. Once on her back, she brought her leg up, hooked her heel around his neck, and pulled him backward off from her then she scrambled to her feet quickly. She ran back to the washing house to look for anything that she could use for a weapon as the man regained his footing.

Sun's day

The Bond

"Good day," Eirik's familiar baritone voice shouted from somewhere behind the man.

"Greetings," Nidpigger turned with a smarmy smile as he greeted him and danced his direction. "Have ye had word as yet?"

"Nay," Eirik said with a scowl drawing his brows together as he dismounted and moved toward him. The horse followed with flattened ears and swung his head as he snorted at the other mount causing it to whinny and dodge away. "I will come ta you, Nidpigger, if needs must," he said as he hastily surveyed Elise standing just outside the bathhouse. He then turned his glare on the man and took three long strides toward him grabbing the front of his cloak within his right fist as his left gestured toward Elise. "She is mine!" he shouted in the man's face and shoved him away from him. Nidpigger stumbled back a few paces from both the shove and the intensity of the blazing look in his eyes. And as Eirik waved his arm out, he said roughly, "Away with you."

The gesture caused Nidpigger's mount to neigh and rear several times before he could get control of it. "Aye, Milord," Nidpigger said lowly and alighted then galloped off over the rise.

Eirik glanced at Elise and tightened his lips as he approached her. "My apologies, Milady," he said quietly and brushed his lips to her head. He could feel her body tremble within his arms and sighed out his breath. "Nary harm befell you, aye?"

"No, I'm all right," she said as her teeth chattered.

"Back ta the house with you then. I'll follow shortly," he smiled as he eased away from her.

Elise let out her breath as she hurriedly gathered up the clothing and went to the house. All kinds of scenarios bombarded her thoughts of what could have happened and was glad Eirik showed up when he did. She would have to keep a better watch on the girls. He had warned her that there were some bad elements here.

Eirik caught up to her before she made it to the longhouse and dismounted to walk with her as the horse went toward the barn. "Mayhap you should carry this while beyond the threshold," he said as he removed his knife from his thigh.

"I didn't realize anyone would deign to do harm on *your* land," she said looking up at him and shivered.

"Aye, methinks 'tis just him, but ta be certain stay close ta the house unless Leif or I be with you."

"You can't be with us all the time, Eirik, you have your own work to do."

"Please...," he sighed out and faced her, "I wish nil harm ta any of you. Mayhap he had nil ill intentions, mayhap so...," he shook his head. "Just stay close, aye?"

"We will, but if you'd just give me a real sword instead of that tiny bug sticker then you won't have to delay your work when we need to wash or get water," she said looking up at him with her brows furrowed.

Eirik glanced down at the knife he held; it was nigh three quarters the length of a sword. And she called it tiny? "Aye, set your clothing aside and we shall see," he grinned at her.

"You're on," she smiled and entered the longhouse to lay out the clothes to dry.

Eirik followed but went directly to the second door on the right, the one between Eirik's and Leif's, and unlocked it before entering. She watched the door as she laid the clothes out and then stood by the central fire to dry a bit. When he came out, he carried two swords with ornate scabbards and shiny hilts.

"You ready?" he grinned, and she nodded.

Once they crossed the threshold, he handed her the swords while he pulled his hair back and tied it out of his way. Elise inspected each sword closely, happy to see they were dulled. Practice swords. She tested their weight in comparison to what she was used to, as well as how well each grip felt in her hand. They both were a bit heavier than her own, which was made just for her, but she thought she could use the one she now gripped and rotated in her hand.

"It's been a few months since I wielded a sword, so start off slow until I warm up," she smiled as she looked up at him and held the other sword out.

"For a certain," he grinned accepting the sword and removed the scabbard as she did the same.

She grasped the pommel and wrapped her fingers around the grip leaving more room between her fingers and the cross-guard than she preferred, but she didn't have a choice. She had to use what was available. As she took a few test swings to become acquainted with it, she kept her eyes on him. He seemed completely relaxed, as if he was simply humoring her. She took her stance, ready for the physical activity to warm her.

Eirik teased her blade a few times, testing her strength and grip on the sword, once he was certain she held it securely, he lunged with a downward stroke, to which she sidestepped, parried, rotated her wrist, and brought the point up to his chest. She backed away and watched for his next attack.

He then brought his sword down, aiming low at her thigh, which gave her enough time to step into his space and block his arm with her own as she brought her sword up betwixt his legs and tapped his inner thighs. She moved off again, not showing the smile that threatened to crease her lips.

With a grin, he lunged forward with a thrust, which she parried, but he returned with another downward stroke toward her shoulder, and she brought her sword up high on the outside of his, pushing it back as she stepped to her left ducking beneath his arm and twisted her wrist bringing her sword forward to stop at his neck. He knocked her sword away with his own, not allowing her to reset as he swung down again toward her left shoulder, but when she advanced to block it with her arm as she had before, he moved quickly to his right and forward bringing his sword down across her back, hard enough for her to feel it but achieved no injury. She pivoted to face him and bent her knees slightly as she readied for his next attack. He whipped his sword down across his body to strike her right shoulder, she blocked and pushed it off to her right twisting her wrist to allow his sword to slide down her blade as she used her left hand to also push his arm to her right to knock him off balance. However, he simply bent his knee and circled his arm high to bring it back toward the left side of her torso, which she blocked once again with an upward stroke. Using her upward momentum, he raised his arm for another downward strike. As she raised her arm to block, he swept his left heel around her right foot and surged forward, effectively sending her to the ground.

Elise held her sword across her body to defend any strikes he may throw while she rocked back up to her feet and advanced on him with his favorite downward stroke to his left, he parried and brought it back with a twist of his wrist to stop at her neck. She smiled and conceded then stepped back to reset.

After several more lengthy sets, Eirik came down with blow after blow in quick succession, which she blocked of course, but he didn't let up, he hammered her sword until she pushed him away from her and dropped her sword to the ground. She held her hands up, to show that she yielded as her breaths came heavily and she felt the sweat run down her back.

"I... gotta... get... dinner," she huffed out between quick breaths and then after inhaling deeply, she finished, "Started." She smiled up at him and nodded then as she turned toward the door, she saw all the others standing there watching them. She had just enough air left to say, "Next," and chuckled as she went through the door.

Eirik was on her heels though, picking up her sword and the

scabbards as he did so. "She did well," he said with a smile to Leif as he passed him.

"Aye. I wonder what she could do with a shield," he grinned as he walked beside him.

"True," he raised a brow at him. "Mayhap on the morrow, we shall see. For the now, take the lads ta the tarn ta bathe and keep a wary eye. Nidpigger was about hunting cats in the wood and is aware of Elise," he said the last bit quietly.

"I've always loved watching her fight," Sara said from behind them, and they turned to look at her. "Believe it or not, she's actually better with a longsword," she grinned.

"Ah, 'twould explain some of her moves," Eirik said. "But where did she learn her skills?"

"She was taught at a training academy. Sometimes she would hold demonstrations at our school too," she said then moved passed them to go to the kitchen while Tristan and Kristin finished folding the now dry clothes.

"Did you know she could fence?" Jesse asked Bo in awe of what he just witnessed.

"Yeah, but I've only seen her do it a couple of times at Festival," Bo replied with a shrug.

When Eirik entered his chamber, he hung the swords on a peg by the door and glanced around the room. Elise was washing her face in cold water from the bucket, not having time to warm it first. "You did well," he said lowly. "I had nary grasped you had skill wielding a sword. Most women use a shield and knife ta defend themselves, if needs must, but very few a sword."

"Thanks for the work out, by the way. I'm a bit rusty, but the more I do it, the sooner it'll come back to me. I don't think I've ever fought someone with your height and strength before; it was a good lesson. And I definitely need to build my stamina," she said and threw the cloth on the table then looked up at him.

"Stamina?" he arched a brow at her as his lip twitched. "'Tis ta be able ta endure longer, aye?"

"Yes, it's something I lose in the winter," she laughed.

He drew closer and pressed his lips to her head as he smiled.

"As we all do, to be certain. I've sent the lads ta the tarn with Leif ta bathe and then after we sup, you and I will accompany the lasses, aye?"

"Sure," she nodded up at him with a smile and moved to the door. After such a workout, him standing that close to her radiating his heat, nearly caused the sweat to breakout across her face again. She needed some distance... for now.

Elise entered the kitchen and began setting out trays to put various foods on and then turned to check on the roast they had started earlier. It smelled divine and she was starving. She also retrieved the cheesecake she had made the day before and jugs of water and beer. Sara came in to get the trenchers and cups then smiled over at Elise.

"I think you made an impression on them," she giggled as she gathered the items.

"Yeah, I don't think he took me serious at first," she laughed. "Warrior women kind of go against their masculine beliefs. You know, we're here to serve them because they don't have the time, they're always off doing manly things," she laughed again. "But at least these two don't seem that way, well, not entirely."

Sara giggled as she carried the plates out and set them along the table then returned for the cups. "You know it makes me wonder what they would think of our archery skills," she said thoughtfully. "Every one of us had to take either archery or fencing in school. I bet they do think we are defenseless."

"We are, Sara, without the weapons, we are. As I found out today. That man had some ugly things on his mind, and I didn't have a weapon to defend myself. I shudder to think what would have happened if Eirik hadn't showed up when he did."

"Well, it was a good thing he did then. I take it lesson learned?" she smiled as she loaded a tray with cups and utensils as well as the two pitchers.

"For sure. No one goes anywhere outside alone. Even tonight after dinner, Eirik's going to escort us up to the bathhouse. He wasn't at all pleased to see this man."

"Did you tell him what happened or was about to happen?"

Elise shook her head, "No, I didn't want to have to clean blood out of his clothes," she grinned, making light of the situation. Sara chuckled and carried the cups out as Elise started cutting up the roast and putting it on a tray.

When Sara returned, Kristin and Tristan came with her to help bring out the food. By the time they had the table laid, the men came in smelling much better than previously, and Eirik was already seated at the table. He lifted a brow at Leif who wore his hair down and unbraided this eve, to which he shook his head and sat across from him then filled his cup.

"'Tis a clear night," Leif said then drank from his cup as his mouth watered at the delicious aroma wafting up from the meat and the lads took their normal seats.

Once the women were seated, they began to fill their trenchers. Leif inspected the cheesecake closely and then passed it up. He would wait ta see what the others would do with it. As they ate, Bo updated the others on his progress with the windmill and said that they should be able to start laying the pipes in a couple of days and then they would have running water near the house and barn, which made everyone happy. After which, their conversation moved from idle chatter to the kid's amazement of Elise's swordsmanship. She chuckled and accused Eirik of going easy on her, to which he denied. When she cut a slice of the cheesecake off for herself, both Leif and Eirik watched.

Just as she was raising her fork to her mouth, she noticed their intense stare and stopped. "What?"

"What is it?" Leif asked and nodded toward her plate.

"It's cheesecake, a dessert... um," she thought for a moment how best to describe it.

"Sweet cheese," Sara said with a smile. "I like it with fruit, but it's just as good by itself."

"Ah," they said in unison then pushed their plates toward it.

Sara obliged them with a slice each then got one for herself and the others, but before she finished, Leif slid his plate back for another slice with a grin.

"I think Leif has a sweet tooth," Elise laughed.

"Aye, 'tis surprising we have any honey at all in the stores," Eirik grinned at her.

After Elise devoured her cheesecake, she rose to take her plate and any others back to the kitchen. Once the table was cleared and the kitchen cleaned up, Eirik and Elise walked behind the girls up to the bathhouse, armed this time, which made her feel better, but she was still on edge. Elise kept her head revolving as she looked for any approaching figures in the moonlight.

Eirik, amused, said, "Nil need ta be worrisome," as he placed his hand on her shoulder, crossing over her back. "I have doubt that he'll return this night," he said quietly so the girls wouldn't hear and pulled her closer to him.

She gave him a disbelieving look and continued to survey the area. "I'm not quite so certain," she sighed and turned to check behind them as well.

"Be assured, Milady," he smiled as they approached the stone house. "I'll rekindle the fire then return." He rounded the small house and blew across the smoldering fire to reignite the flames as he pushed more pieces of wood and peat into the cubby that resided beneath the stone slab aqueduct that funneled the water into the bathhouse.

While Eirik was lighting the fire for them, Elise kept her eyes on the landscape, but had the girls go ahead and get started. Soon she could smell the scent of lavender and smiled as she heard them laugh and giggle while they bathed. It was a good sound to hear after the day she had.

Sara was the first to come out. "I know we brought our own stuff up, but there's an assortment of soaps and oils in there that wasn't there when we did laundry," she said as she smiled at her. "And candles too. He must really like you to spend so much," she nudged her with an elbow.

"Maybe he was just tired of smelling manure," Elise chuckled, and Sara laughed. "Whatever the case, it smells good now."

"Oh, my god, I feel so much better," Kristin said as she emerged from the door.

"Me too, almost human," Tristan agreed as she followed her out.

"Good," Elise smiled at them. "I won't be long," she said as she ducked inside.

"Take your time," Sara said after her.

Elise laid the sword down on the stone bench that ran along one of the outer walls then sat as she unlaced her shoes and unbraided her hair. The fragrance of the room reminded her of the relaxing aromatherapy baths she used to take at the spa near her apartment. She sighed out her breath as she stood to undress, tossing her clothes on the bench before she stepped into the water. Sinking up to her neck, she tilted her head back to wet her hair before washing it, and then sat on the wide bench beneath the water. Just washing her hair made her feel one hundred percent cleaner. She quickly washed her face and body so she could simply relax for the rest of the time she had. Having her back to the wall of the small rectangular shaped pool, she took just a tiny moment and laid her head on the rim and closed her eyes. The water was warm, the aroma relaxing, and the amber flicker of the candles created a most soothing ambiance.

"'Tis pleasing to you?" Eirik asked from behind her.

Elise jerked upright and popped open her eyes. "For a certain," she chuckled, using his phrase. "I didn't mean to take so long, it just felt incredibly good to soak for a minute. Tell the girls I'll be out soon," she said without turning toward him.

"I have accompanied them ta the house. 'Tis nary a hurry," he said as he too undressed and stepped into the warm water across from her then curved his lips when their eyes met. He pulled the ties from his hair and tilted his head beneath the inlet of water, saturating it then smoothed it out of his face before he moved closer to her, sitting in the corner with the water reaching only up to his chest. "'Twas of a purpose. I wish you ta be at peace for a bit, Milady," he said as he reached for her arm, pulling her gently to him, and turned her to lie back against his chest as his left arm rested on top of the surround.

Elise was far from relaxed now. The scene she had just

witnessed could have been performed on the playgirl channel, she thought as she reclined against him rather stiffly, although it was more comfortable than the stone side of the pool. She was alert to every movement when he reached for the soap and then began smoothing it over her arm and shoulder. Was he planning on bathing her? Maybe, but she dropped that worry when he moved her hair aside and his hand began massaging her right shoulder in strong large circles. What she thought was soap must have been oil instead.

"Oh," the moan slipped out before she could stop it, but then she covered with, "That feels wonderful, especially after that workout today."

"'Twas my intention," he murmured as the rotations moved from her shoulder to her neck then down her back before returning to her shoulder.

"Uh huh," she mumbled and closed her eyes, yielding to the intense massage, which progressively pushed her toward his left shoulder with the pressure he used.

Eirik lowered his left arm into the water and encircled her to hold her upright as he applied more pressure, then when he was satisfied her muscles wouldn't be stiff in the morning, he pulled her back against him leaving his right hand on the front of her shoulder curling his fingers around it. With his heart ignited by her nearness, he tilted his head and kissed her neck softly, not wishing to disturb her peaceful countenance. But when she moved her head aside, he believed it to be an invitation, and continued right up to her ear. "'Tis better?" he asked lowly. And of a sudden, her skin broke out into goosebumps, drawing a breathy and private laugh from him in amusement, before he resumed to gently place kisses along her neck. He was encouraged further when she raised her hand to cup his head. Sliding his hand down her arm, he pressed the flat of his palm alongside her breast before gliding down her ribs then returned to cup and caress her ample and malleable flesh, to which she rose to meet. His other hand journeyed further down skimming across her stomach to the apex of her thighs and rubbed along her furrow, causing a gasp to escape her lips.

"Will you stay with me?" he asked in a throaty whisper as he continued to ply her with caresses. He needed to know before they went any further, for as hot as his heart burned for her, he knew it would certainly result in a bonding, not that most bondings happened as such, but he knew this one would. He felt as if his heart reached out to her and if he was to have but one life mate in all his existence, he wanted it to be her. And without her consent, the bonding would nary last, would nary stay true.

Elise, mesmerized by his touch, opened her eyes briefly as his question sank into her numb brain and she could see steam now rising from the water. "On the island?" she clarified before she answered as she floated her hand over his arm and encouraged his calloused hand.

"Aye, 'tis my meaning," he answered just as he engulfed her earlobe.

Her grip tightened briefly in his hair and on his hand that covered her breast. "Yes," she said but it sounded more like a moan.

"As my mate?" he rasped in her ear and then moved toward her trapezius as his fingers worked farther into her slickened opening while his thumb pressed against her rootling.

"Yes," she whimpered and tilted her head back into him as her hand shadowed his.

With her answer and in one swift motion, he stood with her as he sustained his expert massaging. He wanted to take her back to the house where he could lie with her on the comfort of his bed as she so deserved, which was his intention when he stood, but he nary wished to lose his momentum either, knowing the chill night would douse her flame.

She turned to face him and reached up as he inclined his head, both devouring the other's mouth, tongues tangling and exploring. She wanted to climb him like a tree but refrained from doing so when she felt him pull away slightly and kissed her forehead before he embraced her against him and mumbled something over her head. She thought she heard the word Heill.

But all thoughts scattered when he slid his hand down over her ass and gripped her thighs then lifted her off her feet, carried her to the edge, and laid her on top of his clothing on the floor. She felt completely exposed without him against her and fought the urge to cover herself as he stood over her, but still in the pool, staring at her. His nostrils flared slightly as he gazed over her with shining eyes until he crawled forward and settled between her thighs. With one long stroke, he ran his tongue over her folds and lapped and licked at her nub drawing a sighing moan from her lips as her hips tilted to him. He suckled her as he pushed his fingers into her and withdrew them in a sensually slow succession causing her to moan loudly as she closed her eyes and her hands searched for something to grip. She wouldn't last long with his talent, so she reached for him. She could still hear him murmuring as she embraced him, drifting her hands across his back as he eased down paying homage to her breasts. He sucked hard on her beaded nipple and scraped his teeth against it as he rubbed himself against her, drawing soft moans from her, before he returned to her mouth. He wanted ta do so much more for her, but his heart was calling, nay, demanding he create the bond now.

Eirik continued his mumbling chant to form their mating bond as he slowly entered her, and she lifted her legs over him and hugged his body into her with her feet at the small of his back, driving him in farther. "Freya wept," he growled lowly as the feeling engulfed him and traveled throughout his body. She rotated her hips to encourage him, triggering his leisurely insertions to bring them fulfillment.

As he teasingly moved within her, Elise thought she had been set ablaze. At first, it was just where their bodies made contact, but now it flowed like thick molten lava through her veins. She clawed and raked her nails down his back in effort to climb into him as if that would allow her to reach her goal, to become one. The more blissful she felt, the hotter it burned, but it wasn't a bad feeling as it hit the pleasure-pain center in her brain. She needed to be closer to him, within him. She kissed him with everything she had as her hands cupped his backside and pulled him even tighter into her. She might have heard him moan but she couldn't tell for her own gasp was louder.

Eirik quickened his movements at her beckoning as well as his own base needs must urged him farther. He was nigh ta his summit, but would dare naught until she did, but when he felt her essence-flame catch, he groaned as his eyes rolled back and he slowed, going deeper and swived against her, prolonging the erotic feeling. But when he felt her tentacled fire reach out grappling for his and seizing an unyielding hold, he brought her into his arms and kissed her thoroughly as he quickened their pace until their flames burned as one and they cried out together.

As much as he wished to languish in the afterglow, he knew he needed to cool her. After he caught his breath, he stood with her still cradled against him and stepped into the pool. Holding her to his chest, he caressed her face until she became responsive and smiled up at him with shining green eyes. He kissed her lightly then whispered, "You kindle my heart alight."

Her lips softly curved, and she said as she touched his cheek lightly, "Mine too."

"We should abed," he winked and lifted her out of the water with him as he stood.

"Yeah, I guess we should," she chuckled. "The dawn will be here before we know it." She sat on the bench beside him and began to pull her jeans on.

"Nary a need," he said and shook his head, eyeing the breeches as he pulled on his own and laced up his boots. He then brought her a cloak and wrapped it around her shoulders and said, "Gather the clothing into a bundle," he smiled somewhat mischievously.

"You get to wear pants, but I don't?" she chuckled as she did what he asked.

"Aye, you will overheat, if you dress," he said as he glanced over the room then blew out all the candles but the one by the door. "And 'twill take twice as long," he murmured. When she had tied the clothing into his shirt, he handed her the swords and blew out the last one then nudged her out into the night. He swung her up into his arms as he quickly traversed the distance to the house.

"I can walk," she said as she scanned the landscape, it seemed brighter than when they went to the bathhouse. Maybe her internal clock was off.

"Aye, but I can do so faster," he grinned down at her. "My feet know where ta fall without need of my eyes,"

"Ah, I see." And he was right, they had arrived at the longhouse within just a few minutes where he set her on her feet before they entered.

The hall was dark, except for the low embers in the central fire pit, but he clasped her hand and pulled her to his room and through the door with great enthusiasm. He relieved her of the bundle and swords, which clattered loudly to the stone floor. Engulfing her in his arms and lifting her to his height, he said, "Ah, now ta truly pleasure you in comfort," then his mouth overtook hers.

Leif knocked loudly on Eirik's door to announce himself and then entered. The sight of Elise lying on Eirik's chest, with her golden hair spread across her lily-skinned back in wavy tendrils of fine silk, and only covered to her hips, gave him pause. But only briefly, for then something caught his eye and he moved closer. Easing her locks aside for a better view, he saw on the left center of her back was a coiled mark, much larger than that of a simple bonding.

"Raven sigh, Leif, what be ye doing in here?" Eirik growled lowly and pulled the fur up to cover her naked body.

Leif grinned down at him. "You did more than brand her, brother. You've taken her for a mate," he said in whispered tones for he nary wished to wake her.

As much as he tried to keep from smiling, his lips curled anyway as he said, "Aye, needs must keep the others away while she gathers Heill." He carefully eased out from beneath her and went to find clean breeches from one of the chests. "You nary answered me," he quirked a brow at him as he pulled on the pants.

Leif looked from Elise to Eirik and shrugged as he still held his grin, "Seems nary of import now, but the one 'princess' lass – 'tis hard ta tell the difference – Kristin mayhap, requested a few ells of cloth. She wishes ta sew, I believe."

"And for this, you wake me?" he said as he pulled on a serk and tunic, then sat on the bed to don his boots.

"Aye, you are up before now, ahead of the day," Leif gestured toward the cold fire in the hearth.

Eirik glanced at the fireplace and furrowed his brows then at the small window on the outer wall, it was barely twilight. "You know why nil fire was lit. And I be abed yet because I was up late," again he couldn't keep the smile from curving his lips nor his eyes from drifting to Elise. "Aye, I'll get it. What does she wish ta craft?"

Leif shook his head, "I failed ta ask," he chuckled.

Eirik shook his head and herded Leif toward the door, "I'll be out in moments ta get the cloth. You get started on the meal, if the others have yet ta arise."

Leif furrowed his brows at that, and left muttering about having ta do women's work, as Eirik closed the door behind him. Instead of starting a fire, he crossed the room to the small clay bowl, and after filling it with water, he held it in his hands to warm it, then washed up for the day. Before he left his chamber, he pulled the furs down to uncover Elise's back and caressed the small spiral tenderly, pressed his lips to it, then rose and left out the door.

As he went to the storeroom to retrieve the cloth, he saw the high table was already set. After unlocking the door, he selected a few different cloths, not knowing what she planned to craft, and then left the room and locked it once more. He placed the bolts on a table then went to the kitchen to see what needed to be done as of yet. As he entered, he found Sara, of course – she was always the first ta rise – searing pork fat and Jesse dipping slices of bread into a milky liquid and cooking it on a flat iron sheet. He glanced at Leif, who was watching Jesse with interest, and then to Sara with a smile. "Good morn," he said. "Your mistress will nary be supping with us this morn and I have laid out a choice of cloth for Kristin's use. The outwork will nary take long this day so after 'tis done, work on the windcatcher can begin. Needs must, has your mistress taught any of you her skill with the sword?" he was looking at Jesse but glanced at Sara, just in case she too had such a skill.

"I'm good with a bow," Sara grinned, "But I'm not very good with a sword."

"I'm not as good as Miss Thornson is at fencing, but I'm not bad either," Jesse answered as he put the bread on a platter and began another round.

"I think Tristan and Kristin are good at archery too," Sara looked at Jesse to confirm but he shrugged slightly.

"Bo may do archery, because I don't recall seeing him in fencing class," Jesse said.

Eirik looked to Leif with an arched brow of surprise, who wore the same look on his face, and then smiled. "'Tis good for all ta know how ta defend, although a bow will nary do well up close. Hand weapons, knife or axe?" Sara shook her head. "Mayhap after the chores, we will see to that, aye?"

"Um... sure," Sara said, flicked her eyes to Jesse briefly, then to Eirik. "Is it because of that man that attacked Miss Thornson yesterday the reason that you want us to be able to defend ourselves?"

Eirik tighten his lips as his jaw clenched and his brows creased. Just bringing Nidpigger up gave him an ill feeling, however he nary knew that he had attacked her. "'Tis so, aye," he admitted. He then gestured to Leif to take over for Sara and then said, "Sara, I wish ta speak with you," and went through the door.

As Sara came out, she eyed Eirik's awkward behavior and smiled. "What's wrong?" she asked.

Eirik filled a cup with mead before he looked at her. "I have asked your mistress ta stay with me on the island and she consented," again the smile broke through, even as he tried to cover it with his cup. "She had mentioned your desire ta also stay, aye?" he asked to confirm before he continued.

"Yes, I told her that I did," she said warily.

"I can grant you permission ta do so, but I wish ta know the thoughts of the others. I have talked with Elise on this, but she was reluctant ta pass on the knowledge I gave her to the lasses and lads."

"We can't get off the island, can we?" Sara went straight to the point.

"'Tis uncertain. As you wish ta stay, I will share the knowledge I had imparted on her." He then told her about the bond that is shared with the island, receiving Heill, and that 'twas uncertain where the ones go that choose not to stay.

"Are you saying that if they choose not to stay, they die? Or is it possible that they return from whence they came?" Sara asked.

Eirik shook his head and said, "I know naught, but I have told Elise that we will search for ways to return the ones that wish ta go. 'Tis our hope ta return them to their own time, should they nary wish ta stay. 'Tis unfortunate that we have but less than a fortnight ta do so," his face looked doubtful though.

"That is a problem. Maybe Bo can work on it? He's the smartest person I know," she offered him a smile. "But since I've decided to stay already, I was wondering if there was a potter here, perchance?" she asked.

"Nary as of yet. 'Tis a bowl or such you need? We can acquire one from the first ship ta port."

"No, no, no," she chuckled. "I can make pottery, if I had the right equipment, like a wheel and a kiln," she grinned.

"Mayhap, 'twas nary chance that brought you to the island," he returned her smile. "As for your bonding...we can make it so when you wish, but 'twould prefer ta wait till Elise can attend. She worries greatly over you lot and I wish her ta worry nil longer."

"Why is she not able to eat with us this morning anyway?" she raised a brow at him.

"She be gathering Heill," he said and looked for the words to explain further. He cleared his throat. "She made her bond last eve, but also... um... became one with me." He raised his eyes to hers then lowered them quickly, clearly uncomfortable with the subject. "'Tis quite different than the bond with the island, to be certain," he said to set her at ease, but when he chanced another look, she was grinning.

"Well, that's good to know," she chuckled. "So... are you telling me that you are now life-mates?" she asked using the term she had heard him use.

He grinned, couldn't help it. "Aye, we are. Now must needs ta find Leif a mate," he teased, "Of interest?"

Sara laughed, "I'm pretty certain that I'm not his type, but Kristin may be, eh?"

"Leif nary has spoken of any interest, but mayhap," he smiled. "I must need ta ask, is Elise a völva? She bears the totems on her jewelry," he indicated to his right thumb.

Sara arched her brows at him and smiled. "I'm ah... pretty sure she isn't. I gave her the one with Odin's horns on it because she was my favorite teacher, and I valued her wisdom. And she's my friend. I guess she bought the other one herself," she shrugged.

He nodded his understanding. "'Twill look in ta getting you a wheel and kiln for your craft, but may take some time, aye? We mayhap ta build it ourselves. Nary a doubt that Bo would know how," he chuckled, "'Twould seem he has the knowledge of an elder."

"He's just really good at figuring out how things work, you know? I kind of hope he decides to stay, his ingenuity would come in handy, like the windmill. To be honest, they all have skills that I think you would consider profitable, except maybe Jesse. Although he *is* a great cook! Better than me anyway," she laughed.

He raised a brow at her, still finding the concept a bit odd. However, he did note the slight flush in her cheeks when she mentioned him and smiled. "If it pleases you, I must need ta attend ta Elise before we break our fast, aye?" She nodded and returned to the kitchen as he went to his chamber.

Mani's day

The Arrow

Elise woke to the soothing caresses of someone laving her back and arms, and on occasion swabbed across her forehead and face. She blinked several times until she came fully aware that she was nude and was being bathed while she laid on her stomach in bed. "What...?" she said as she started to turn, but felt a hand gently press against her to keep her in place.

"Hush and be still, heartling," Eirik said softly. "Methinks 'tis nigh complete."

"What is?" she asked sleepily from her prone position.

"The mate-bonding," he said as he continued to smooth the wet cloth over her.

"How long have I been asleep? I should get up to start on breakfast," she said a bit groggy as she tried to rouse herself to move, but the energy just wasn't there.

"Nay, the others will tend ta the meals. You just rest a bit longer," he said quietly, and she succumbed to sleep once again.

After the morning meal and the chores were finished, Eirik did as he said while Leif and Bo worked on the windcatcher. He had retrieved bows, axes, and knives, as well as dulled practice swords from the stores and set up a training field between the longhouse and the barn. He first wanted to see their skill with the bows before he assessed their skill with hand weapons. As expected, all but Jesse were proficient with the bow, but with more practice even he would improve, and as he said, he had rudimentary skill with a sword. Once Eirik showed him how the weapon was intended to be used, he improved greatly. However, the lasses nary had the strength to wield the sword, so he moved on to knives and then to axes. He found that both the twins were highly accurate using them as projectiles, but again lacked the strength to fight off an attacker. However, Sara showed great promise with a knife and could slip out of many holds when grappling. As well as Jesse was suitable with both axe and knife, wielding them like the sword. Given his size and muscle mass, he would do just as good with a hammer also. He didn't show any of them shield tactics though. He felt that they wouldn't have one nearby if taken by surprise. It would be a lesson for another day. They just needed to know how to defend their own body, not attack another. When he was satisfied, he dismissed them to begin the evening meal, but told them to keep practicing, then went back in to check on Elise.

As he entered his chamber, he glanced over Elise before he poured more water into the bowl and began washing up then with fresh water, he bathed her once again. While he washed her down, he noticed her mark had taken on an unexpected shape and size. 'Twas more than he'd hoped. It had changed from its initial spiral into one that twisted and folded about itself, taking up nearly half her back now. He could even make out the head and six limbs. He pressed his lips to her back as his smile grew. She was to be as he.

While they ate, another exotic meal of spiced roast meat instead of boiled, Eirik somewhat listened quietly as he ate. His mind was on other things if the crease of his lips were any indication. His anticipation of Elise wakening was most distracting, until he heard Bo ask about her. Eirik flicked his gaze to Sara and then to Bo before he answered. "'Twas hoping afore now that your mistress would have told you, but as it stands, she'll nary be able ta tell ye." He took a healthy drink from his cup.

"What do you mean?" Bo's concern showed in the furrow of his brows.

"I told your mistress days ago, methinks that mayhap you can nary return. But 'tis your choice ta stay and consent ta the bonding, as Elise and Sara have. Although should you choose ta go, I know naught where you will go," he said and pulled another draught from his cup.

"You've chosen to stay here?" Bo turned on Sara.

"Yeah," she said with a snort. "What do I have back home? Nothing, that's what. Besides, Eirik has assured me of a place here and not as a slave." She glanced to Jesse then back to Bo. "I like it here. I can be myself and not nearly as invisible," she said the last part quietly.

Bo held her eyes and then nodded as he understood her meaning and tightened his lips and then looked at his other classmates' grave faces with a lifted brow before looking at Eirik and sighed. "So, what are our choices? Stay here or what? Die? Return home?"

"I know naught, the others vanished," he said with a shrug. "But you must make your choice within the fortnight."

"So, it could mean they returned from wherever they came from. Or it could mean they dropped out of existence," he sighed.

"Well, I'd rather stay than die," Jesse spoke up, his eyes darted to each of the others. "Our chances are better here than the unknown, right?" He received quiet nods from the girls and Bo. "Then maybe we should just choose to stay, huh?"

"Won't you miss your family?" Kristin asked softly.

"I guess I would," Jesse shrugged a bit. "But really this isn't a choice, it's life or death. One hundred percent chance of life or what? A fifty percent chance? I'm not a mathlete, but even I can figure this one out," he said, but he had other reasons besides the threat of death to stay and he unintentionally glanced at Sara before moving to look at the others.

"Well, I'd miss my family," Tristan said, "But at least I do have my sister here, unlike the rest of you."

"I don't want to die, and Tristan's right, at least I do have her," Kristin said as if she just came to her decision.

Bo scanned the faces of his classmates and sighed heavily. "Then we are all in agreement? We stay and become our family?" They each nodded and then he looked back to Eirik. "What does the bonding entail?"

"'Tis a bond between each of you and the island, once the agreement is established, I or Leif here will brand you."

"Branding?" Kristin said quite shrilly.

"'Tis more of a skin discoloration," Leif said and patted her hand.

"Like the tattoo on your back?" Bo asked.

"Nary as quite," Leif said and chuckled. "'Tis much smaller and may appear anywhere," then he held up his thumb and index finger about two inches apart.

"Well, that's too bad, your tat is absolutely legit," Jesse said grinning.

"Okay, so, all we should expect is a small tattoo somewhere on our bodies, right?" Bo confirmed.

"Aye, you may also feel overwhelmed by awe when the Heill begins ta fill you," Eirik said with a shrug as if it was nothing.

"Do you still want us to wait until Miss Thornson can join us?" Sara asked.

"Aye, methinks she'll nary be pleased that you each have decided to stay, and I feel she'll wish ta ... um...," he paused, stuck on vocabulary. He rolled his hand through the air then said, "Witness?" He arched a brow at Sara.

"More like supervise," Sara chuckled. "She is a bit overprotective, but I think you're right, she will want to make sure that this is our choice and that we aren't hurt." She nodded her head in agreement.

"If she's going to freak-out, maybe we should do it before she can stop us," Jesse said.

With a lifted brow, Eirik asked, "Freak-out?"

Sara clarified, "Um... berserk," she then chuckled.

"Ah... Nay, I intend ta keep my honor and methinks she would find it dishonorable ta proceed without her knowledge, aye?"

"Okay, so when will that be?" Bo asked with a furrowed brow, again he was worried about something, but Eirik couldn't figure out what.

"Tyr's day eve," Eirik said. "She gathers Heill," he said as if that explained why she wasn't available.

Even Leif raised a brow at that, to which Eirik shook his head, willing him not ta ask in front of the others, but...

"What causes her bonding ta take as long?" he asked anyway.

"Is it because you are life-mates?" Sara questioned.

"What's that mean?" the twins asked in unison.

"They're married," Sara grinned.

"Oh," they said, again in unison, but the others looked to Eirik for explanation.

"She is unique," Eirik said and tightened his lips to keep them from curving but gave Leif a pointed look. Again, Leif responded with arched brows, but said nothing. "She requires more Heill than a simple bond as you each shall have," he said hoping that satisfied their curiosity. He then said, "Ingrid should return in the morn ta resume her duties in the kitchen, so that should leave you lasses with a bit more time ta work on other... tasks.

"You mean we don't have to work in the kitchen anymore?" Kristin said excitedly.

"No, that isn't what he means," Sara said. "He means with her help, our job should go faster," she smiled.

"Oh," she said downheartedly.

"If that be all, I should attend ta your mistress," Eirik said as he rose from his seat and started toward his chamber, only to be caught by Leif before he entered.

"What makes her unique?" Leif asked in lowered tones.

"I know naught. Come see," he grinned and eased opened the door.

Elise was as he had left her; still lying prone and covered to the hips, indicating that she hadn't moved. As they approached, he could see that it had grown but a smidge more and yet had a bit more definition.

Leif stretched out his hand to touch the mark, but Eirik

smacked it away. "'Tis a dragonling," he said, astonished by the discovery.

"Aye," Eirik grinned proudly. "Mayhap 'tis why the calling was so strong with her. Methinks 'tis why they were brought here, leastways her. The others, time will tell."

"Ah, brother, I can see how pleased you are, and I join you in your happiness. But will she be as pleased?" his lips quirked at the corners.

"She will. By her own admission, she has voiced her love for dragons. Why do you torment me so?" he said the last as he cuffed him on the shoulder.

Leif squatted closer and whispered with a degree of reverence, "What kind do you suppose she'll be? Fire? Ice? Forest? Alf?"

"I know naught, but whatever she turns out to be, she'll nary be pleased with you so nigh," Eirik said as he grabbed him by the arm and lifted him to his feet.

Leif grinned and said, "She'll nary, or you'll nary?" as he faced him.

Eirik furrowed his brows. "For a certain. Now be on your way," then he smiled and locked the door behind him.

He removed his serk and tunic soon followed by his boots and breeches as he stalked closer to his bed and his heartling, Elise. He had two more nights for his mating ta be complete and he meant to see it fulfilled, he thought as he pulled the furs from her, exposing her entire body to the chill of his chamber. He was purposefully gentle with her on their first mating for 'twas about her pleasure, but this night, 'twas about his and was nigh certain he be nary likely restrained.

As he sat on the side of the bed, he picked up the vial of oil from off the floor and uncorked it, dripping it down her back, and then watched as her skin heated it causing it to stream in a thin rivulet into her cleft. His brow flicked along with the corners of his mouth. Then he poured some in his hand and rubbed them together before spreading the slick scented liquid over her back in large swipes from her shoulders down and over her perfect round arse, paying particular attention to the valley between and betwixt her thighs. He let out a soft growl of anticipation. Pouring more of the oil in his hand, he grasped his throbbing phallus and applied it in long slow strokes from root to crown as he gazed at the woman who would be his forever. He would make it so. She consented and he was going to take full advantage of his privileges with her. His lips curved and his eyes shimmered at that as he crawled over her with a knee on either side of her legs and his arms braced beside her shoulders, keeping his weight from her. He bent and whispered in her ear.

"Heartling," he nuzzled and sucked her lobe in his mouth as the crest of his erection skimmed lightly over her arse.

"Hmm?" she mewled and stirred slightly.

"Wake," he murmured as he pressed his lips to her neck and right shoulder and lowered himself to allow her to feel him gliding along the channel dividing her arse. "I want you."

Elise moaned softly and slid her hand up to touch his face and curl around his head as her hips tilted toward him rising to greet him.

He readjusted himself downward to where his pulsing shaft slid along her folds only brushing her bud to further entice her. "Heartling, I need you," he whispered roughly as his desire grew near to desperation and lowered his chest to her back, skimming his hand along her ribs and beneath her to slide over her mons and into her furrow, spreading her dew around her folds but circled several times over her rootling.

She writhed against him as she arched her back and slid her knees forward, pushing back against his hardened shaft and then forward into his hand as her breathing became more pronounced in sultry pants. Eirik encircled her waist and lifted her higher as he slowly pushed his crown into her opening, stretching it wider to accommodate his girth, taking pleasure in every blissful inch of her embracing sheath until he was tightly pressed against her and so deep his tip tantalizingly brushed the back wall of her womanhood. They fit so perfectly together. He held her there momentarily as he scraped his teeth against her shoulder and resisted the urge to bite down. "Freya wept," he growled softly as she gasped and seized his wrist that held his weight and fisted her other hand in his hair.

He eased out at the same leisurely pace then glided forward once again, holding her in place as they rocked forward with much more force than before and a rolling grunt like distant thunder reverberated from the depths of his throat. His instinct pushed him into more powerful dives within her and hers aggressively met his fierce insertions, thrust for thrust and let out short moans with each stride. His essence-flame flared as he opened his mouth over her shoulder and pressed his teeth against her skin. The taste so sweet to his tongue his chest vibrated with an echoing rumble. And as he felt her heart blaze into a conflagration, he bit down and quickened his movements as his arm tightened around her. His body tensed with each vigorous shallow thrust, urging and coaxing him closer to his summit. Faster and harder he moved. He couldn't get enough of her as their flames consumed them until he suddenly sat back on his haunches, bringing her with him, and snarled into her shoulder as she cried out with her climax. As he felt her contractions, he held her in place with both arms wrapped around her while his seed spilled into her, and her head lulled back against his shoulder. He could feel each moist heavy pant expelled from her mouth as it blew across his ear before she pressed her lips to it.

He gently released his bite as his breath still rumbled out of him and kissed and licked at the wound he'd made. Bending forward with her, he laid her back on the bed before he pulled out and moved to her side. He continued his laving until he was certain it was healed then rolled to his back as he regained his breath and pulled her over his chest, kissing her head, and softly stroked her back. He was contented for now, if the purring rumble emanating from his chest was any indication.

Leif left Eirik's chamber, still grinning, and turned to his own but then he saw Kristin near the central fire trying to sew by the dim light. "I can make it burn brighter for you, if it pleases you?" he asked her from the opposite side of the pit.

"Oh, could you? This light will ruin my eyes, but I wanted to get this part finished. The day goes by so fast here, ya know?" she smiled up at him.

"Aye, 'tis much ta fill it," he said then squatted down, added a few more logs before he blew across it and caused it to flare to life. "'Tis better?"

"Yes, thank you," she smiled again.

"What is it that you craft?" he asked as he couldn't make much sense out of what she was holding, although it resembled something between a serk and a tunic.

Well, I thought I'd try my hand at a shirt. When we were washing, I noticed that several of your undershirts were ripped from where there isn't enough give between your belt and your arm. I'm trying to fix that with this fabric," she held a square swatch of cloth out to him.

He came around the pit and pulled it from her fingers. It was rather thin and soft. "'Twill nary stand the stress any more than the linen," he scoffed.

"Pull it, stretch it," she coaxed. He did so as he sat beside her. "Now imagine it in your armpit, here," she said as she put her hand under her arm. "It's either that or remove all the sleeves from your shirts," she chuckled. "Because something's got to give. If it's mended repeatedly, it will rub a sore, and you wouldn't want that."

"Aye, 'tis so, but why just my serks and nary Eirik's?"

"His isn't torn," she chuckled. "Maybe he doesn't wear his belt as tight, huh?" she giggled.

"You say I'm fat?" he said affronted, "We are nigh the same girth," he furrowed his brows and tightened his lips.

She chuckled at his reaction. "No, I'm saying that you tighten your belt much more than he does... for whatever reason."

"Ta keep my breeches from falling passed my arse," he laughed.

"Then maybe you need tighter breeches, at least around the

waist. I'll look into it," she smiled.

"I'll leave it ta you," he returned her smile. "But you should not be up late for the morn comes as quickly as the day goes by, as you say," he said as he stood to go to his chamber.

"All right. Good night," she said and went back to her sewing.

"Good eve," he mumbled thoughtfully as he went through his door. She was making him a serk? That meant she was of interest in him but was he of interest in her? He did not feel the calling as described by his brother, although he found her pleasing to the eye as with her sister. He also found Sara intriguing as well. He rolled his eyes. Perhaps the winter has been too long. His head swam with thoughts as he removed his tunic and serk, dropping them to the floor. He ran his hand over his stomach and side, checking for fat, but all he found was hardened muscle, and nodded his head in satisfaction. He needed to clear his head of these thoughts and pulled his serk back on as he went back out his door and on out into the night without even glancing in Kristin's direction, purposefully so.

He made his way to the barn, then on around it to the back where he proceeded to remove his clothing before allowing the Heill to flow through him. With one deep breath as he drew in the Heill, he stretched his arms out slowly then snapped them. Suddenly, he transformed in a blink and then shook his head and that of his grey scaly body all the way to the tip of his thorny tail as he stretched his bat-like wings out. With one powerful stroke after another, he lifted his body from the ground and ascended away from the farmstead. He soared the skies over the small island, and it felt good to be in this form. He could see every night creature scurry about as he flew over the forest and one particular that shouldn't be. He could easily sense the malign Heill within him in this form as he drifted lower to the ground and only hesitated for just a moment as he felt the sharp sting of an arrow pierce his shoulder. He swung at it with a heavily clawed hand, breaking it off and then turned back toward the farmstead, pushing his wings to take him higher.

He transformed in the air as he came closer to the ground and landed behind the barn, taking the few extra steps that forced him forward. Quickly, he pulled on his breeches and boots before he headed to the house holding his left arm in close to his body and the massive arrow protruding through his shoulder. He rushed in and went straight to his chamber, only glancing at Kristin when he heard her gasp. He grabbed his wash bowl from the table and dipped it in the bucket then got out a clean cloth to clean his wound, but he froze when he heard his door open.

"Kristin, please go," he said as normally as he could without looking at her.

"Let us help, Leif," her voice was soft with concern.

He turned toward the door and saw she wasn't alone, Bo stood next to her. "You can't take that out by yourself," Bo said as he came toward him. "Let me look."

With a sigh of resignation, Leif sat on the stool in front of his table and allowed the lad to examine the wound. Kristin lit a few candles and brought them closer then moved his water kettle over the fire before she left to get bandages.

As Bo pressed gently around the wound on the front, he asked, "How did you manage to get shot in the middle of the night?" and then did the same on the back before he looked at Leif awaiting his answer. Leif tightened his lips as he furrowed his brows. "You're right, the how doesn't really matter. What does matter is that the arrowhead has gone through completely, but we have to push through the shaft without causing any more damage to your muscles. I'm not sure how, but it missed your clavicle, however it might have nicked your scapula. Any thoughts on how to get it out?"

Kristin came in with several strips of cloth just as Leif put both hands on the end of the broken shaft and pulled them toward him, effectively pushing the arrow through till his hand laid flat against his shoulder. She let out a gasp and bit her lips together as she brought the bandages to Bo.

"Now pull it free, Lad," Leif said in a tight voice. "Without delay."

Bo shook his head in awe. "Kristin, hold him still, please," he said as he gripped the arrow.

"How do I do that?" she said wide-eyed.

Leif grabbed her hand and drew her in front of him then placed both her hands around his neck. "You pull as he does," he said then lowered his head to brace for the extraction as he raised his right arm around her, fisted his hand, and sucked in a deep breath... of her.

"Leif, you need to relax your muscles, so we don't cause more injury," Bo said as he looked at Kristin and nodded. Leif uncurled his fingers, laying them out flat across her arse and slowly drew in another breath. Then Bo pulled the arrow straight out, not giving Leif the chance to tense up again, who in turn released a growling complaint and tightened his arm around Kristin with his head still bowed into her chest.

"Whoa there, big guy," Kristin yelped when he squeezed her into him. "He's going to be all right, isn't he?" she asked Bo as she held Leif against her.

"Yeah, but we need to clean and dress the wounds. Did you find any triple-antibiotic in my things?" he asked as he started cleaning the wound on his back.

"Just this one," she said as she pulled the small tube from her pocket and handed it to him then replaced her hand to Leif's head.

"It'll have to do." He then put a small amount on a cloth he had folded and pressed it against the puncture.

"Leif," she said softly. "The worst is over." She tilted his head up and smiled when he looked at her. "Let's get this dressed and then you can pass out in bed," she chuckled.

He nodded and leaned away from her so she could clean the injury. His gaze wondered over her as she knelt in front of him, between his knees. Huh, her bodice was cut low and gaped a bit. He hadn't noticed before now. Nay, now he could easily see the top curve of each breast and the valley between even as her undergarment held them firmly in place. He licked his lips then raised his eyes to her face. When they reached her eyes, her lips curved then she continued with her task as he glanced away. She smelled of lavender and arousal. Nay, nary could it be. His nostrils flared as he drew in her scent causing his mouth ta water and he swiped at his lips again. His heart ignited and he fluttered his eyes closed and kept them locked down until they finished.

When she had the folded cloth over the front of the wound, both her and Bo wrapped the longer lengths tightly around his shoulder and chest to hold them in place.

"What I wouldn't do for an adherent cohesive wrap or even an Ace right now, huh?" she chuckled.

"No doubt," Bo mumbled. "But this will due." He checked to make sure the bandage was secure.

"I do have a sports bra, but I think it'll be too tight on him," she giggled.

Bo gave her a lopsided smile. "I recommend that you don't use that arm for a while and allow it to heal," he said to Leif as he came around and looked at him. "And I would tell you to stay in bed, but you probably won't. So just keep your arm immobile."

Leif nodded as he stood. He looked down at Kristin, ran his hand across the bloodstain on her shirt by her hip, and tightened his lips before he turned and made his way to his bed and dropped down on it. He just couldn't understand how the arrow penetrated his scales. He never used to have to worry about being harmed on the island before, but whoever that was, was out to kill them, that was for certain. He needed to let Eirik know before he too got hurt. First thing in the morn, he would tell him. Just then did he notice Kristin straightening up his room and picking up the discarded cloths from where they cleaned his wound.

"You nary have ta do that," he said lowly. "Ye nary be my servant. I'll get it in the morn." He continued to watch as she finished her task.

"You need to rest," she said as she blew all the candles out, but one, which she set near his bed.

"Thank you," he said, "For everything." Then bit at his lip in restraint of saying or doing anything else.

"Sure thing," she smiled, "Now get some sleep." She then turned to leave but stopped to pick up the bloodstained cloths before she stepped out the door.

Leif eased down in his bed, lying on his back with his left arm crossed over his chest, and closed his eyes against the pain. Now that Kristin wasn't near to distract him from it, he felt every throb of his heart in his shoulder. He allowed his mind's eyes to wander over Kristin again, hearing the soft lilt to her voice, and the decadence of her scent, even the firmness of her arse came to his fingers, all to keep his mind busy. Although it did give rise to another issue to which he couldn't assuage. And now, he wondered how she tasted. With his senses sufficiently distracted, he drifted.

It seemed as if only moments had passed before he heard his door open, and someone came in. He refused to open his eyes for fear of losing the vision of Kristin he had keeping the pain at bay. He heard the stool scrape on the stone then placed closer to him and someone sat heavily upon it. The aroma of lavender and arousal wafted to his nose. It had to be him dreaming.

"'Tis bad, aye?"

Eirik's baritone voice shattered his vision and he scowled up at him as the scent too was tainted by his brother's own spicy one. "'Twill heal enough ta fly by the turning," he said roughly and resisted the urge to cover his face.

"Where were you?" Eirik placed his hand on his arm and allowed his heat to radiate up to the injury.

"'Twas flying over the wood when I sensed malign Heill," he said. "'Twas of a purpose ta maim, for a certain, if nary ta kill."

"Aye," Eirik sighed, "I've seen the arrow. 'Twas made ta burrow through and too large for any game in the wood."

"Aye, methinks 'twere made for us," Leif said and then shrugged off his hand. "Thanks, but if I heal too quickly, 'twill raise suspicion."

Eirik nodded his head and folded his hands together. "I'll send someone in with food and ta change that," he indicated toward his wound.

"And go bathe. You smell like you've swived six ways ta Freya's day," Leif growled.

Eirik grinned and wiggled his brows. "'Tis because I have," he said then rose and left out the door.

Leif scrubbed a hand over his face, wishing he could regain the vision he had, but his brother had ruined it for him. He sat up and sighed heavily as he glanced out the small window then growled at seeing the sun was fully up. Him and Bo were going ta start laying the pipes today, but he had slept in. He pushed off his bed and then plopped back down, gritting his teeth. The door opened and he looked toward it.

Kristin came in with a tray of food and a pouch slung over her shoulder. She smiled when she saw him sitting up. "Good, you're awake. I thought you might be hungry, and I need to change your dressing," she said as she slid the tray on a nearby chest. "What would you like to do first?"

Leif peered up at her and licked his lips. He knew what he'd like ta do. His lips curved. "I need ta piss," he chuckled.

"Okay," she giggled. "Do you need help with that or...," she glanced around till she found his chamber pot.

"Nay, just ..." he shook his head and then lifted himself off the bed and moved toward it.

Kristin busied herself with adding water to the kettle over the fire and fanning the flames while she put some wood and peat on it then opened her pouch and set out the clean bandages on the table, all the while trying not to look his direction.

"That must've been uncomfortable," she said over her shoulder.

"What?" he asked from behind her, perusing over the tight breeches and bodice she wore this morn.

"Sleeping in your pants... breeches, I mean," she said and cleared her throat as she turned to look at him.

He shrugged before moving the stool back over to the table where she had set up with her bandages and eased down on it in front of her. "What would *you* like ta do first?" he asked lowly and brought his eyes up to meet hers.

"If you'd like to wash up before I change your dressing, we can do that... or rather you." She cleared her throat again. "You can do that." She bit her lips together then smiled.

He grinned and winked. "Nay, change the dressing and I'll wash up after," he said.

He inhaled her scent when she leaned closer to remove the old dressing and it made his eyes roll once again. "Mmm," he moaned softly. It wasn't so much lavender this time but another flower with an undercurrent of her as well as that of her arousal. "You smell like a goddess that's been rolling in a field of flowers," he said over her shoulder in a rough whisper.

Kristin froze briefly before peeling off the cloth from his back then leaned back to do the same with the one in front and curved her lips as she glanced up at him. "I'm glad you like it," she said then straightened to get the hot water to clean the punctures.

A soft growl escaped his lips as he drew his hands into fists. He didn't know if this was the calling or just plain man woman attraction, but it was going ta drive him berserk. She came back with the bowl of hot water and began cleaning his front wound.

"This doesn't look too bad," she said and leaned over to do the same with the back one. She then reached back to get the two cloths she prepared earlier and pressed them over each injury. "I'm going to need a little help here," she said and glanced up at his eyes. "Just hold this one while I bind them into place." He nodded and slid his hand over hers. "You're not usually this quiet, Leif. What's wrong?" she asked as she wound the cloth around his chest and over his shoulder.

"I have nil words for you," he said then grunted as she cinched it tight.

She raised her head and studied his eyes for a moment before she bit her lips together and straightened then began gathering her supplies into her pouch. "I'll leave you to it then."

He was certain he had just caused her pain but knew naught how so. "I meant nil offense, Kristin," he said as he curled his fingers around her wrist to turn her. "You ease my suffering but cause me so much more, I have nil the words ta tell you."

She gasped. "How do I cause you to suffer? I only want you to get better," she said softly.

"Oh, lass, you're well aware the effect that you have on men, for a certain," his lips curved as he spoke. "As I am aware of the effect that I have on you, but only as of late."

"Oh, um… honesty, now I'm speechless," she chuckled dryly. "Um… well, I'm sorry if I cause you … um… discomfort in that department. That was not my intention." She smiled feebly.

"Are the men nigh as honest where you be from? Jesse and Bo seem honest," he creased his brows.

"Those two? Yeah, they're honest, but most others not so much," she shrugged.

He tugged her a step closer, right between his knees. "What might be your intent, if nary ta cause me discomfort?" he asked as he focused on the last part of her statement and began circling his thumb over her inner wrist in featherlight strokes.

A knock on his door sounded then it swung open as Eirik came in. "'Twas seeing if you had been attended, for I failed ta ask someone ta do just that," he said and grinned.

Leif dropped his hand to his lap and lowered his head shaking it. "Aye, brother, I have clean dressing and food," he said then raised his eyes to Kristin's and winked then nodded, dismissing her. "Thank you for your kindness," he smiled.

"Sure thing," she returned his smile then turned and grabbed the pouch off the table and left.

Eirik watched as Kristin left then closed the door behind her before turning on his brother with a grin. "'Tis a good mate for you," he said as he drew closer.

"Mayhap yea or mayhap nay, I may ne'er know," he sighed and looked upon his brother. "For a certain, nary afore the turning."

Eirik lifted a brow. "What be amiss? 'Tis nary the lack of attraction, for a certain."

"'Tis timing," he shook his head then peered up at him. "'Tis the last eve of your mating this eve," he chose to shift the focus to him. "Does she still gather Heill?"

"Yea, but she still be responsive ta the mating," his lips curled at the corners. "'Tis as if... I know naught. I have nary the words."

"She'll be nigh starved by Tyr's day eve, perhaps we should prepare a feast in honor of her becoming, aye?" he lifted a brow at him.

"'Tis a grand idea and we can brand the others just after, aye?" he grinned.

"Yea, 'twould set me at ease ta know they be safe from the influence of others. Ye be keeping them close, eh? Within the threshold?"

Eirik chuckled. "Yea, 'twould nary dare ta let harm come ta any of them while Elise is indisposed. And for as much as I wish a mate for you, I'd much rather that wait till then as well," he flicked a brow at him.

Leif chuckled, "Nil worries there, my brother. As I said, time runs against me for the now."

"I nary know your meaning, but 'tis naught ta rush. Once bonded, the mating could happen at any time thereafter. Mayhap I should brand Kristin though," he said the last thoughtfully.

Leif drew his brows together as he stood quickly and took a step toward Eirik. "Nay, she's mine," he growled out. He hesitated momentarily then turned to where she had set the tray and began eating. He was uncertain where that reaction came from, but he shouldn't have used such a tone with his brother.

Eirik closed in on Leif and laid a hand to his shoulder infusing it with his healing fire. "I have nil interest in your Kristin," he spoke softly. "'Twas just a thought ta stave off an unintended mating, but I see how strongly you feel for the lass. My wish is that her heart aligns with yours. Aye?" He removed his hand and nudged him to face him. "Once you have a mate, this..." he indicated to his shoulder, "And this," he indicated to his scowling face, "Will be nil more. We of an alike mind?"

With a heavy sigh, he nodded, but then tilted his head. "What does one ta do with the other?"

Eirik chuckled. "Your mate can heal your injuries and any other ailments you may suffer from," he said and winked as his lips creased. "Now, I must away and you," he scanned his appearance, "You need ta clean up, if you wish ta sup with the rest of us." He then turned away and left Leif to his thoughts.

Tyr's Day

Dragons

Elise woke and stretched her arms out lazily and even pointed her toes. She felt like she had slept for eons, and she really had to pee. It was so dark in the room though that she was afraid to move from the bed for fear of stubbing her toes. The only light she could discern was from the shaft of moonlight streaming through the tiny window. Not even an ember glowed in the fireplace, and she wondered why. Eirik had always kept it going. Maybe something happened to him, to all of them. She stood up and carefully made her way to the chamber pot and as she peed, she searched the floor for her purse. Finding it, she then rummaged through it till she found the familiar shape of a book of matches and a tissue. Having that taken care of, she made her way back to the bed before she struck the match and lit the candle setting on the chest.

Now she could see. Picking up the candle, she went to the hearth and loaded it with kindling and a bit of peat then lit it. She checked the kettle for water than swung it into place. The first thing she wanted to do was brush her teeth and wash her face, but she had to wait for the water to get hot. Therefore, she fanned the flames to be sure the peat caught before the kindling burned away. As it burned brighter, she looked about the room and stood to brush her teeth while she waited. Thankfully, it wasn't long before she heard the small pot spitting and roiling.

As she filled the bowl with water, she was careful not to drip on the fire, then she found a cloth and washed herself down, beginning with her face. She felt so much better, well cleaner anyway, but then her energy was waning. What was wrong with her? Why was she so tired all the time? She didn't know, but felt she'd deal better with it and all her other questions in the light of day as she curled up on the bed and pulled a fur over her. "Where was Eirik?" was her last thought before drifting back to sleep."

Eirik opened his chamber door and paused at seeing the fire lit then closed and locked the door behind him before he stalked closer to his bed. Standing at the foot, he shrugged his tunic and serk off and tossed them on the closest chest then removed his knife and axe before his belt. He sat on the edge of the bed and unlaced his boots as he gazed at Elise in wonderment. She had to have lit the fire, but he knew she wasn't cold, so why did she? He chuckled to himself as he removed his breeches. He didn't bother with the oil tonight for she was most responsive a night ago that he wouldn't have needed it then either, but it made it interesting, for a certain. Tonight, would be about them both, not one or the other, but both as it will be hereafter.

He lifted the fur away and laid on his side, turned toward her propped on an elbow and his knee raised out of his way. He sniffed, detecting the mint with which she brushed her teeth as well as the clean smell of soap. Pulling the hair away from her face, he kissed her cheek softly as he trailed his fingertips down her side and over her hip then returned. Even in her sleep, she consumed him with desire and set his heart alight. He encircled her waist and pulled her against him as he kissed her neck and shoulder. Ah, her beautiful shoulder. He scraped his teeth against it as his hand slid up to caress her breast at the same time she reached back and pulled his hip into her. A soft growl escaped his lips. He would get to that, but for now, he nudged her onto her back and engulfed her breast in his mouth, swirling his tongue over the nipple, and then sucked hard on it, drawing the sweetest moan from her lips. Then he reached for the other and laved it with his tongue before he took several long pulls on her hardened nipple and grazed it with his teeth.

Elise laid her hand to his cheek and drew his face to hers as he continued massaging her most supple flesh. She brushed her lips to his and as her heart was set alight, she pressed harder to separate them as he did hers and then glided her tongue between his lips. While their tongues enticingly explored, she followed his side down to his thickening shaft and stroked it lightly with her fingertips from crest to root and beyond. He nigh lost his rhythm when she rasped her nails across his ballocks, but caused his phallus ta jerk ta full erect, for a certain.

As his essence-flame flickered higher, he smoothed his hand down her stomach and over her mons to slide within her furrow. She moaned into his mouth as her hips rose to greet his hand and her leg slipped over the edge of the bed as she continued her stroking, although not as lightly. Finding her dew dripping from her channel, he pushed two fingers in, keeping his thumb pressed to her rootling as he kept rhythm with her leisurely strokes on him. He felt the overwhelming need to taste her alluringly sweet dew. Giving her a slight squeeze before he withdrew his fingers and gently disengaged her hand from him, he then turned upside down on the bed alongside her. He grasped her leg and scooched her down to him before he bent over her and lapped at her dew with a rumbling purr.

She gasped out as his tongue did magical things, ever tightening her arousal tension and sending her flame skyward. Sliding her hand along his leg, she grasped a hold of his ever-hardening shaft once again, and her tongue lashed out stroking across his tip, invoking a growl from him. She opened her mouth and sucked him in, feeling him jerk involuntarily into her mouth as she did so and then she drew even harder on his crest as she moved her hand along his shaft.

Eirik rumbled against her then slid his arms beneath her and rolled to his back, pulling her over on top of him with a thigh on either side of his head, he curled his hands around each cheek and sank his tongue in as deep as it would reach. Elise, in turn, ran her tongue down his entire shaft before pulling him into her mouth and lowering her head, taking him in from crown to root.

Then slowly she rose back up as she sucked in while she fondled his ballocks and applied a bit of pressure just beneath them at the same time causing his hips to thrust up toward her mouth.

"Freya wept, woman," he snarled, tilting his head back attempting to restrain himself longer. His essence-flame soared, and he was nigh ta his summit. He needed ta align them to burn as one before he found release.

Elise had freed her hold on him as she jumped, startled by his outburst and then, after a moment, she gradually crawled down his body until she felt his upstanding member brush against her. She burned for more and obviously so did he. Rising on her knees, she deliberately rubbed her mons against him.

Eirik, grasping her notion, clasped her hip with one hand and guided his throbbing shaft into her. As she eased down on him, they both moaned out in pleasure. Yea, this could be what does it. He could feel her essence-flame flare and he smiled as his hands tightened slightly on her hips, holding her in place.

She could feel him pressing against her uterine wall and it caused her to contract sending waves of pleasure throughout her body then she ground against him triggering another wave. "Oh god," she moaned out as she felt the lava once more course through her veins setting her body to blaze.

Eirik clasped her around the waist with his huge hands and lifted her just a bit as he bent his knees spreading hers even farther apart, then he began thrusting into her, slowly at first then more rapidly until she cried out his name in extasy. They were close, but not as one yet. He then sat up and encircle her with one arm as he pitched them forward, catching them with his other, and resumed his thrusts. She rocked back into him as she panted heavily and lowered her chest to the bed with the weight of him on her back. Her body was a firestorm and she thought she would literally burn from the inside out, it felt so good. She gasped when she felt his teeth sink into her trapezius and flooded her with a whole new level of extasy as he pulled her back upright with him, holding her there. Once again, they were of one flame, now and for always. She hugged his arms that surrounded her as she rested her head on his shoulder, feeling her contractions still tremble around his undulating shaft.

Eirik disengaged from her shoulder and licked it clean before he eased them back on the bed and withdrew from her as he rolled to his back, heavy breaths heaving out of him. She turned toward him and kissed his chest as he draped his arm across her back and pressed his lips to her head. "Rest now, heartling," he mumbled and squeezed her into his side. Then as she started to fall asleep, she heard him emit a purring rumble from his chest.

Elise slept well into the next day before she woke alone and naked with not even a fur to cover her. She wasn't certain what time of day it was, but at least it was daylight. And Eirik was gone again, but she expected that he was off doing his chores. Chores! Her eyes opened wide as she remembered the kids. She had been so out of it that she didn't even know what day it was. She jumped out of bed and quickly began her morning routine. As she washed her body, she saw what appeared to be a clawed foot tattooed on each of her sides and on the outer most portion of her shoulders, as well as a scaly tail that wrapped around her left leg and the thorny head of a dragon rested over her right shoulder ending just above her breast. She stroked her fingers over the dragon head as she thought about the glimpses of waking moments. She didn't remember getting tattooed, and one this big would take days to create, not to mention would be extremely painful. Shaking her head to dismiss it for now, she continued getting ready. She dressed in jeans and a lightweight blue blouse with an open neckline and that draped passed her hips. She braided the sides of her hair and pulled them back to encircle her head but left the rest loose in long wavy tendrils. She straightened up the room before she applied a bit of lip gloss and stood before the door.

Suddenly she was nervous about seeing the kids. She knew they would have questions, but she didn't have any answers, however she would get them today. Sucking in a deep breath of courage she grasped the handle on the door and pulled it open. Eirik stood there with his hand on the frame and his head lowered, that is until the door opened. He looked impeccable in his tightfitting breeches and belted blue tunic with silver threading woven through the silk edging, and his hair shined blue-black and hung loose except for the braids at the side.

He raised his head slowly, taking in her appearance as he did so, and smiled when their eyes met. Licking his lips before he spoke. "My lady," he said and lifted his hand out to her. He wanted to draw her into an embrace and kiss her glossy lips six ways ta Freya's day, but the others were waiting.

Her lips pressed into a smile as she took his hand and stepped out into the hall. Eirik pulled the door closed as her eyes scanned the large room that smelled of fresh threshes, baked bread, roasted meat, and cinnamon, but she saw the high table was laden with food and the others stood waiting around it. She glanced up at Eirik, who smiled reassuringly as he slid a band of silver onto her finger and then nudged her forward.

He sat her in one of the two remaining seats as he took the other, then the others took their seats. She glanced at each of their smiling faces and took note that they sat in different places than before. Sara now sat beside her and across from Jesse, who sat next to Leif with Kristin and then Tristan to her other side, and Bo now sat to Eirik's left. Then she noticed Leif's arm in a sling and crinkled her brow with concern. "What happened?"

"'Tis nil ta worry, for a certain," he said and smiled. "You must be famished," he nodded to the food that sat in front of her.

She nodded, seeing he didn't want to talk about it, and tightened her lips before glancing up at Eirik, who was filling her cup with mead and winked. "I feel like I'm missing something," she whispered to Sara, who grinned at her.

"'Tis a day of celebration, heartling," Eirik said quietly.

"What are we celebrating?" she asked.

He chuckled. "Our joining as mates, for one," he indicated to the large torch above and behind them. "The other will be discussed after you have had your fill."

Elise looked behind them and saw the large torch flanked by

seven other smaller torches, but only the two next to the main was lit. "Oh," was all she could manage as she peered down at the ring that he had given her and saw it had a circle with the same stylized dragon on it that the broaches and cloak pins did. Then the aroma of the food reminded her that she was starving, and as she began to eat what Eirik had set in front of her, the others started filling their own trenchers.

They seemed to burst to life after that, eating ravenously and chatting with excited voices, even Bo didn't seem as brooding as he was, which made her smile.

"Is that your brand?" Sara asked quietly.

Elise looked at her and furrowed her brows. "Brand?" she asked.

"From the bonding. Eirik told me that when we bond with the island, we'll receive a brand. Well, they call it a brand, but from how they describe it, it sounds more like a tattoo. Is that yours?" Sara gestured to the dragon head peeking from beneath her blouse.

"I suppose," she said and raised her hand to it, pulling her shirt out briefly as she peered down at it.

Sara gasped. "I thought it'd be smaller," she said and smiled. "And not so real looking. Yours looks like Leif's."

"Leif has one like this? I thought only Eirik did," she said and bit at her lips thoughtfully.

"He said you were unique," she grinned at her.

Elise brought her cup to her lips and drank deeply. She knew it was mead, but she felt she might need it to get through dinner. She then ate hungrily, not even saving room for the sweet bread that someone made, and before she knew it, the dishes were being cleared away, all but the cups and pitchers.

"Are you well sated?" Eirik asked with curved lips. "With food, 'tis my meaning," then his smile grew to a grin.

She chuckled and elbowed him lightly. "I'm full as a plump tick. Now will you tell me what's going on?" she asked.

"Aye, when the lasses are finished."

"Okay, how about explaining my tattoo?" she glanced at Leif

then back to him.

He tightened his lips briefly before they extended into a smile. "I see it has grown ta maturity," he indicated toward her chest.

"Oh yeah, it has. It covers nearly half my body." She pulled her neckline to the side, exposing the entire head and neck up to where it disappeared over her shoulder.

Jesse took in a sharp breath as she revealed the dragon's head. "That is awesome," he said in amazement.

"Aye," Eirik said as he worked her fingers loose and covered her tattoo. "She be unique, as I said," he winked at Jesse then gazed at Elise. "'Tis a discussion for after, aye?"

Elise huffed out her breath. "Can I get any answers?" she looked to Leif.

"Aye," he chuckled, "When the lasses are done."

"Well tell me something. How long was I out? What day is it? How's Astrid doing? Something," she said with frustration.

"The windmill pipes are nearly laid. We should have running water in a day or two," Bo said from the other side of Eirik.

"That's wonderful, Bo. How did you manage to do it so fast?"

"'Tis Tyr's day, heartling," Eirik said lowly. "Astrid has recovered and doing well."

She peered up at him as her mouth dropped open, at which he closed gently and leaned in to whisper, "You ought naught make such expressions for it causes my fire ta rise within." He chuckled lightly as he saw her cheeks flare in color.

She lowered her head then reached for her cup and finished it. She was about to ask if there was any progress in them finding a way home for the four kids, when Sara, Kristin, and Tristan came in, each reclaiming their seats and filling their cups. Good, now she could get some answers.

Eirik cleared his throat and licked at his lips before he looked at her. "All five have decided ta stay. They were nary coerced nor threatened. 'Tis of their own choosing. This eve we bond them with the island," he said then lifted his cup in the air, followed by all six of the others and waited, looking at her. She reached for her cup and raised it, then lowered it as she frowned.

"Are you all certain?" she asked as she refilled her cup.

"Yes," they said in unison then laughed.

She was about to raise her cup again but paused. "What about your families?" she asked looking across the table at Jesse, Kristin, and Tristan.

"We've already talked it over at length and we're all in agreement," Bo said and peered around Eirik to see her. "This will be our family now," he circled his raised cup to indicate to all of them and smiled.

"I see," she sighed and raised her cup then said, "But...," then stopped as she heard the resounding groan. "Okay, okay," she chuckled and lifted her cup as high as the others.

Once her cup was raised, they drank simultaneously. Both Eirik and Leif then stood and went to the edge of the dais as the others lined up in front of them; Kristin and Tristan in front of Leif, and Sara, Bo, and Jesse in front of Eirik.

Elise got up and moved to the side to watch as Sara sucked in a deep breath and stepped closer to Eirik. He raised his hands to her shoulders and asked, "Do you freely consent ta the bond which the island offers?"

"I do," she said confidently and smiled up at him.

He nodded and placed his hands on either side of her head as he closed his eyes and inhaled deeply, drawing the Heill into him then tilted his head to hers and sliding his right hand to her exposed sternum as his left pressed against the back of her neck to hold her in place. As his hand heated, he then transferred the Heill into her indicated by the bright red glow where his hands touched her and then streaked in luminated veins throughout her body. When the transfer was complete, he held her close as he sat her on the step then straightened and prepared for the next.

While Eirik bonded the lads, Leif did the lasses and gestured Kristin forward. She looked up at Leif and tightened her lips causing him to smile. "Nil worries, dearling," he said as he caressed her cheek lightly and drew her closer into him. As he embraced her, he whispered, "Do you give yourself freely ta the bond in which the island offers?"

"I do," she said quietly into his chest.

He held her tightly within his right arm as he gathered the Heill to transfer then bent and inclined his head to her lips, breathing the Heill into her mouth as they kissed. He drew back when he felt it ignite and move throughout her, giving his eyes a silvery sheen. He eased her down to his feet and beckoned Tristan forward.

Each one was given the Heill by different transferals, Elise assumed it had some significance, but she couldn't really figure out how. Even her own differed from any of theirs, but she figured that had something more to do with the mating. When they were finished, the brothers returned to the table and downed their drinks and refilled everyone else's, as the kids sat on the step with a look of elation on their faces. She too returned to the table and took her seat.

"Are they going to be all right?" she smiled as she brought the cup to her lips but paused. "They all look... um... euphoric," she chuckled then drank deeply.

Eirik narrowed his eyes at her as he tried to make sense of the word she used until he asked, "What is euphoric?"

She smiled and flicked her eyes at Leif then back. "What you feel after sex." However, by the look on both their faces, 'sex' wasn't part of their vocabulary. If they didn't know the word sex, any other word she had wouldn't be of any help either. "Hmm, it's the feeling after two people... um...," she kind of gestured with her hands as she said, "Making love? It's the afterglow."

Eirik quickly grasped her hands, and his cheeks reddened a smidge as Leif uttered quietly, "Swive," then lowered his head but lifted his eyes to her to see if he understood right.

Elise burst out laughing at their reactions. Eirik certainly wasn't shy in bed, but to talk about sex in the open embarrassed him and Leif to no end. "I'm sorry for laughing," she said. "I had no idea what word you used for sex. And you shouldn't be embarrassed either," she smiled up at Eirik.

"You should hear what word they use for 'hit'," Jesse said as he dropped into his seat at the table. "Fuck," he chuckled, and she smiled. "Imagine my surprise the first time Eirik told me to fuck him when we were sparring in the courtyard," he snickered.

Elise grinned, "Did you enlighten him to its meaning for us?" She couldn't quite keep the smile from her face, especially when she felt Eirik's hand on her knee and she flicked her gaze his way to see he was bright red.

"Oh, yeah," Jesse said still snickering. "He ended the match rather quickly."

"What does it mean for you?" Leif asked but could probably guess by the look on Eirik's face.

Elise tried to soothe Eirik's embarrassment by clasping her hand with his, but then looked at Leif and said, "It's kind of a catch all word because it can be used in place of any word, but initially its meaning was the same as the act of sex or in your case the act of swiving."

"Bragi wept," Eirik muttered and closed his eyes as he put his head in his hand.

"Although now I can see how the word has evolved into our meaning. It must be through kennings. It would seem they elude or imply through short phrases of things they don't say in the open. It's kind of poetic. Kennings such as sword-dew or even woman's dew, is pretty easy to figure out..." Eirik's hand tightened on hers in warning as he peered back at her beneath the hand that hid his face from the two that sat across from them. "Maybe I'm wrong," she said then continued, "Maybe there are just some things they don't discuss at all, at least not in mixed company," she smiled.

"Do you ever get tired of teaching," Sara grinned at her as she sat down.

"Not really, no," she chuckled. "I like to understand, and I guess that I assume others do too."

"Well, as much as I'd like more understanding, I'm feeling quite tired," she smiled at her then rose to go to bed.

"Me too," Jesse agreed then started for their room.

"Maybe we should get the rest of them to bed," Elise said as she too rose and saw Bo splayed out on the floor.

Eirik was more than happy to depart from the others as he moved toward Bo and heaved him over his shoulder and took him to the guest chamber. As he laid him out in his bower, a niggling sensation struck him. He flipped him over onto his stomach and lifted his shirt then pulled it back down quickly before any others saw. He straightened and looked to Elise, who was standing in the doorway watching Leif carry Kristin to her bed and Jesse did the same with Tristan.

"Sara," he said loud enough to get her attention. "Where be your brand?" he asked quietly when she approached.

"I don't know, I haven't looked. Why?" she asked with creased brows.

He moved closer and pulled her into an embrace as he concentrated on the Heill within her. With a sigh, he released her and said, "I need you or Jesse ta undress Bo and mayhap the lasses before you abed." Then he turned to find Leif, who was crouched to reignite their fire. "Let it die," he said then moved to the door. He grabbed Elise's hand and dragged her behind him back to the table where he downed what was left in his cup.

"What's wrong, Eirik. You're scaring me," Elise said as she clutched his hand in both of hers.

He smiled down at her as his eyes shimmered silver. "'Tis nil wrong. 'Tis…"

"Why nary a fire?" Leif asked as he drew closer.

"'Tis for the same purpose I let the one in my chamber die," he quirked a brow at him. "As much as I wished it, 'twould seem you are nary the only ta be unique," he peered down at her and grinned.

"What does that even mean?" she said with furrowed brows.

Leif nodded his head to the door of the longhouse and Eirik pulled her toward it and all the way to the barn. Once inside, he released her hand to remove his tunic and serk. She took several steps back when she saw Leif was doing the same, unsure of their intentions. When Eirik had everything but his breeches removed, he came toward her and grasped her hand and pulled her near the fire where Leif stood. "Trust me," he said and slipped his hands beneath her blouse then lifted it away.

Leif turned away from her and began untying his wrapping as Eirik turned her to face Leif's back. She could see what appeared to be a dragon similar to the one on Eirik's back, but slightly smaller. "Dragon," Eirik said.

"I can see it's a dragon, Eirik, but it doesn't explain anything," she said as she reached her hand toward it. Even though it seemed to be bound by his bandages, she could still see its head and other appendages. As the binding loosened, she helped him remove it and pulled the cloth from his shoulder. Oddly enough, the wound on Leif's shoulder appeared to have penetrated the dragon's shoulder too. She traced her finger over the nearly healed wound.

Eirik turned her gently to face him and said, "Dragon," as he pointed to himself and then to her. "Dragon," he said lowly and rubbed his thumb over the head of her tattoo as if he was petting it.

"I still don't understand," she said looking up at him.

Eirik nodded and began unfastening her jeans – he had learned how to use the odd fasteners – and tugged them down. "Trust me," he murmured as he felt her resistance and then skimmed them down her legs. Before he straightened, he hooked his fingers around her tiny garment she called panties and lowered them as well, then he stood and unhooked her breast-binder and slipped it from her shoulders.

He quickly shed his breeches and pulled her toward the back exit followed by Leif in the same naked state. Eirik held her against his front with her back against him as he allowed Leif to pass them. "Dragon," he muttered and indicated toward Leif, who stood with his head bowed but gradually raised it along with his arms, and then with a final snap of his hands, he transformed.

Elise gasped loudly and tried to back up as a massive scaly tail came down toward her, but Eirik held her solid as he watched the tail whip and then curl around the beast in front of them. "Dragon," he whispered in awe. He then kissed her head as he released her and moved alongside his brother, then proceeded to do the same, except he faced her.

When he transformed, he shook his entire gargantuan body, half again larger than Leif's and darker grey nearly black, then lowered his incredibly huge and thorny head to the ground in front of her and snorted, blasting her with hot air sending her hair up into a flurry. She let out a small laugh and reached out toward his snout. She glided her hand over his nose ridge, up between his silvery blue eyes that gleamed at her, and along one massive horn that her fingers wouldn't even reach around. She then curled her fingers around another thorny protrusion and lightly stroked behind it but stopped when he began that growling purr that she had heard him do before. "Sorry," she chuckled.

He snorted at her then carefully nudged her to the side of him with his snout as he stretched one giant clawed paw out to her. Drawing all the talons back but one, he gently pressed the curve of it against her chest.

"You want me to turn into a dragon?" she laughed at the absurdity. "I don't know how." She heard Leif snort and growl from somewhere behind Eirik's mass. She sighed heavily and closed her eyes. Eirik moved to give her more space, shoving Leif over as well, then he waited with great anticipation. He felt her drawing in the Heill as she lifted her arms and then it expelled with the snap of her hands. She transformed into a magnificent white beauty with sleek iridescent scales glinting in the moonlight, thin needlelike spines ran down the ridge of her back, white leathery wings, and large crown horns like his own, but was now flailing about and sounding off in short moaning roars. Eirik leaped onto her and spread his wings to help pin her down. Leif was quick to her other side, both pressing against her with their entire bodies.

When she calmed down and stopped moving and was vocalizing a mournful whine, they cautiously eased away from her. She was somehow on her back with one wing trapped under Eirik and the other folded around her. Eirik snorted and backed up, moving his feet with care, but Leif stayed close, and when he was certain Eirik was off her wing he shouldered her over to set her right. He quickly pressed low to the ground as she extended her wings and flapped them a couple of times before she folded them into her sides. That was Eirik's cue to approach and he nuzzled along her neck to under her head as he purred proudly.

Leif grunted and shouldered her again before he turned toward the open field, indicating for her to follow. Taking a few paces out, he unfolded his wings and within a few strong strokes, he was hovering above it. Eirik nudged her forward into the field, urging her to do the same then gave her plenty of room to do so. Elise opened her wings, flapped them a few times then swung her mighty head back towards Eirik and tilted it. He gave her a snort before he spread his wings out and up then hopped as he brought them down in a strong stroke.

Elise followed his instruction and before she knew it was off the ground, but soon back down again. She stood there in thought for a moment, of planes, helicopters, and rockets. She understood the hop would give her lift, but it wasn't strong enough to keep her there. She then hunkered down and sprang from the ground then unfurled her wings to catch her, giving several powerful strokes to keep her lifted. Now she was hovering, but she wouldn't be able to maintain this for long. How does she go higher... and forward? Feeling pressure in her midsection, she gathered enough courage to peer around herself and saw she was much higher than she thought, but still hovered above the same area from which she bounded. She also noticed Eirik below and just to the right of her. He must have helped her go higher, she thought.

Birds! Several images of birds taking off and in flight flashed through her mind and then she let herself fall, but at an angle, propelling herself forward. Within a few more strokes, she was flying. She was actually flying! But now her arms... um... wings were getting tired. She wondered briefly if she was high enough to glide. She was. However, now she was just going in a straight line and running out of land below her. If she didn't do something soon, she'd be out over the ocean.

Just as panic began to set in, she felt a nudge beneath her right wing that tilted her towards the left. Ah, she understood. Then she felt something bump her tail. That caused her to bank even more sharply. As understanding set in, she swayed first one way and then the other, using her tail like a rudder in conjunction with the tilt of her wings. Of a sudden, Leif swooped up past her, right in front of her face, and went skyward. As she lifted her head to watch him soar and gave her wings a flap, she followed. This is how she went higher. He was teaching her and Eirik stayed on her right to help with minor corrections.

With that understanding, she followed Leif through the darkened skies and copied each movement he made until she felt she had mastered each one, that is until he came at her, straight as an arrow. How was she going to dodge him? She began flapping as hard as she could to stop her momentum and hovered. Then she lowered her head and began falling, much like he was doing. As the ground loomed closer she spread her wings and raised her head to slow and then when her feet touched the ground, she tumbled head over ass across the field, landing on her back. She laid there, unmoving for a moment until she felt the gentle nudging of Eirik's head coaxing her up. She righted herself with a snort then rose to her feet. She was tired.

Leif once again bumped her and gave her a snort intending her to follow him. With a grumble she did so. When she was close enough, he opened his mouth and blew out his dragon fire across the field, then swung his head to her and nodded toward the burning field.

Elise raised her head with her emerald eyes wide and looked at Eirik who also encouraged her to try. She slowly moved forward as Leif stepped back, not knowing yet what her element was, and nary did he want to be wrapped in vines or doused by water. Eirik chortled and swung his head at Leif. She took in a deep breath and closed her eyes, having no idea what she was doing, she opened her mouth and exhaled sharply, a bolt of lightning ejected from her mouth. She yelped and sprang backward, bowling over the other two as she kicked her powerful legs to scramble away and then to right herself. Once again, Eirik pounced on her to hold her down before she got hurt. He slowly backed off her and bumped her forward as he heard the lamenting growls and chuffs from Leif below them. He chortled again as he moved to the field with her.

Rubbing his head along her neck and against her head, he coaxed her to do it again and as she opened her mouth, she sent out a new streak of electricity then snapped it closed. He nodded then turned her back to the barn. As they approached, Leif was standing outside in human form and dressed in his breeches and boots with his serk in his hands. He smiled up at them as he held the serk out to Elise. She lowered her head to it and sniffed then snorted before she transformed back to human. He dropped it over her as she raised her arms and it drifted into place.

"I'm in awe, Lady Elise. I have ne'er seen a skyfire dragon," he grinned down at her.

She smiled shyly up at him. "What did I say about that? I'm not a lady in that sense of the word."

"Aye, you are now," Eirik said as he stalked toward her and guided her inside with a hand to the small of her back.

"Huh?" she glanced up at him.

"When you became life-mates with Eirik," Leif said as he followed them in.

She reached down to pick up her clothes and slipped her shoes on. "Is there anything else that you haven't mentioned?" she said as she waited, holding her wadded jeans and underthings against her side under her arm as if she was carrying a football.

Eirik belted his breeches in place and laced up his boots as he peered at her thoughtfully. He then held his left palm up to her. "'Tis a summoning. Every spring, Leif and I are forced to change.

We usually go help the king during that time because this island can't sustain us for long in that form unless we go elsewhere ta hunt."

"So, you're going to leave us? For how long?" she asked as a bit of panic contorted her voice.

"I nary wish it ta be so, heartling," he said as he grazed the back of his fingers over her cheek. "But if needs must, I'll see ta hiring help." He tried to reassure her, but the look in her eyes nigh broke his heart. He grasped her hand and started back to the house.

"What about the kids? Are they going to be dragons too?" she asked as she glanced up at him then over to Leif, who shrugged.

"I know naught. 'Twas a surprise ta me that you are. Bo will be... something else, nary a dragon though nor Sara, but those are the only two I was close enough to sense. Leif? What of Kristin?"

"'Tis hopeful, but I know naught," he said and bit at his lip.

Elise eyed him with a raised brow then looked back to Eirik. "Do the other people here know what you are?"

He nodded. "They do."

"Are they dragons too?" she asked a bit apprehensive at the answer considering they would be left to defend themselves while they were away.

"Nay, but there be one you should be wary of, 'tis Nidpigger." He tightened his lips and regarded her as he wondered why she ne'er told him that he attacked her.

"Oh, I'm well aware of him," she chuckled. "Is he the one that shot you?" she asked Leif.

The two men glanced at each other. "'Tis possible, but I know naught. I nary saw, I only felt the tainted Heill."

Elise let out a sigh as she worried even more now and felt Eirik's hand tighten on hers and looked up. "We have more ta show you," he said as his lips curved. He then guided her into the hall and came to a stop in front of the door that he kept locked.

As he unlocked it and swung it slowly open, she could see the room was filled with things, but there wasn't enough light to see exactly what they were. Then suddenly there was a flare of light as Leif lit a torch with his dragon fire. She could now see the room had many treasures; weapons and shields lined one wall; bolts of cloth were stacked on shelves; large ancient vases, midsized urns, amphorae of multiple proportions, and small ampules lined the back wall of shelving; and mounds of furs and rugs piled on the floor.

Leif handed the torch to Eirik as he closed the door behind them and locked it before Eirik tugged her toward the back corner closest to Eirik's room. He then descended into a narrow stone stairway and pulled her in behind him with Leif following. The lower she got, the more of the room she could see, and it seemed to be as large as the entire longhouse not just the room above. It too was filled, but with more precious treasures than what was above. The firelight glinted and sparkled off every surface. Eirik put the torch in a wall mount aligned with large, polished trays reflecting the light throughout the room. She gasped as her eyes drifted over small silver overlaid chests overflowing with jewels, ropes of pearls and gems, and gold coins. There were even larger chests containing more of the same. In the center of the room stood a pedestal with a large golden crown perched atop it and a smaller circlet beside it. She reached her hand out toward it but hesitated to touch it.

Eirik cleared his throat. "'Twas our father's and mother's," he said lowly and looked away. "This," he said louder, "Is our trove and now 'tis yours as well." He rolled her hand over and placed a key within it.

"Oh, I couldn't," she said and started backing away, but his hand tightened on hers as Leif pressed a hand to her back.

"As his life-mate, you are entitled," Leif said from her other side. "Just as my life-mate will be as well." His lips curved slightly as he glanced down at her. "Someday," he said as his brow flicked.

"Oh," she said softly and peered around the room as the enormity struck her near dumb with the implication of what they were saying. "You're a king!" she blurted out and stared up at Eirik with wide eyes.

"Nay," he said and smiled gently. "Mayhap once I might have been, but nary now. Our people have been hunted ta nigh extinction and have scattered ta the winds." He shook his head.

"You give us hope, Lady Elise," Leif said quietly.

"Me?" she asked then widened her eyes briefly as she understood what he meant. "Oh, you mean…"

Eirik chuckled and squeezed her hand. "We live very long lives, even more so here. 'Tis time enough for that. Let's abed."

Leif snorted softly as he turned back to the stairs. "Seems you be well on your way ta doing just that," he grinned.

Eirik cuffed him on the shoulder even as he too grinned and followed him up, removing the torch and carried it with him. When they left the room, he locked the door once more then pulled her toward their chamber still grinning.

Odin's Day

Broken Bond

Elise woke early the next day after her nearly continuous sleep for the past three days and her lips curled at hearing Eirik's purr vibrating against her ear as she laid on his chest. She reckoned that was what the sound was that emanated from him when he was contented. Then she wondered if she too made that noise, although she had never heard herself do it. She giggled softly at herself and licked at her lips. She was happy. She hadn't really ever given a thought to a lifelong commitment before and she gave it easily, not to mention quickly, to Eirik. But then again, she had never been so drawn to a man as strongly as she had been to him. It felt... right. Then her thoughts turned to what Eirik had told her last night about them leaving and it soured her mood.

"What be amiss, heartling?" he asked in a soft whisper as he slid his arm up her back and curled his fingers around just under her arm and squeezed.

She was so buried in her thoughts that she hadn't heard him stop purring. "Nothing," she said on a sigh. "I was just thinking," she said dismissively as she smiled up at him briefly and grazed her hand over his chest absently.

"'Tis nary true. We burn as one. 'Tis concern within," he said as he peered down at the top of her head then tilted her face toward his gently with his other hand.

"I guess I'm just nervous about being left here alone with the kids, protecting them... And I don't want you to go, if I'm completely honest with you as well as myself," she said after a moment of hesitation.

He smiled and leaned to kiss her lightly. "'Tis my thoughts as well, but nary so much on your defense. Three days hence, we'll know for a certain what Bo will be. Methinks he'll be of much help. And I have tested their skills in battle. I have nil worries of that."

"Well, I'm glad you don't," she chuckled wryly.

"Leave it be for the now, heartling. 'Twill do your heart nil good ta dwell on it." He then bent forward and pressed his lips to hers as he pulled her more atop him to deepen the kiss. And even more so when he rolled them onto her back.

Elise quietly opened the door to the kids' chamber and closed it just as silently behind her. She wanted to check on them and see if any of them was awake or needed tended to since none of them was up for breakfast and it was now midday. She slid the small torch into place then turned to check on Bo first. Kneeling beside his bower, she touched her hand to his head. He was just as hot and sweaty as the little girl in the village. She tightened her lips then went to move to Sara's bower but saw Jesse sitting on the floor with his back against the front of it. She stepped over him to check on Sara. When she reached her hand out to her, she rolled to her side.

"I think Bo's sick. He's been restless all night and running a pretty high temperature," she said and sighed out heavily. "I'm feeling kind of run down myself."

"It's the bonding, honey," Elise whispered. "I think it's what Eirik refers to as gathering Heill. I'll go get you some water and some cool compresses to help. Do the others feel like you do?"

"I don't know. Jesse helped me undress them and then we both sacked out. I only know about Bo, because he's right next door. When he woke me up, I got up to check on him, but couldn't get enough energy to do anything about it."

Elise patted her gently. "Just rest, honey. I'll see to him. I'll be right back with that water." She stood and hurried out the door.

When she returned, she carried a tray of cups and two pitchers of water, but Eirik and Leif were right behind her with buckets of water. They sat one by each of them and Elise handed them a handful of cloths before she filled each cup with chilled water. She went to Sara first.

"Here, honey, drink this," she said softly as she helped her up and put the cup to her mouth. Sara sighed out in relief and Elise smiled. "I'll leave it right here for you. And here," she had dunked one of the cloths in the pail and wrung it out then handed it to her.

"Thanks," she said and laid it across her face.

Elise chuckled then moved in beside Eirik, who was tending to Bo. "How's he doing?" she whispered.

"He'll be all right," Eirik replied as he moved the cool cloth over his face and neck then dipped it back in the water and did the same to his chest. Tossing the cloth in the bucket, he then rolled Bo onto his stomach and repeated the process on his back. Then he pointed to the tattoo. "See his brand? 'Tis different from how yours began and yet alike."

Elise looked at the brand on the upper left center of his back, and to her, it looked like an embryo with an extended tail that curled around it. "What did mine look like?"

"'Twas like this," he said as he drew a spiral on Bo's back with his finger.

"Hmm," she said as she stood and went back to Jesse to get him moved to his bower after leaving a cup of water for Bo. "Hey, honey, wake up," she said as she submerged a cloth into the pail and ran it over his face. "Let's get you back to bed."

"Yeah, I'm up," he said sluggishly and started to lay over to go back to sleep.

"No, let's get you back to bed," she chuckled as she urged him to his feet and then guided him to his bed.

"Here, I brought you some water to drink and a cool compress. Do you need anything else?" she asked as she held the cup out to him.

He took the water and drank deeply from it then shook his

head. "Nah, I'm good." She smiled and started to back away when he grabbed her hand. "Hey, how's Sara doing? She looked like she was going to collapse when we were putting the others to bed. And then I found her in the floor last night."

Elise smiled and patted his hand. "She feels about the same as you do. Now get some rest." Then she rose to her feet and stood beside Eirik as he watched Leif tend to both Kristin and Tristan thoughtfully. Tristan first and now Kristin.

They watched as he took his time laving her with the cool compress with one hand and clasped her hand with his other. Then he turned and looked up at Eirik with tightened lips and concerned eyes as he shook his head slightly. "I feel nary the bond as I did with Tristan," he said lowly.

Eirik squatted next to him and placed his hand over theirs. As he concentrated, he sighed out heavily. "She has bonded with the island," he said then peered over at Leif. "Nary so with you."

"She consented, for a certain," Leif argued.

"Mayhap, nary wholly so. 'Twill be all right. Once she awakens, needs must a bit more convincing till she feels it so here," Eirik said as he gestured toward her heart. He then squeezed their hands and rose glancing at Elise before heading out the door.

She turned to follow him with creased brows. "What's wrong with Kristin?" she asked before he got too far away from her and tugged on his arm to halt him.

He scrutinized her as he thought of the words he needed to explain. "I fear she was nary ready for the bond as the others were." He swiped at his lips. "She spoke the words of her consent but was nary certain of her decision. 'Twas intended for her ta bond with Leif, so nil other could lay claim. As I did with you..."

Elise's eyes widened as she said, "As a life-mate?" then scowled up at him, fiercely so.

"Nay, heartling, nary as yet." He shrugged slightly as he lifted his hands to her upper arms. "Sara, Bo, and Jesse are bonded ta me for their safety. Tristan and Kristin were ta be bonded ta Leif for theirs. 'Tis a high obligation ta undertake and nary made lightly. She be bonded ta the island, but still can be claimed by another should she so consent ta the other, whereas you five are safe from any other on the island."

"I don't mean to be thick here, but I don't understand. I thought the intent *was* to bond them to the *island* so they would stay and not vanish," she said with a bit of venom and continued to scowl up at him as her hands balled into fists at her sides.

"Aye, as well as with us, so none other could claim them. So, they would nary be thralls, as *you* wished," he said a bit louder as his brows drew together then tightened his lips to keep their shared anger at bay, but his breathing became heavier as hers did.

She stared at him as her eyes widened. "No, now they're *your* slaves, that's what you're telling me," she nearly yelled.

"Nary... are... ye... slaves," he said clearly and harshly. He inhaled deeply and pulled her into an embrace then calmly said, "'Tis the way of the island. I have bonded many ta the island, some with consent and some nary so, but all are given the choice ta stay or nay. I create the bond with the island through the transferal of Heill. I create the bond with me with the consent. I nil longer transfer Heill without consent for it leaves them open ta become bound ta another. With Kristin, if she should go ta the thorp and someone there convinces her to consent, then she would be bound ta them thereafter. Ta do their bidding, enforced by the will of the heritor, for she would have nary a choice. I am the heritor of many, but nary do I force my will on any, heartling."

Elise huffed out her breath. "To make sure we're on the same page here, you have enthralled them, but you won't force them to do anything against their will, right?"

"Aye, ta be under my shield and none other would trouble them. You five may roam the island as you wish. But be warned, those that be nary bonded ta me, mayhap will test my leniency."

"You mean that the ones that aren't your thralls may try something? Like 'long winter, one slake-whore' kind of something?"

"Aye, 'tis my meaning. I have heard of such crimes at our spring and fall things and would have ta set recompence. I have yet ta have one of mine be taken in such a manner. Ta be fair, I have but a few females." His lips curved as he gazed down at her, but it wasn't returned.

"You have female thralls?" she asked looking up at him.

"Aye, as you well know. 'Tis Ingrid, Astrid, Sara, Jasmin, you, and but a few others," he said still smiling.

"Who is Jasmin?" she asked since she was the only other one that he cared to name who she didn't know.

"'Tis the slake-whore," he grinned.

Her eyes widened once again. "The slake-whore is yours?"

He chuckled at her reaction, extremely amused, if not pride-broadened. "Aye, 'twas her trade afore I brought her ta the island and I did so ta keep the men happy for I've had less crimes as such since. She keeps all earnings, for a certain."

"Well, if Ingrid is yours, then why is she so nervous around you?" she asked as she loosened her fists and slid them around him.

He shook his head, still smiling. "I know naught. She has always been so. I have ne'er mistreated her nor any of them."

She tilted her head against his shoulder and sighed out her breath, then, after a moment, she said, "So, it's really important to get Kristin to truly consent to Leif before something happens?"

"Aye, nil worries. I know my brother well. Leif will see it through," he said then squeezed her into him and pressed his lips to her head.

In the deepest darkest depths of the night, when the hearth fires burned low and the occupants of the longhouse were swathed in slumber, six figures crept through the entrance draped in shadow. The head of the column paused at each door before coming to the last and stealthily slipped inside followed by the rest. They spread throughout the chamber, but the leader of the others moved quickly but silently from one bower to the next, stopping once he found Kristin. He carefully rolled her into his arms, and preceded by one, escaped back through the door as the others waited to see if any stirred, then one by one, left as quietly as they came.

The girl was bound over the back of a horse, in front of the rider, a thick leather collar was placed around her small neck and locked before being carried off, swallowed by the night as they and the four other mounted figures, raced northeast around the rise. The leader watched as they disappeared then mounted his own horse and went southeast.

Kristin rolled to her back and let out a small moan as she felt the biting stone cut into her tender skin, but she was barely aware of her surroundings. Her mind refused to keep any focus as it dimmed to silence once again.

Eirik was awakened by the incessant pounding on his door and the bellowing of his brother, his mind jerked alert. He rushed to his door to release the lock and was pushed backward as Leif burst in. "She's gone," he growled. "She lay nary in her bed consumed by Heill fire as the others."

"Settle, brother," Eirik said as he hurried to dress. "We'll find her. Prepare the horses."

"I should have abed her with me," Leif mumbled as he retreated to do what Eirik had told him.

Elise, too, dressed hastily as she looked to Eirik with concern. "Where would she go?" she asked.

"She'd nary go anywhere," Eirik said as he placed his axe in his belt and strapped his knife to his thigh. "She's been taken."

"Who would take her?' Elise didn't understand why anyone would risk stealing into *their* longhouse and kidnapping Kristin. Everyone knew that they were not only dragons but also, they pretty much ruled the island. They would respond with a vengeance. Eirik with the anger provoked by the insult and Leif fueled by his affection for the girl. Elise almost felt pity for those that took her, but it was so fleeting that it was as if it hadn't existed at all, once her own anger took over.

When she was dressed, she swiftly entered the kitchen and loaded a leather bag with food and skins of water and mead. She wasn't certain how long the search would take, but she didn't want them deterred by hunger or thirst. Having it filled, she ran to the door where Eirik was about to exit, carrying two swords.

"Take this," she said breathlessly. "It's food. Find her quickly," she smiled slightly in hope that what she said would be true.

He bent low and pressed his lips to hers and then said, "Keep safe."

She watched as he tossed the sword to the awaiting Leif then alighted his mount, securing the bag to his saddle, and then she breathed out heavily as they rode off to the southeast.

When Kristin next woke, it was so dark that she was uncertain she had even opened her eyes. Her nose was assaulted by revolting odors of rot and excrement that caused her to gag and gasp, scraping her delicate skin against the floor, and she could hear the scurrying of tiny feet somewhere out there in the blackness. She felt the stone floor beneath her and sent out her hand in search of something, anything. Disappointingly, nothing but the stone floor surrounded her, she found as she sat up to her knees, feeling straps tighten around her thighs with the movement and the distinct sound of metal dragging lightly on stone. She didn't explore any farther than her immediate area for fear of what she might find. "Hello?" she called out timidly into the dark, receiving no answer. "Is anyone there?" she tried again. Where was she? She knew this couldn't possibly be part of the bond, Leif would have told her, she was certain. She rubbed her bare arms with her hands in the chill darkness and they drifted over bands around her biceps then down to her wrists and she felt another one around her waist. She didn't understand. The bond was supposed to allow them to live freely on the island, not this, whatever this was, she thought as she crossed her arms over her chest and felt yet another strap under her breasts and crossing between them over her shoulders to her back. Just then did she realize that she wore no clothing, not even her bra and panties nor her nightgown or t-shirt, just these leather straps around specific parts of her body. She slunk down toward despair as she fell back to the stone floor.

She didn't know how long she had laid there deprived of sight, huddled into herself, and shivering against the unforgiving and ruthless surface before she heard the rasping footfalls of someone coming. Angling her head toward the sound to where she could see, she waited. A light dimly brightened across from her outlining a crude stone opening but didn't illuminate any farther as two hulking silhouettes came toward her. She cried out in fear as a hood was dropped over her head. Then she heard the clinking of chains rattling all around her and roughly being attached to each of the bands on her limbs, the last she heard near her head beneath her chin. The room illumed more from what she could see of the irregular floor beneath the loose-fitting hood. She whimpered at the state of herself, as she peered down her body, bound in chains and saw several pairs of booted feet around her, one pair much finer than the others. Slowly, she felt each chain tighten and pull where they attached to the bands, but the first was the one at her waist, just under her ribs then nearly simultaneously the one that crossed her chest. Hearing a low rumble of masculine laughter and feeling calloused hands pinch and squeeze roughly at her breasts, smack at her backside, and bite at her skin all over her, she screamed out in horror for what they had planned and struggled against her restraints. No one spoke a word, just gravelly giggles and gritty laughter answered her screams.

As she hung suspended vertically, the belts at her waist and ribs supported much of her weight, she swung gently from her tired struggles and whimpered. Then as she heard a low murmur across from her, but couldn't understand what was said, the chains jingled over gears and her head tilted backward as her legs were lifted into a horizonal position and turned upward. Tears now soaked the cloth hood from her sobs as her fear rose up in her again and she screamed hoarsely. When she stopped moving, she felt tension on her legs pulling them farther apart. "No, no, no," she cried out and tried to squeeze her legs back together. "Please, no," she wailed as she felt a hand slide along her thigh and the heat of a torch near her. She continued with her pleas as hands grasped a hold on her thighs and then she felt the scrape of teeth right before they bit down, and she screamed with the pain. Then the wet slickness of a tongue laved over it and then continued to slither up her furrow and within her several times before a finger was forced into her opening and worked in deeper then stopped suddenly and withdrew.

She was then raised upright again, to her relief, but then was tilted in the other direction, now she faced the floor. Hearing the jingling chain on the gears a bit more, she was adjusted lower to the floor. More whispering came from a distance. She heard someone distinctly say 'no' and then followed by another voice saying, "I command ye to..." and the rest was muttered where she couldn't hear. Hanging as such, she could see her body now and the jaggedness of a cavern wall, but nothing else until the lower half of the man with shiny boots appeared within her field of vision. She began crying louder as she could see the man loosen his belt and lower his breeches as he came up behind her. The chains jiggling a bit more causing her knees to move outward and more up beside her then lower till she could see only from his knees down. And his shiny boots. He slapped and pinched at her buttocks causing her to yelp and screech each time his treatment stung or bruised her skin then he took his time smearing something thick and greasy over her backside, within the crease, and made several swipes around her puckered rose-colored aperture. Another man stepped up to the side of her and began fondling one breast as another did the other, both coarse with their handling. One even bent across her back and bit her in hard nips. She sobbed and whimpered as her body was abused, she had no more strength left to fight the restraints. Then her entire body tensed and drew into itself as she felt the man behind her rub up against her with his phallus coating himself in whatever it was that he had applied to her.

She held her breath and she squeezed her eyes closed, bracing for what he was about to do, but then she heard the slap of fists hitting flesh and the laughter was replaced by shouts and hollers of complaint. Groans and moans accompanied fighting sounds, the crack of crunching bones, and the dull thud of bodies landing on the floor. When the room had quieted, she was lowered to the floor and the chains swiftly removed then wrapped in a cloth and carried away just before she passed out.

Kristin woke again, but instead of the harshness of cold stone beneath her she was surrounded by the warmth of furs and sighed out feeling the softness of the mattress beneath her, which she quickly identified as down, not straw. Her entire body hurt reminding her of what had happened, and she began to weep. She also felt the thick collar still around her neck although all the others had been removed and she still was naked. How could he do this to her? She thought he had had feelings for her, but this? This was savage. Maybe Tristan was right about alpha males. She sobbed anew.

"Hey, hey, hey. Nary do this. Ye be safe now," a soft masculine voice cooed from beside her, though at some distance. Startled, she peered around wildly then recoiled from the large man that came toward her from a chair across the room. "Just rest. Ye have been through quite enough," he said kindly.

"Who are you?" she croaked with a husky voice, warily watching him as he stopped just a couple of feet from her and poured some water into a cup. His long, strawberry blond hair hung smoothly straight around his head and stopped between his chest and waist, and he was dressed in dark colored breeches and just a stark white serk, no tunic.

He held it out to her as he said, "My name be Faolan. Drink this, you must thirst." He gently smiled at her from beneath his meticulously trimmed beard that came to a point, elongating the sharp features of his face into a triangle.

Kristin cautiously reached out a hand from beneath the fur and slowly wrapped her fingers around the cup, never taking her eyes off him. Then quickly brought it to her lips and drank deeply. She was so incredibly thirsty, and the water was sweet, soothing to her throat.

"Slowly," he warned and reached for the cup too late. She started coughing and noisily inhaling, trying to catch her breath and then it came back up as she swung her head over the side of the bed, splashing the liquid on the wooden floor at his bare feet. He eased her back on the bed and poured her another cup. "Slowly," he said again and smoothed her hair away from her face. "Would you like some food?" he asked still squatting beside her and tenderly adjusting her hair.

She nodded slightly, and he straightened, walking across the room then disappeared as he descended the stairs. What was she doing here? This was not the farmstead. The room she was in was more of a loft and she could see all the way across the ceiling beam to where it ended on the opposite end of the house. She guessed the area below was one big room, much like the hall at the farmstead. He had chests that set along the opened end of the room and one that sat beside the chair he had been sitting in as well as one by the bed with a candle burning on it.

When he returned, he padded to her and set the tray on the chest next to the water pitcher. It held a few slices of cheese and a hunk of bread. As she held the fur against her, she snatched the bread from the tray and brought it to her mouth, taking a small bite. It hurt to swallow. "Where am I?" she asked.

He squatted beside the bed and wiped at the floor with a cloth. "My home," he said simply and creased his lips into a smile. "Ye were in need of some care after..." He lowered his eyes and glanced away. "'Twas unlikely the rogues would find ye here."

"Who were they?" she asked as her eyes glassed over with the memory and her hand went to the collar at her throat.

"Nithings, rogues who somehow escape the justice of the lords." His slim brow flicked. "My apologies for the collar," he said as he tilted his head toward her. "It seems ta hide ye Heill from others. I feared, should I remove it, they would find ye."

"Why me?" A tear escaped and dripped down her cheek.

He reached out and tenderly rubbed his thumb over it, and said, "Because you be unclaimed by any other. 'Twas careless of the lords ta make ye so. 'Tis nigh a beacon ta those that wish ta be the heritor of another, but also nithings such as they, would have nary fear of retaliation from another heritor, as ye be unclaimed. Aye, 'twas careless indeed." He tightened his lips as he sighed.

She scrutinized his face as she deciphered his words. Careless? That didn't really coincide with the brothers. They said that she'd be safe. Unclaimed? What did that mean? Unclaimed by a man, not married? "I don't understand," she said as she shook her head. "They said that if I consented, I would be safe."

"Ye consented?" he asked as his brows folded into a frown. "But ye remain unclaimed. Ye were nary ready for the Heill then. Careless," he said and looked away as the corners of his lips quirked nearly imperceptibly as he fought the grin. "Ye should rest," he said as he swung his head back to her and smiled softly, cupping her head. He then rose, extinguished the candle and turned.

"Don't leave me alone," she whimpered, which caused a thrilling shiver to rise up his back and over his skin then sink low in his loins.

He lowered his head as he drew his fingers into a fist then flexed them before he turned slightly back to her. "I have but one bed, milady," he said lowly.

She stared at his silhouette as she considered what he said. Being left alone in the darkness or share the bed with this kind man that saved her from the disgusting vile monsters. "Don't leave me alone, please," she repeated having decided.

"Aye, but needs must ta dowse the torches below," he said then continued to pad to the stairs and on down.

She watched as the amber glow gradually dimmed beyond

the chests until only a flickering illumination played on the slanted ceiling, then a darkened shadow rose from the edge and moved toward her. "Faolan?" she asked timidly and retreated from the advancing being.

"Aye, 'tis me," he said quietly and removed his serk and breeches before he turned to her, lifted the furs and slid beneath, turned on his side away from her.

"Thank you," she whispered and tilted her head into his back, just to have contact, some sense of safety.

"Rest, milady," he murmured as he slid his hand over his stomach and slowly down along his extended phallus, torturously so for he would have no relief this night if he wished her to consent to him. She needed to be carefully moved to align with him, but he felt he had sufficiently put himself in a better light as he reduced her perspective of the lords. His eyes rolled back, and his hand tightened on himself when he heard her whimpering in her sleep as she undoubtedly relived what he and his men did to her. His intention, and that of his men, was to have her every way possible, forcing her to consent just for the reprieve as he had done to others until he discovered she had never been had by a man, then his tactic changed. However, the sweet taste of her furrow still lingered on his tongue and the tightness of her sheath on but a single finger and nary even his largest, excited him beyond reason. His hand quickened its strokes as he recalled the memory himself until they both jerked. He in release and her awake with a gasp. He froze and waited, not even breathing as she put her hand to his back and up to his shoulder then her breaths evened out as she fell back to sleep. He rolled slightly as he reached for the cloth he had left on the floor and felt her hand clutch his shoulder. He cleaned himself of his seed and dropped the cloth back to the floor before he pressed his hand over hers in comfort as he silently admonished himself for nearly ruining what he had gained.

Kristin woke alone and her eyes darted fearfully around the room. Seeing no one around her she calmed down and scanned the room more thoroughly. She saw Faolan had laid out a white serk for her and brought her water, now cold, to wash with as well as a tray of food, which she ate hungrily before even dressing. After washing quickly because she couldn't stand to see the many bruises and bite marks that marred her body, she peeked down over the side into the lower part of the house. It was vacant. He had left her alone, all alone. What if the rogues found her? She eased backward till she was sitting on the bed, and she drew her knees up to her chest as fear overwhelmed her once again. She still couldn't believe Leif would do this to her. She knew he was attracted to her, but maybe that's as far as it went. Maybe she had only imagined that he felt something for her because she wanted it so much. But to do *that* to her, was savage in the strictest sense of the word. That kiss during her bonding, she didn't imagine, that's for sure. Maybe he didn't have anything to do with what happened to her. Faolan said it was careless of him to let her remain unclaimed which was the reason for what had happened. Surely, he would have known it too. So why didn't he claim her? Did he claim Tristan? Is that why she's not here with her? Did he find her demur innocence more attractive than her own bold aggressiveness? Oh, poor Tristan, she will hate being claimed by him. Her vision blurred with the unshed tears for her sister. How will she ever endure?

Unaware of the time that passed while she was lost in her thoughts, the sound of the front door caused her to jump backward on the bed and huddle into herself. She heard it close and then footsteps move around below her. Her body shuddered violently as she heard the heavy footfalls ascend the steps. As she recognized the outline of the dimly lit figure, she sprang from the bed and threw herself at him.

Faolan caught her within his arms with a quiet grunt and held her until she was ready to let go. "Shush, milady," he cooed softly as he held her head pressed against his neck and rolled his eyes. "Ye be safe with me."

"You left me alone," she mumbled against his skin.

"Only ta retrieve food and ta hear word of the rogues," he

said with creased lips as he felt her squeeze him tighter with the mention of the rogues. "'Tis word they be hunting for ye, so best ye stay hidden till they yield the pursuit, aye?" he said to embellish the lie and to be assured she stayed within the threshold.

She eased back away from him and nodded as she looked up at him, just noticing the bruising stark against his light skin. She lifted a hand to his face and tightened her lips. "Thank you for what you did," she said as a tear spilled over her lid with the memory.

He rubbed at the wetness and smiled gently. "'Tis nary a need for gratitude, milady," he said although he felt he'd soon be well rewarded for his efforts. "Ye have slept a might. Allow me ta fetch ye some food and drink," he said as he backed away from her and went down the steps.

She went back to the bed as she waited for his return. He was so kind to her, and he had taken quite a beating when he rescued her, she had now realized. She would have to find a way to repay him, somehow.

When he returned, he carried a tray heavily laden with meat, cheese, and bread, but also a long skinny vase and two metal goblets and set it on one of the chests near the stairs. He went to the chest that was by the chair and hauled it to the center of the floor then he tossed two large pillows beside the chest and moved the tray onto it. As he poured a dark red liquid from the vase into the goblets, he glanced at her from beneath his brows with a small smile. "Come, join me," he said as he eased himself down carefully, almost painfully, against one of the pillows and began removing his boots, which he flung away from him before he leaned back. He reached for the goblet and held it out to her.

Kristin came toward him and folded her legs to the side of her as she sat on the floor before she took the cup from him. "What is it?" she asked curiously as she brought it to her mouth. It was sweet.

"'Tis wine from the south," he smiled as he sipped at his own hoping the intoxicating liquid would work its wiles on her.

"It's good, thank you," she said then drank deeply from the small cup.

"'Tis my intention 'twill ease the pain for ye," he said then relocated the food to between them.

"And for you too?" she asked and gestured toward his mid-section.

He chuckled. "Aye, mayhap," he said as he ran his free hand over his ribs.

"Let me see," she said as she set her cup on the chest and moved closer.

"Nary a need, milady. 'Twill be all right with another cup or two," he smiled and finished his goblet then reached for the vase and stopped with a grunt.

She raised to her knees and got the wine then filled his cup. "Let me see," she repeated.

He pulled his serk over his head and threw it the way of his boots, and she let out a gasp as her hand stretched toward him. On the left side of his defined abdomen was blemished with several shades of purplish blue and lightened toward the edges as it extended toward his pectoral and around his side. As she peered at him, she wondered what he did to keep so muscular.

Faolan clasped his hand around her outstretched hand and pulled it toward him. He could see that she wavered between the pain he must have endured to save her and the attractive massive physique he had purposefully worked his body into. But was it enough? He thought not. He placed her hand delicately over the bruising and left his hand over hers. "'Twas worth it," he whispered as he grazed his fingertips over her cheek.

Kristin flicked her eyes to his as she silently licked her lips and shook her head ever so slightly. He gently eased her back to her seat and creased his lips as he maintained his eye contact and he too licked his lips. "Eat, milady," he said lowly. "Ye should regain ye strength." Ye 'twill be needing it, soon enough, he thought.

She lowered her head and began eating, seeing the bites on her bare legs. He had pushed her away. Who would want a woman with such as that covering her body? She drank again from her goblet. She chanced a glance up at him. He was slowly chewing as his eyes was cast down at her legs as well. She drew them closer and tried to cover them with the tail of the shirt.

He looked up at her and tightened his lips. "My apologies, milady. I intend nil offense," he said quietly. "'Twas just wishing I had arrived earlier," he said and glanced away. Although he recalled some of those were his, one in particular was placed on her inner thigh nigh to her apex.

"I'm just happy you came," she said shily and then finished her cup.

"Take ye mind away along with the pain," he said as he refilled it and nodded his agreement then sat back once again and finished the food.

To that she drank deeply. "I hope it works," she whispered and then returned her gaze to him. She could see at least one rib was either broken or possibly cracked. They were probably protected by the overabundance of muscles covering them. He was nearly irresistible to look at, she determined by the way her eyes kept traveling to him and over the expansive chest, thick arms, and massive shoulders. He was probably not much older than herself.

"Let us abed," he said softly and rose to his feet. He held his hand down to her, and as she took it, he pulled her up and she stumbled against him with the strength in which he did so. He then maneuvered her to the bed before he turned to extinguish the candle. He had had his fill of her wandering eyes for it caused him discomfort within his tight breeches. He did nary wish for her to see his arousal, just yet, but soon she would feel it, he promised himself.

He relieved himself of his breeches and lifted the furs ta lie beneath, but merely sat on the edge. "Remove the serk," he said lowly. "I have but the one for ye," he explained further. Only when he felt her movement and then settle back down, did he then lie down beside her. He was so very tempted to turn on his side and repeat his activity from last eve, but he chose to stay on his back when she slid her small hand over his shoulder and felt her lips press against his skin. She was close, he thought. He lifted his arm up and placed it around her as she moved her head to his shoulder and scooted closer to him. However, when she grazed her hand over his chest, he snatched it into his own. "'Tis only a certain amount one man can control, milady, and ye be quite desirous. Please, I beg, nary tempt me further," he stated tightly, then after a moment, laid her hand down on his pectoral, but left his hand over it.

"I'm sorry," she whispered.

"Rest," he said simply, but then allowed himself a prideful grin in the darkness. On the morrow, he would have her.

Freya's Day

Rescue

Just before dawn, a thunderous sound rattled Faolan's door bringing them both awake with a start. He sat up and hastily dressed before he turned and looked at the terror in her eyes. He gently caressed his fingers to her cheek and said, "Stay here till I see who it be." She nodded silently as her eyes glassed with unshed tears.

He pressed his lips to her head before he rose from the bed and padded quickly down the steps, lighting several torches as he moved toward the door. He wanted her to be able to see who was there to cultivate further the fear she was already feeling. He opened the door.

Eirik and Leif stepped in and scanned the lodging as he moved to the side. "Milords," he said reverently and bowed his head slightly.

"Nidpigger," Eirik said curtly as his eyes flicked up to the loft seeing a flash of blond hair. He then glanced at Leif and nodded to the loft. "Seems you have what nary belongs ta you," he said lowly as a soft growl reverberated from his throat.

"She was unclaimed," he said as he met his eyes accusingly, as if to blame him as well as state that he had every right to her.

Leif skirted them and hastily moved toward the stairs, climbing them by threes, then paused as his eyes found her huddled in the corner with a fur wrapped around her. He wanted to rush to her, but he took deliberate steps as he felt the fear roil around her and heard her whimper and cry. "Kristin," he whispered and knelt near her extending his hand.

She cried out at the gesture and turned her face to the wall, sobbing, "No, no, not again."

Leif gritted his teeth as he forcefully lifted her from the floor into his arms. She beat her fists against him and struggled to get loose from his hold, but he held her tightly as he descended the stairs and continued out the still opened door.

"What was done?" Eirik demanded as his glare landed on the smaller man.

"I sheltered her. Protected her as ye should have done," he said and clenched his jaw to keep himself from furthering his insult.

Eirik growled as he turned and left. He angrily alighted his awaiting mount and raced to catch up with Leif. He shuddered at what Nidpigger must had done to her to make her react so to Leif, mistreated, for a certain.

"Did they find her?" Sara asked as Elise came in the entrance of the hall with a bucket of water and headed to the kitchen.

"Yes," she sighed out then dumped the water in the caldron. "Wake Tristan and have her go to Leif's chamber. I'm afraid she's going to need some TLC," then she gave her a pointed look.

Sara gasped then turned and left to get Tristan. When she entered the hall, she saw Leif carrying Kristin into his chamber, but she struggled against him. She frowned as she opened the door to the guest chamber. She gently shook Tristan awake and said, "Tristan, wake up. They found Kristin."

Tristan sat straight up and then rushed to get dressed, not stopping to brush her teeth or hair even. "Where is she?" she asked.

"Leif's room," Sara said.

"Why there? Why not put her in her own bed?" Tristan asked with a frown of confusion, to which Sara shrugged and shook her head. Tristan rolled her eyes and quickly went out the door. When she opened the door to Leif's chamber, she found him restraining her within his massive arms. "Let her go!" she shouted and ran toward them.

Leif loosened his grip to release her and received a cuff to his nose just as he did so. With a startled growl he turned and left his chamber. He glanced back to see them clinging to each other and sensed her fear subside. He nodded to himself as he held a hand to his nose and went to the kitchen. "'Twas worth the fuck ta see her fear subdued," he mumbled as he snatched a cloth from the table without meeting anyone's eyes, then retreated to the hall and sat heavily as he cleaned the blood from his face.

Eirik poured his cup full of mead as well as his own as he scrutinized his brother. "You all right?" he asked.

"Yea, much better than she, for a certain," he said as he glanced up at Eirik.

Eirik nodded. "She still be unbound," he said lowly in hope to bring some comfort to him.

"Yea, I felt it so when I removed the collar that strangled her Heill." He shook his head and growled out his anger. "I can nary fathom how ta regain that which she felt before the thralling. 'Tis nigh a loathing now." He clenched his jaw and huffed out his breath.

"'Twill be difficult, aye. Mayhap over time she will come ta trust once more, eh?"

"We nary have what time be needed," he said harshly as he thrusted his left hand toward him, displaying the brand on his palm.

"Mayhap afore, but certainly after," Eirik smiled sadly.

Then they both turned as the door to Leif's chamber opened and Tristan came out. She paused as she stared at them with reddened eyes, wet cheeks, and wrung her hands together, uncertain what to do.

"Lass?" Eirik said softly.

She took a hesitant step toward them and then another. "She…," she bit her lips together and glanced around the hall.

"Come, lass," Eirik encouraged her further.

"She… told me… what happened," she stuttered out and another tear slid from her eye. "They molested her," she said quietly as if spoken any louder would cause it to happen to her too and looked at the floor.

Eirik could tell the word she said held a heavy implication, but he could nary fathom its meaning then he saw Elise step through the door to the kitchen and hug the girl. She knew its meaning and then he knew, and he glanced at Leif. "You say they?" Eirik questioned her, having thought Nidpigger was the only one.

Tristan nodded as Elise pulled away from her. "She told me there were five or six, but she didn't see their faces because they kept a hood over her head. She's covered in bites," she wailed as more tears drifted down her cheeks. Elise gasped and held her close as she eyed Eirik with furrowed brows.

"'Twas nary just Nidpigger?" Leif asked.

"No," she shook her head, sniffled, and wiped at her tears. "She said a man named Faolan saved her and took her to his home."

"Aye, Faolan Nidpigger," Eirik clarified, and Elise inhaled sharply at hearing his name. She had no doubt he had something to do with it. "Aye, I as well, heartling. He be involved, for a certain. Needs must proof for a judgement."

"I should...," Tristan said and gestured back to the room and received understandable nods, but then she paused and looked at Leif. "I'm sorry about your nose," she said and grazed her hand over her blackened knuckles then turned back toward the door. Pausing once again, she said, "I borrowed one of your shirts for her to wear. She felt so exposed and seeing the bites just reminded her..." she couldn't finish.

"She may have all I have, anything she needs will be hers," Leif said then hurried toward the exit to the hall. Eirik rose quickly and followed, hoping to curb his anger before he did something that he couldn't retract.

As Tristan disappeared beyond the door, Elise saw Sara standing within the threshold of the kitchen. "I don't believe Nidpigger was her savior," she muttered to her then started a tray to take to them.

"Where does he live?" Sara asked distractedly.

"I have no idea," Elise said on a sigh. "Why?"

"He lives ta th' nort of the thorp, jus' ta the eas', milady," Ingrid said as she prepared their morning meal.

"Hmm," Sara uttered as she gathered the place settings and carried them out to the hall then went looking for Jesse.

"Ye should nary go nigh him," Ingrid said lowly with a shudder, or so Elise thought.

"Why do you say that, Ingrid?" Elise asked gently seeing the woman gave her the same fear-respect that she afforded the brothers.

She glanced ever so briefly up at her then back to her task. "'Tis but idle chatter," she shrugged.

"What do you know, Ingrid?" Elise smiled when her eyes flicked to her once again.

"Jasmin tol' me of some… unnatural things he wished her ta do, but I nary know what. I nary wished ta know an' thought she be teasing me. She likes ta do just so. I ne'er took it for truth. Oslo said he had a… hmm," she paused as she tried to think of the word her husband used. "What word is used when a man is the heritor of many women and lies with a different one each night?"

Elise looked at her as many words came to her mind, such as asshole, polygamist, sadist, asshole, womanizer, lothario, and asshole, but the word she thought she may be referring to was, "harem?"

"Aye, 'tis th' word he used," she smiled and nodded.

"Really?" she said surprised they were talking about the same man. The man that crudely attacked her, and now Kristin, could hardly have the charisma and skills to gain a harem of women.

"Aye, Oslo would nary tell me a tale as such lightly. He did so as warning ta keep li'l Astrid away from him, for a certain. 'Tis but three or four, he said, but 'tis two or three too many," she said the last with a critical nod.

"I agree," she smiled and winked then turned to take the tray to the girls.

She passed Sara and Jesse on her way, who were standing in the hall with their arms stretched out, he behind her, and it looked almost as if they were dancing as they swayed and moved their hands about so gracefully it reminded her of a ballet she had once seen. And Sara no longer wore her glasses. When did that happen? She shook her head and continued to the chamber.

With a light knock, she opened the door and entered. She backed up against the door and the tray rattled when she jumped seeing a rather large black leopard lying in the middle of Leif's bed and a huge black bird perched on the mantel.

"Ah... girls?" Elise asked timidly and took a step forward.

The raven made several popping sounds before a loud guttural caw as it flapped its wings, however the panther simply batted its eyes slowly and swished its tail.

"Okay... Well, I brought you some food," she said and set it on the nearest chest then escaped the room closing the door a little too hard according to the cawing commotion within the room. She let out her breath and scanned the hall.

Jesse and Bo sat at the table but also looked at her with the slamming of the door. "Is everything okay, Miss Thornson?" Bo asked then tightened his lips in a thin line of concern.

"Yeah, just... don't go in there," she nearly chuckled as she glanced at them, then with a slight tilt to her head she scrutinized the pair of them. "Did you two get tattoos?"

"Not as cool as yours," Jesse said as he patted his chest and smiled, assumedly where his was, but Bo merely nodded.

She lifted a brow at him. "Bo? May I see it?"

Bo sucked in a healthy breath and tugged on his turtleneck sweater until it popped off his head then he pulled off his t-shirt and glanced up at her. His began at the front of his throat with the hooked beak of an eagle and then split to either side of his neck with the profile of the bird, but as she circled around to his back, she could see the feathers gave way to golden fur over the main body of the animal and black and white feathers for the wings. She could see how its great paws clawed around him and into his chest as if it was holding on for dear life and the rear legs disappeared below his waistline.

"That's just fucking awesome," Jesse said lowly as he came to stand beside her. Elise glanced at him, unable to tell if he was impressed or... jealous?

"I agree," she said and understood its meaning. "That's a gryphon," she said as she smiled.

"Whatever," Bo uttered as he pulled his shirt back on followed by his sweater.

She sat beside him with furrowed brows. "What's wrong?" she asked.

"It was supposed to be no more than two inches, not this," he said a bit disgruntled.

"Mine's bigger than that and I think both Kristin and Tristan have ones like ours," she spoke softly. His head came up at Tristan's mention, but he didn't speak. She then looked at Jesse. "What were you and Sara doing earlier?" she changed the subject for Bo's benefit.

"It's going to sound crazy, but she said she was trying to locate something on the island. There's something wrong with it, like a corruption or something," he said as he slid his hand over the left side of his chest. "We can feel it."

Elise's brows were much too high as her eyes opened wide then she blinked. "Did you... find it?" she asked.

"More than one," he said and licked his lips. "Mostly on the far side of the island though." He cleared his throat. "I think I'm going to see if I can help with breakfast," he excused himself and went to the kitchen.

Bo studied her for a moment before he too cleared his throat. "After your bonding," he started then licked his lips. "Did you feel... I don't know how to describe it... unsettled, maybe? Like a battle was going on inside you."

"Come with me," she said and rose from her seat and waited for him to do the same. When she seen that he was going to follow, she continued then stopped in front of Leif's door and listened. Hearing no sound, she cautiously opened the door and peeked her head in. She then opened it a little further for him to see the cat still laid on the bed and the bird was shredding some kind of cloth.

When he looked in, the Raven sounded a shrill alarm and the cat leaped from the bed and slowly brushed its body against the door, forcing it closed. "What the hell?" he exclaimed. "I thought Kristin and Tristan were in there."

"They are," she chuckled. "Although I don't know which one is which. That's why I said I was certain they had the large tattoos as well."

He snorted and shook his head. "What are you trying to say, Miss Thornson?"

"Panther and raven," she indicated to the door then pointed to the entrance of the hall and said, "Dragons." She then tapped her own chest and said, "Dragon." But when she placed her hand on his chest, she merely lifted her brows at him.

"Gryphon," he whispered, and she nodded.

Just then the door opened, and Tristan squeezed through the opening as she held the door close to her. "Um... sorry about that, but she's a bit of a man hater at the moment," she said and grimaced at Bo. "I don't blame her really."

"I don't either, but she's going to have to realize not all men are that way, certainly not Bo," she said as she raked her eyes over him then looked back at Tristan with a scowl.

"I know it, but it *will* take her some time, even if she says nothing but good things about Faolan," she shrugged.

"Oh, that's got to change. *He* is not a good man, Tristan," she said adamantly then bit her lips together and turned away and headed back to the kitchen.

Bo and Tristan looked at each other with lifted brows. "I think there's something she hasn't told us," Tristan said quietly.

"I think there's a lot they all haven't told us," Bo agreed and sighed out his breath. He licked his lips as he gazed down at her then said, "So a panther, huh?" She nodded a bit uncommittedly. He tugged at his collar enough to expose the eagle's head and said, "Gryphon, supposedly."

"Wow, something mythical," she smiled up at him as she

could swear the eyes followed her when she swayed to see both sides of his neck. Then she pulled her sleeves up to show him the paws not only covered the back of her hands but followed the length of her arms. "As far as I can tell, it covers the whole back side of my body, like I was wearing a skin. It's not too weird, right?" she chuckled.

He grinned at her and shook his head. "Not at all. Not any weirder than having a huge beak sticking out of your throat."

She giggled. "I better get back in there before she destroys all of Leif's clothes," she said.

"Why is she so angry with him? It wasn't his fault that she was kidnapped," he said before she could leave.

"No, it wasn't his fault any more than the rest of us. But you just don't know, Bo. Those men did some horrific things to her, and it shames her even though I told her she shouldn't feel that way. She refuses to come out of her raven form because she can't bear to see the bites and bruises left by them."

Bo nodded his head as he sadly gazed at her. "Maybe she just needs to be treated with kindness by us?" he suggested as he patted his chest.

"Maybe," she said, "But not yet," she smiled weakly and opened the door, sliding between the narrow opening once again.

After breakfast, the boys went out to tend to the animals and finish laying the pipe and Elise and Sara helped Ingrid in the kitchen and then sent her home when they had their evening meal prepared to cook ahead of time. Although she was reluctant, she left with the convincing argument from Elise that they were capable of finishing and that her wage wouldn't diminish for leaving early since she had to cook for eight now instead of just two. Elise told her it would remain this way hereafter, but she would also be compensated for any extra work that they may need in the future. Elise was certain that Ingrid was feeling as if she was being set aside due to the many females within the household now, and she tried to reassure her as well as she could that it wasn't the case. They hadn't seen the brothers all day.

As they laid the table with dinner, Elise's concern deepened, though she tried not to let it bother her. She had convinced Tristan to talk to Kristin about joining them at the table and she did so. They all ate quietly, unsure what to say.

"By tomorrow night, we should have water to the house," Bo said and smiled, hoping to break the uncomfortable silence for Kristin's sake. "And then I thought a hot water heater should be next." He glanced at the others. "Then maybe a bathtub?" He grinned trying to get some positive reaction from one of them.

"Oh, that would be marvelous," Tristan said also smiling. "No more Saturday only bathing days, huh?"

"That's what I was thinking," he chuckled.

"Soon there'll be no reason to go to the tarn at all, and that'll be a good thing, huh?" Sara said and glanced at Elise.

"Yes," Elise sighed out.

Bo looked from Sara to Elise and furrowed his brows. "What happened at the tarn?" he asked.

"You didn't tell them?" Sara asked Elise. "Not even now?" She clenched her jaw in disapproval as she stared at her.

"You're right, Sara. I'm sorry. I guess I should have said something before now," Elise said and flicked her eyes ta Kristin then at the others. "Last washing day, remember when I rushed you girls off to the house because someone was coming? That someone was Nidpigger. He tried to..." She lowered her eyes.

"He attacked her and if Eirik hadn't showed up when he did, he would have succeeded," Sara said venomously. She carried a healthy hatred for the man.

Kristin shook her head. "That can't be true," she said as her eyes welled.

"Why else do you think Eirik got out the swords and made sure we could defend ourselves? He was worried that he wouldn't be here if something happened again."

"Well, he *was* here, wasn't he? They both were. Are each of you claimed by Eirik?" she asked looking to all of them but Tristan. They sadly nodded. "Yeah, and Tristan is claimed by

Leif. That's why they took me, because I was carelessly left unclaimed, unwanted," she said as she tried to keep the tears out of her voice even though they spilled down her cheeks. "Leif should have just claimed me, whether he wanted me or not," she burst out and stood. She then turned and ran back to his chamber but paused when she seen them standing at the entrance, then continued and slammed the door behind her.

Leif looked at Eirik, handing him the heavy bag he was holding, and took deliberate steps to his door, but before he opened it, he looked at Tristan as a silver sheen cast over his eyes and said, "Stay." After she silently nodded, he opened the door and closed it behind him. He stood in front of the door with his arms crossed over his chest as he gazed at her flung across his bed and sobbing into his pillow. He approached soundlessly and sat on the side, hesitant to touch her.

"Kristin," he said softly and licked his lips. She gasped hearing his voice and he placed a gentle hand on her back. "What you said is untrue, dearling. 'Twas you I wanted most."

She turned her head to look at him. "Then why didn't you claim me? Especially if you knew I'd be open to attack if I wasn't claimed," she said harshly.

"I be uncertain of what you've been told, but the claiming is more about the one giving the consent than the one claiming," he swallowed hard. "I wanted you so that Eirik nigh made the bond with you, so I would nary make a life-mate bond without you fully aware of it. 'Tis the extent of the want I have for you," he said as he patted his chest. "It nigh extinguished my essence-flame when I grasped that we were nary bound for it signified you were uncertain of the bond." He tightened his lips and looked away. "And then ta find you missing when I came to move you to my chamber..." He shook his head. "I should have done so as soon as the broken bond was discovered."

"Why didn't you?" she asked looking up at him.

"I thought you'd be safe among the others, at first, but then the overwhelming feeling of dread consumed me, and I rose ta bring you in," he said and lifted his hand to caress her hair away from her face. "I ask for forgiveness, dearling, although I feel unworthy of such."

"You feel guilty? You just told me that I was the reason we didn't bond, so why do you feel guilty?"

He gave a soft wry snort. "Because I didn't move you, dearling, as I wanted to. I also felt your mistress would nary approve of me doing so," he said with a slight chuckle. Finally, she smiled at him.

"She is overprotective, isn't she? Turns out, she had good reason," she said and lowered her eyes.

"Nay," he tipped her head back up. "'Tis difficult ta predict the future?"

"Did you know she was attacked at the tarn?"

He nodded, "Eirik said he had suspected though she ne'er told him so. 'Twas Sara that alerted him."

"Yeah, I don't think Sara believes in keeping secrets, among her friends anyway. Honest," she smiled.

He nodded and sighed out his breath. "Honest," he returned her smile. "You may stay in my chamber for as long as you wish it or until you are safely bound," he said and kept his eyes trained on hers.

"What about you?" she asked.

"If nary welcomed ta abed with you, I shall sleep across the threshold. I nary wish for anything more ta happen ta you." He lowered his eyes.

Kristin studied his face and felt he was being honest with her. All she wanted was to feel safe and she believed that was what he was offering her.

Following Kristin's outburst, Sara tightened her lips and began clearing the table. She felt she'd said more than perhaps she ought to, given the frowns she was given in return by the others. Sure, she might have been a little tough on Kristin, but someone needed to tell her the truth about her 'savior', however she didn't expect that she'd blame Leif. Secrets! There were far too many among them and she certainly didn't see them as necessary. Not among them anyway. Even now, she felt there were secrets being kept. Feeling an overwhelming surge within herself, she pressed her hands flat on the table as she took in a deep breath and closed her eyes. A surge of what, she was uncertain.

"Relax," Jesse whispered quietly from behind her as he put his hands on her shoulders then smoothed them down her arms to rest upon each of her hands. "I feel your turmoil. Clear your negativity before it consumes you." He continued speaking softly over her shoulder as he laced his fingers with hers and brought them around her midsection. He began to slowly sway with her. "Think of peace within and that which you desire the most at this moment. Feel it. Visualize it as if you have it or that it was already done." He slid their conjoined hands up to lay over her heart and tapped out a slow rhythmic cadence which kept time with his swaying as the other pair remained around her waist.

After several moments, Sara began to feel other things stirring within, but knew she had other duties to do before bed and thought she should get on with it. He had sufficiently distracted her from her thoughts, but now he was being a distraction from her cleaning the kitchen. Sometimes it sucked to be responsible, she thought as she sighed out her breath.

"Thank you," she mumbled just before she tilted her head back to see him.

At that moment, Jesse released her hand at her waist and spun her around to face him. Catching her against his chest, he raised their still entwined hands to lay on his own heart before he released it and brushed his own down her back stopping at her waist. He smiled down at her briefly as his eyes darted over her face then landed on her lips.

"I want to kiss you," he whispered in both a declaration and uncertainty, as if asking for permission.

Sara felt her stomach flutter and her heartbeat gain momentum as she stared up at him, her lips curved slightly. "What are you going to do about it?"

As if that was all he needed, he lowered his head and gently moved his lips across hers several times sweetly before adding just enough pressure to open her mouth as he pulled her tighter against him. Pressing into her, he angled his head just so and flicked his tongue across her teeth, sliding deliciously alongside hers. He moved forward to gain that pressure, that friction... As his breathing became more rapid, he felt as though... As if he could... He eased back, but kept her tightly embraced, pressing his mouth to her head.

He let out a throaty chuckle, which caused Sara to stiffen a bit. "Oh my god," he breathed out on a sigh. "I about got out of hand, didn't I?" his voice huskier than she recalled. "But I won't apologize," he whispered.

Sara pushed back on him to see his face and smiled. She then glanced around them at the room, noticing it was much darker than the kitchen. They were no longer in the kitchen but in the guess chamber right near her bunk. "Uh... Jesse?"

"What did you wish for?" he chuckled, scanning the room.

"To be honest, I wished I had the kitchen cleaned already so I could go to bed," she too then laughed. "Do you think... Wait, what did you wish for?"

He gave her another throaty chuckle as he licked his lips. "How do you suppose it happened?" he said distracting her from that thought. "I mean, teleportation."

"I don't know, but it has to have something to do with this," she said as she tapped on her chest. "Yikes!" she squeaked out.

"Oh, fuck. I'm sorry," he chuckled out nervously as he released her and sank down on the side of her bed with his head lowered to his hands willing himself not to look at her.

Sara quickly found her sleep clothes and hastily donned them then went to the other side of the room to get his before anyone came in. "Get it under control," she said as she held his shorts out to him.

"I'm trying," he chuckled as he pulled his shorts on. "But you do make it hard...uh...difficult."

"You're scattered. Focus," she said as she sat beside him

and turned his head to face her. "You can't let your emotions run with the Heill. I think we drew it in earlier and now it needed used. But that's only a guess. Maybe it's always with us. Regardless, it can't run amuck." She grazed her hand over his cheek. "Now scootch over. I'm tired."

Jesse stared at her momentarily before he moved in behind her and stretched out on her bunk and opened his arms to her. Several thoughts ran through his head in that moment. First was that she had intended on him sleeping in her bower. Secondly was the motives or intent of having him do so. Third was that he could hold her in his arms... all night.

When she had settled in beside him, he pulled her up tight against him and said, "You don't have to worry, I've got you," then he squeezed her gently.

"They've been in there a really long time," Elise said as she chewed on her thumbnail nervously watching the door as Eirik finished eating. Sara and Jesse were cleaning the kitchen while Bo was instructed by Tristan to pack up Kristin's things and had set them by the door, but she didn't feel like she could move from where she sat.

"'Twill take some time, heartling," he said as he emptied his cup and pushed his plate away. "'Twill wager neither will appreciate such idle speculation of what happens beyond," he smiled down at her teasingly. "We should abed," he said as he rose. "Ye two as well," he directed toward Bo and Tristan.

Tristan turned and looked up at him, shaking her head and opened her mouth to speak when Leif's door opened, and he came out. He went right to Tristan and bent to one knee in front of her with a bowed head and an uplifted hand stretched out to her, palm up. "I wish for your forgiveness," he said without lifting his gaze.

She grasped his hand and said, "Of course, but for what?"

He swallowed hard and glanced at Eirik before her then said, "Commanding you ta stay."

Elise inhaled sharply and hardened her face, but Eirik simply lifted her into his arms and stalked off to bed. "'Tis nary our concern, heartling," he mumbled.

Leif brought her hand to his lips then released it as he stood. "We had much ta discuss and 'twas of great import ta have her sole attention without interruption. I will nary do it again, aye?"

"Sure thing," she smiled and stood. "She's... um... better now, so we're cool. Her things are right there," she indicated toward his door then turned and headed to the guest chamber, followed by Bo as he stared at him with his mouth agape.

Having not eaten in what felt like forever, Leif went to the kitchen and made a tray then returned to his room, a smile playing on his lips, with only the most fleeting of thoughts at the two piles of clothes on the kitchen floor. He set it on the table before he swung his kettle over the fire and then went to move her things inside the door. As he settled down on the stool, he glanced at Kristin and asked, "Would you care for some food or drink?" while he removed his boots and tunic.

She shook her head. "No, I'm fine," she said from below the furs.

He quickly ate but took his time washing up as he felt her eyes on him the entire time. When he finished, he blew out the candle and moved to the bed. He slid between the furs next to her and raised his arm indicating for her to lift her head. When she didn't do so right away, he said, "Have nary a fear, dearling. I shall ne'er touch you without being agreeable ta your needs as well." She lifted her head then and he embraced her tightly into him and pressed his lips into her hair. "For a certain," he whispered.

"Leif?" she said timidly after several moments had passed.

"Aye?" he answered sleepily.

"If I consent to you, will I be safe from those men?" she asked at nearly a whisper.

His eyes popped open. "Ye be safe with me, dearling. If you consent, you must feel it here," he said as he slipped his hand beneath the furs and grasped hers that laid upon her hip and put it on his chest. "If you nary feel it strongly, 'twill nary bond true.

I wish it ta bond true, dearling. Nary out of fear, but out of want, aye?"

She nodded her understanding then slid her hand up and curled it against his neck, keeping in mind what Faolan had said about a man's control. She swallowed hard as she thought about him. It was hard for her to believe what Elise had said. The thought that he had attacked her was ridiculous. Why would he do that to Elise but then save her from the same fate? However, if it was true, why hadn't the brothers gone after him? Why wasn't it reported to a magistrate or whatever law types they had here? She sighed out heavily.

Leif crossed his hand over his chest and cupped her head. "How can I help," he whispered.

She shook her head. "Help with what?" she asked, but she knew.

"With your restlessness. Nary do I believe 'tis fear keeping you from sleep. What may I do for you ta help you be at ease?" He kept his voice low and hugged her against him.

"I don't know," she sighed. "Is there a masseuse on the island?" she chuckled.

"Mayhap, what be a masseuse?"

"Someone trained in the art of massage," she said again on a sigh, knowing full well there wouldn't be.

"Yea," he whispered, "Turn about." He reached under his bed then rolled toward her and pulled the furs out of the way as she laid on her stomach. He held the vile in his hand as he blew gently on it to warm it and then said, "'Tis much need for massage following battle ta keep the muscles loose." Then he uncorked it and poured it over her back. Replacing the cork, he set it back from whence it came then smoothed the oil over her back before he sat up to work it into her muscles. He rubbed her shoulders and neck firmly as he had his brother's and she flinched; he froze. Remembering the bruises and bites, he rose and stoked the fire to burn brighter before he returned. He needed more light, and the added heat would assist him in his efforts. "You certain this be your wish?" he asked.

"Yeah, just be careful," she said and sighed out her breath.

"For a certain," he mumbled as he inspected her back. Now that he could see clearly, he saw the body of a large black bird with its talons curled into her back and a wing crossed over her shoulders. When he leaned to his left, he saw the other wing stretched down her arm and the head disappeared over her shoulder beneath her. She was to be a bird of some sort which made him smile. He then proceeded with softened caresses, which would never reach her muscles, but it was difficult to avoid the tender flesh. He hoped it would still have the same effect as he moved his hands gently in spiraling circles over and over her back until, eventually, he felt her body lose all tension. She was asleep. He moved back beneath the furs that were just covering her lower half now and carefully rolled her to her side. He bit at his lips to keep a gasp from escaping as he was hit hard with a mixture of emotion between sympathy and anger when he beheld the front of her body. Her breasts were obscured with overlaying rings of ovals and so discolored he wondered how she would ever heal. However, it didn't end there, the same such rings continued across her stomach, and he was certain even further down. He pushed his arm beneath her head as he pulled her into him until she was lying nearly as she had been before. As he dragged the fur over her and held her close, he closed his eyes and silently wept into her hair.

Washing Day

Mending

Leif woke with Kristin still in his arms, but not as human. She laid alongside him between his side and his arm with her head on his shoulder. He ever so gently smoothed his palm over her head and smiled. "'Tis all right, dearling. If this form suits you then keep it until you be ready," he said softly. She made a few quick knocking noises and pressed into his palm. "I nary speak raven," he said as his lips curved, and he slid his thumb along her beak and across her feathered face. "I hope you slept well." She popped a few more times and snapped her bill closed. "'Tis time ta rise, but I shall stay with you or you with me till your bonding," he promised and eased away from her, but before he stood, he drew the furs over her.

Leif filled the small kettle and swung it over the fire which he stoked as he began his morning routine without a shred of modesty. At one point, he glanced her direction and saw she had returned to human which made him smile. It gladdened his heart to see her comfortable enough with him to come out of her raven form, although she remained covered to the chin beneath the furs.

Once dressed and prepared for the day, he sat on the bed next to her. "If you wish it, I will bring you food, but I prefer if you would join us ta break your fast this morn."

She nodded. "I'll come out," she smiled slightly. Then she disappeared below the furs and shortly thereafter the furs moved about, and she cawed alarmingly.

He chuckled and threw back the furs. She righted herself then hopped up on his arm and on up to his shoulder. "Very well, dearling," he murmured and stood. She curled her short talons into his shoulder and flapped her wings a couple of times to gain her balance. When he felt she was settled, he proceeded to his door.

He first attended to the central fire then moved to the kitchen and found Ingrid was already there trying to make sweet cakes without success. "Good morn," he said cheerily.

She bowed her head and mumbled, "Good morn, milord."

"What be amiss?" he asked taking in the situation as Kristin made a sound something like a hissing laugh.

"I fear I be lacking the skills milord requires," she said lowly.

"Blessed Ingrid," he chuckled. "You lack in nothing. If you wish ta make the sweet cakes the outlanders make, then ask the one who makes them ta show you, eh?"

She nodded and looked about her. "'Twas hopin' ta master th' task afore they awoke."

"'Tis for certain," he smiled. "Let me fetch him," he said then turned and headed for the guest chamber.

He went directly to Jesse's bower and found it empty, then he checked the others. First Tristan's, which contained both Tristan and Bo, to which Kristin made that popping knocking noise. Then he went to Sara's, which is where he found Jesse and he shook his shoulder gently.

"Jesse, I wish you ta rise and assist Ingrid," he whispered so he wouldn't wake Sara.

"What's wrong with Ingrid?" Sara said as she rose to her elbow with alarm.

"Nil, that a cooking lesson would nary cure," he snorted.

"All right," Jesse said sleepily. "I'll be out quick as I can," he mumbled, but squeezed Sara into him with a sigh.

Leif nodded then rose to his feet and left with a grin. When he had the door closed, he whispered, "Seems your friends have paired." To which she made that same knocking sound of approval and rubbed her head against his cheek. "This makes you happy?" he asked her and received a quiet gurgling caw accompanied by the knock. "Good," he smiled. "But seems we have much time afore we can sup. What say you, we tend ta the stock while we wait, aye?" he said as he headed to the entrance of the hall.

Upon entering the byre, he lifted his hand to her feet then extended his arm upwards. She flapped her wings a few times then alighted into the air. He laughed as he watched her fly around him and then landed up in the rafters. As he attended to the horses first, he could hear her calls and wings as she tested what the new body could do. Leif's mount, Stormbringer, nickered as he approached, he ran his hand along his jawline then bowed his head toward his. "Greetings, my friend," he mumbled. Then he fed him as well as the others and continued with his chores.

When he was finished, he raised his hand into the air without calling for Kristin for he knew she'd be watching. He steadied his arm to catch her when she landed on it and set her on his shoulder. "'Twas enjoyable ta take wing, eh?" he asked with a chuckle and continued to the longhouse. She rubbed against his cheek as she knocked a few times just before she let out a shrill shrieking caw and flapped her wings wildly. "Easy," he cooed. "I see him," he whispered and continued on to the house.

They could see in the dimly lit dawn a mounted figure slowly approaching the house. He could clearly see it was Nidpigger and growled deeply though quietly. "What brings you," Leif bellowed before he got any closer.

"'Twas my intent ta see how the girl be faring," he said as he adjusted himself in his saddle. "Tell me, does she remain unclaimed?" his grin gleamed in the failing light.

"'Tis nil concern of yours, for a certain," Leif said then clenched his jaw. "She be mine," he growled with a echoing rumble.

"Nay, milord, she be unclaimed. Keep a sharp eye on the delicate morsel," he warned and licked his lips then rounded his horse and spurred it into action.

"Shh shh shh, dearling," he said softly as he gently coaxed her out from under his hair. "He'll nary lay hand ta you again," he rumbled quietly then went inside nearly running into Sara.

"That is one evil man," she said lowly as she watched him ride away.

"'Tis the feeling I be grasping as well," Leif muttered then closed the door.

"I was just coming out to get you," she said as she smiled up at him.

"You should nary go beyond the threshold without another with you," he said as he moved with her toward the high table.

She furrowed her brows briefly then said, "Kristin? Is that you?"

"Aye," Leif answered as the raven rasped a low caw.

"Absolutely amazing," Sara chuckled and reached her hand out toward her then thought better of it as the bird eyed her.

"Aye," Leif agreed and grinned at her as he took his seat at the table.

He poured his cup full of mead then held it up to the raven. She swished her beak in it a few times then lapped at the liquid before withdrawing her head and fluffed out her feathers as she shook her entire body. He chuckled and wiped the splatter from his cheek then brought the cup to his own. He then poured water into the cup set out for her and dipped what Elise had called a napkin in it and smoothed it over her face and head.

"Methinks mead 'tis nary good for bathing, dearling," he chuckled. "'Twill make your feathers stick together, aye?" She issued the repetitive hissing sound and nibbled at the curve of his ear with her tongue carefully not to scrape her beak against it.

When the others were seated and the table laid, he filled his trencher with mostly meat but also a large stack of sweet cakes and poured a generous amount of what they called syrup over them. He gathered some of the meat in his fingers and held it up to her as he cut into his sweet cakes and began eating, not noticing or uncaring that the others watched in stunned silence.

"Sara tells me that we had a visitor this morn," Eirik said casually as he, too, ate.

Leif nodded as he looked over the table at him. "Yea, he made threats," he said then jerked his fingers away from the raven as he felt the razor-sharp beak poke his now empty fingers. He picked up more meat and held it up to her. Tristan giggled, and he grinned at her.

"We need proof of his crimes, nary just words," Eirik said then drank deeply from his cup.

"I feel like either he's the cause of the tainted Heill or maybe he's been corrupted by it," Sara said then tightened her lips.

"I'd have to agree," Jesse said with a nod. "It comes from his side of the island."

"How do you guys know that?" Elise asked.

"It's the bond we have with the island. Almost like GPS and storm trackers," Sara explained.

"Yeah, instead of gaining the cool-ass shapeshifting abilities the rest of you obviously got with your fucking awesome tattoos, we got Heill GPS sensory and maybe a few other skills," Jesse shrugged.

"You can have mine," Bo said quietly and Eirik peered down at him.

"You and I must have words," Eirik said with a nod then turned to Jesse. "You be very green, my friend. Release your jealousy and embrace the Heill within as Sara has done. Then you will amaze even yourself with your skill, aye?" Jesse nodded with just the slightest of smiles curving his lips. "Mayhap work with Sara ta search what more you can do?"

"For a certain," Jesse mumbled and winked at Sara.

"You seem very at ease with all of this," Elise said to Eirik.

"Aye, the island chose ta gift the lot of you for a purpose. I know naught what it is, but 'tis nil a mistake."

"Maybe it was because of the tainted Heill," Sara suggested. "She's sick and needs help to heal."

"Mayhap," he nodded at her. "Methinks we should search the areas you said had the maligned Heill today ta have a better grasp," he said to her then looked to Leif with a glance to Kristin. "You should go ta the wood, where Nidpigger's been hunting." The raven cawed shrilly at him and flapped several times before Leif lifted his hand to her with an open palm to calm her, but he nodded at Eirik.

"Then I'm going too," Tristan said with furrowed brows.

"Aye, 'twill have Bo with me," he then turned to Elise. "You stay here ta defend the others," he winked and nearly purred.

"With all that I am," she smiled.

After the table was cleared and the kitchen cleaned, Sara and Elise worked with Ingrid once again and Eirik, Jesse, and Bo finished the piping while Leif, mounted on Stormbringer, Kristin, as a raven, and Tristan in her panther form went to the wood.

As they drew near the small forest, Leif slowed his mount to a walk and Kristin landed lightly on his shoulder. Tristan slunk ahead of him cautiously weaving in and out of the trees and sniffed at the ground. She paused midstride at one point as her golden eyes landed on something and she chuffed quietly. Stormbringer stopped when she did as Leif peered around him then followed Tristan's gaze. Kristin took wing and landed on a branch high above and somewhat ahead of them then issued a low rasping call. The horse and the panther moved forward slowly until they came to an outcrop of stone with a large long-haired mottled grey cat sitting in front of it.

"'Tis just a cat's den," Leif said as he scanned the woods around him then dismounted. Kristin came back to his shoulder as Tristan moved forward and touched noses with the significantly smaller cat, though a third the size of Tristan, then lowered her forehead to the cat's and chuffed. After a moment, she swung her head back to Leif and made a growling whine noise. With raised brows he moved forward and squatted in front of the cat, extending his hand toward it as Kristin hopped from one shoulder to the other displaying her agitation without voicing it.

"Greetings, my small friend," he said softly and waited for the cat to accept him then ran his hand over its head and down its back. "I ne'er knew you were tamed so," he chuckled and glanced inside the den seeing several other heads peeked out at them.

Tristan butted his shoulder with her head nearly knocking him off balance then laid her paw on the hand he pressed to the ground to catch himself. The cat moved forward and tapped its paw on Tristan's then extended its claws into hers, and in turn, she did the same to his hand.

"Hello?" he heard a voice in his head. "Can you hear me?" Leif nodded slowly. "Good," the voice said. "I'm Grimal."

"Leif," he breathed out then regaining his wits, he said, "Tristan and Kristin," nodding toward each respectively.

"I'm aware of who you are, though you might have forgotten me. I came here many years ago, much as your friends here did, but, as I understand it, did not make my decision in time to remain human. Thus..." The cat swished its tail.

"I ne'er knew of what happened ta those who vanished. I feared they extinguished," he looked appalled at the cat and then his face blanched white. "Nidpigger's been hunting you," he whispered then shook his head. "My apologies for allowing such an atrocity. 'Tis horrific."

"Indeed," the voice said. "The island weakens with each death. As a lord of the island, you must rectify." The cat then retracted its claws and headbutted him then walked back to its den.

"If e'er in need of shelter or assistance," Leif started, "Come ta the homestead, Aye?"

Grimal turned and winked its eyes closed briefly then continued into the den.

Leif rose to his feet with a heavy sigh and then quickly mounted. "We must scout the forest before we return," he said aloud then Stormbringer rounded and galloped through the trees picking its path carefully so as not to dismount Leif. Kristin took to the sky as Tristan sprinted beside the horse.

When they were satisfied the woods were clear, they returned to the house, stopping just outside the entrance. Leif dropped from the horse then loosened the saddle before he went in, and Stormbringer went to the barn. When he opened the door, Tristan pushed passed him and Kristin and ran toward the guest room. He scanned the hall but didn't see anyone around. Checking each room, he found no one then called out to Tristan.

"I'm coming," she said as she came out of the room pulling on a jacket. "I think they're in the barn."

They both rushed out and made their way to the barn. Kristin flew ahead giving a cry of warning to the others before they entered. They both stopped short, and Leif eased Tristan behind him as he whistled shrilly for Kristin to come to him. He caught her gently and folded her into him protectively as he beheld the great golden gryphon standing near the center of the barn. At hearing the whistle, it spun around, stepped in the low embers of the central fire, and leaped in the air to escape the burning sensation as it screeched with the pain. Startled yells sounded as the others dodged wing and tail, but mostly claw as it rebounded off walls and stalls causing a cacophony of alarm from the other animals in the pandemonium. When the great beast finally settled and the others rose to their feet, only then did he notice the others scattered around it, but Bo was missing.

"Ah," Leif uttered as he grasped the situation. "'Tis Bo's form," he said then set Kristin back on his shoulder. "Stay close," he whispered as he stepped closer.

"'Tis his first turning," Eirik said as Leif drew even with him. "He fought with the thought of turning into an animal. Many thanks ta Sara, he came ta terms and was ready," he smiled.

Tristan moved ahead of them and continued closer as she stretched her hand up toward the massive animal. "Bo?" she said as she smiled up at him. He turned, causing Jesse and Sara to duck beneath his half-extended wings. "Easy," she cooed and gestured for him to come closer. "Calm down, it's okay. Just let it fill you," she soothed.

The gryphon lowered its body gradually to the ground as it swished its tail wildly, but even it slowed to a gentle flick when

Tristan came forward and hugged its neck. Then he lowered his head over her back and emitted a sound something between a purr and the repetitive coo of a pigeon.

"Nice, we've been trying to calm him down forever," Jesse said from across the barn.

"Tristan, teach him to turn back. We have much ta discuss," Leif said then gave Eirik a grave look before he turned and went to Stormbringer's stall and picked up the saddle, setting it where it belonged then exited the barn.

As each joined Leif at the high table, he passed the pitcher of mead to them, but didn't speak until all were present. "'Tis tragic news we bring from the wood," he started. "Nidpigger, as we know, has been hunting the cats that dwell there for their hides. We discovered this morn that all we thought had vanished from the island ne'er vanished at all but were turned ta these cats." He then drank heavily from his cup.

"How do you know that's what happened to the ones that vanished?" Elise asked, remembering the two cats she had seen dangling from Nidpigger's saddle and had been appalled by the fact they had been hunted at all, but now to know they were once human, sickened her.

"Grimal told us. He said that as each one dies the island weakens," Tristan said as she tended to Bo's burned hand.

"'Tis been many years since I heard that name," Eirik said and lowered his eyes. "He was one that nary chose ta stay, but nary left either till after one and twenty days."

"You didn't know," Elise said quietly.

"Aye, but I knew they'd be nil more," he said as he glanced down at her and tightened his lips.

"Okay, so, we just need to prevent them from being hunted, right?" Jesse said.

"They require justice as well," Leif said looking at Eirik.

"They shall have it. I shall post a ban on hunting the wood, for the now. It'll nary cease his poaching but make him a nithing should he do so."

"And we'd have legal charges brought on him," Elise said.

"Aye, but 'tis nary enough ta rectify for what's been done," Leif interjected.

"No, but it's a start while we search for proof of his other misdeeds," Elise said to soothe him. He nodded at her. "I know it's only rumor, but Ingrid told me that he has a pretty bad reputation amongst the villagers." She lifted a hopeful brow at him then peered up to Eirik. "You should talk to Oslo and Jasmin about what they know."

"Aye. 'Twas going ta search the tainted area ta the north across the valley before nightfall, but 'twill do that afore," Eirik conceded.

"I shall talk ta Oslo and Jasmin, if you wish ta begin the search," Leif said, and the raven issued a shrill caw. He cupped her head and said, "Both be of import."

"Aye, return by evening meal," Eirik said with a nod. "All else, stay within the threshold till we return," he said and curled his fingers around Elise's arm. "You as well."

"Why can't I go search one of the other areas?" Elise asked with a look of determination within her eyes.

"'Twill have Bo with me, which leaves only Jesse here ta defend Sara and Tristan," he replied with a scowl.

"Oh, you mean Tristan, the panther and Sara, the grappler from hell, with only Jesse, a great weaponist to protect them? I think they'll do fine. Besides, if Kristin is with Leif and stays in her raven form, what reason would he have to come here?" she argued.

He clenched his jaw as he studied her features. "Mayhap so. You'll nary have the darkness ta hide you so stay high so nil arrows may reach you, aye?" She nodded and grinned then kissed him quickly before she ran off to their chamber. He then stood, avoiding the eyes of the others as his face flushed a bit, he cleared his throat and said, "Bo," then headed toward the exit.

With a plan set, they each went their way. Using two leather packs, Eirik instructed Bo to put his weapons in it along with his clothing before they transformed. Then they took to the skies with Eirik teaching Bo how to use the wind in which to glide so he wouldn't tire from the constant use of his wings. And to use his tail much like a rudder of a boat in conjunction with his wings to guide him in the direction he wished to go. He even showed him how to lift or lower his head to help ascend or descend. Then he showed him more complicated maneuvers, such as banking, hovering, barrel rolls, and pulling out of deep dives. When he was confident, they then soared over the blight sensed in the northeast.

Bo let out a screech to get Eirik's attention as he circled back toward a simple structure hidden among some boulders and descended. He gently landed on one of the giant rocks and folded his wings in as he opened his beak and tasted the air. As Eirik landed, he scanned the surrounding area then transformed still holding the two packs. He quickly took out his sword and then his clothing to dress. Bo waited until he was finished before he too transformed and began dressing.

"There's an opening beneath the roof," Bo said as he tied the knife to his thigh and slung the sword over his shoulder.

"I be nary certain how you could see such from the height in which we soared," Eirik snorted in amazement.

Bo's lips creased into a grin, and he gestured to his face as he said, "Eagle eye," then joined him at the entrance.

Eirik entered first as Bo cautiously followed. They came into a small windowless room with bedrolls scattered about on the dirt floor and remnants of discarded food. But also, there was a small container holding several snuffed torches and a doorway cut into the stone with rough-hewn steps leading down into darkness. Eirik picked up a torch and lightly blew his dragon fire across it till it flared to life then he lit another one from it and handed it to Bo before they descended the stairs.

As they neared the bottom, it turned and then opened into a large cavern. They both grunted and covered their faces with their hands as the stench hit them. "Smells like shite in here," Eirik uttered as he moved the torch around.

"And rot," Bo said as his eyes went straight to the chains hanging from the ceiling and followed them as they wound around spools and across toward a complicated apparatus near the entrance. He studied it as he worked out its use then looked to the chains that hung from the ceiling once more, giving his focus to the ends with a cuff of diverse sizes attached to each. "It's a torture chamber," he breathed out.

"Aye," Eirik said as he handed off his torch then gripped the chains in his hands and pulled with all his great strength until the spools came crashing to the floor. Then he did the same with the device on the wall. With a huff, he pushed Bo back out the entrance then filled his lungs with air and exhaled his dragon fire over the entire room, burning anything that could burn and melting the chains to the floor.

Bo hurried up the stairs, soon followed by Eirik but stopped just before he crossed the threshold. He could hear voices. Eirik pulled him back as he eased forward and peeked around the corner. He could see the small room was still empty and heard the voices were just outside. He then rushed across and flattened himself against the exterior stone by the opening as Bo peeked around to watch for the men. He then nodded at Eirik as a man started into the opening.

Eirik waited for him to pass then grabbed him from behind and pulled him to the side and down to the floor. With a knee to his sternum, he held him in place as he glared into the man's eyes and whispered, "Stay and be silent." The man nodded as Eirik rose and glanced at Bo, who could see the silvery sheen cross over his eyes then looked back to the opening as another man came through. He nodded. Eirik did the same to this man, but followed up with, "How many?"

The second man stared at him wide eyed and slowly held up three fingers. Eirik sighed out heavily and backed against the wall once again and waited. When the third entered, his sword was drawn, but it didn't matter as Eirik wrapped his arm around his neck as he kicked at the bend of his knees causing them to bend and he fell backward with Eirik to the ground. Once he lost consciousness, Eirik bound his hands with a strip of cloth from the man's own tunic.

"Bind them," Eirik said to Bo as he gestured toward the two men who stared wildly at Eirik but didn't move or make a noise.

Bo did what he was told, but said, "What are we going to do with them?" as he tore a strip from the first man's tunic and began tying his hands.

"Take them with us," he said as he scanned the area outside the opening. "They brought horses." He then searched the horses for anything helpful, but all he found was a length of small link chain in each of the saddlebags, a bit of rope, and a blacked sackcloth hood. He pulled out the rope and went back inside. He looked at the two still lying on the floor and said, "Follow me," as his eyes shimmered silver once again. As Eirik hefted the limp body of the third over his shoulders, the two men stood and followed him out to the horses where he flung the man over one and secured him to the saddle.

"Can everyone do that or is it unique to you and Leif?" Bo asked once they were headed back toward home.

Eirik shrugged as he glanced at him. "Methinks 'tis just us, but I know naught truly. Most heritors have control over their thralls though."

"Have you ever used it on any of us?" he asked thoughtfully.

"Aye, but twice. On you on our first encounter at the kirke and then on Elise when needs must for truth," he said and kept his eyes on their path.

"So, it's not an island thing it's a species thing," Bo muttered distractedly.

Eirik lifted a brow at him but didn't speak. He had used yet another word which was unfamiliar to him. He hoped that someday their languages would merge, but it seemed that would not be for quite some time.

"If that's the case, then Miss Thornson will have it too. Hmm," he continued to mutter as he thought about the implications of that.

"Perhaps 'tis time ta cease using that title. Hush now," Eirik said softly and nodded slightly behind them to the men that followed.

Bo looked back and saw the men were still silently following them, but they carried hard scowls on their faces as they did so. He didn't know if they had heard him, but they certainly weren't happy. He straightened in his saddle and sighed out his breath.

They were nigh home when Eirik stopped his horse abruptly and jerked his gaze off to the southeast as his heart sank. He dismounted hurriedly and looked at Bo. "Take them ta the homestead. Go straight to the house. Leave them bound 'til I return."

"What's going on?" Bo asked, wide-eyed with worry.

Eirik didn't reply, he just quickly moved to the two men walking and, after catching their eyes with his own, said, "Do nil harm and follow Bo. Do ye understand?"

He waited until each nodded before he began to remove his clothing. He gave Bo his weapons and stuffed his clothing in a saddlebag. After walking out a few paces, he raised his hands slowly and gave them a snap. His glorious dragon form appeared with an angered bellow causing the two men to gasp.

Bo turned toward them and said, "If you don't do what he says, he'll eat you."

The men blanched white and nodded frantically, then Bo moved his horse forward and collected the reins of the other two horses before he looked over just in time to see Eirik take off.

Leif rode leisurely to the thorp as he watched Kristin soar through the air. He knew the enjoyment of doing so as he wished to be up there with her, but it would nary do to speak with Oslo and Jasmin. So, he rode. As they came closer, he whistled for Kristin and held his hand aloft to catch her. She landed lightly then promptly jumped to his shoulder and nuzzled his cheek. They stopped by Oslo's first and instructed him to post a ban on the forest before setting off to Jasmin's with Oslo not having any new information.

They came to a stop in front of a smallish two-story building with colorful scarves and lanterns hanging from the eaves. Leif dismounted, careful not to upset the raven on his shoulder and strode toward the door. Just as he was about to knock, the door tore open and a petite woman with exotic dark eyes and long curly black hair rushed into his arms with excitement.

"'Tis been many moons," she said as she held to him tightly.

Leif cleared his throat and set her back away from him as he uttered, "Aye. 'Tis nary the reason for the visit."

She looked up at him with hurt-filled eyes then glanced to his shoulder where a large raven stood bent forward staring at her quite menacingly. She brushed it off. "Then what brings you, milord?" she asked as she drifted her hand down his chest and pulled slightly on his tunic before she turned to reenter her home. He followed, after glancing in either direction. Inside was a plethora of brightly colored carpets, pillows, cushions, and fabrics, all arranged around a hookah, and small brazier to warm the immediate space. Beautiful intricate lamps hung over the area giving it a rather subdued lighting, one would say romantic even. She gently tugged him down to a mound of pillows with a soft inviting smile curving her lips.

Leif sat and reclined back against the pillows as he thought best how to ask her what he needed to without being too indelicate. "Needs must ta ask about a visitor of yours," he said as she pushed a chalice into his hand.

"Of whom do you inquire?" she asked in a sultry voice, one he was certain convinced many out of their coin.

"Nidpigger," he said, and her entire demeanor changed. Her nose crinkled and her brows crossed above hardened eyes.

"What of him?" she asked as she drank heavily from her own cup.

"I've heard tale that his tastes are… different, aye?"

"Aye, I dread his visits greatly, but he supplies the most coins. Thankfully, he visits rare, nowadays. I've heard tale he gets his pleasure from others he's trained to his wants. What be your interest?" she asked eyeing him with a smile caressing her lips.

"There's been a complaint of a young woman being mistreated by him along with a few other men. Do you have knowledge of such?"

Jasmin went pale of a sudden and stared wide-eyed at him. "'Twas a thrall of his or another?"

"Another," he said tightly, getting the feeling that Nidpigger does this often with his own or even mayhap with her.

Jasmin's hand came up to her mouth as she mumbled, "He nary said 'twas nary a thrall."

"Who be he?" Leif asked with furrowed brows.

"Torvald. He came to me shaken by actions he was forced ta endure... to inflict on another. He was told he would be forced to do so 'til he could enact on his own. Torvald is a gentle soul, nary one to behave with cruelty in bedplay or otherwise, but Nidpigger has forced him to act against himself. Even now, he hides from him and suffers from his latest actions. 'Tis disheartening to see such a soul destroyed by another." She tightened her lips as she brushed the tears from her cheek.

"Where be he?" Leif asked gently as he cupped her face.

"He be in the loft," she said and nodded in that direction.

"Have him come ta the homestead for his safety as well as your own, aye?"

She fell against him in an appreciative embrace as she mumbled, "Oh, thank you. Thank you." Then she kissed him. Nary the sweet brush of lips, but the full-on, slanted heads, open mouthed, enduring kind of kiss. 'Twas then that Leif heard a raven's caw and the flap of wings as it alighted into the skies, and with it his heart sank to his stomach.

He jerked away from her and stood abruptly. "Get your man, I'll take him myself. Without delay, woman," he said rather harshly.

"Torvald! Gather your things. The lord will give you sanctuary. Make haste!" she yelled from where she stood looking up toward the loft.

Leif could now see the blond headed man moving about in the loft. He didn't look any older than those at home or even perhaps himself. Fact was, he likened to himself a great deal, lacking in the height and breadth a bit from his own. His brow rose at Jasmin when he got a full view of the lad as he came down the ladder from the loft.

"Come, lad," he said without remarking on their likeness.

"Thank you, milord," Torvald mumbled as he bobbed his head at Jasmin and followed Leif out the door.

As soon as Leif exited the house, he scanned the skies above in every direction, but mostly toward home. He couldn't see her. "Do ye see her?" he whispered lowly and Stormbringer nudged him gently as he nickered. He alighted his horse then held his arm out for Torvald. Once gripped, he swung up behind him and Stormbringer was away racing off toward home barely giving Torvald time to seat himself.

Leif kept his eyes trained on the sky as they traversed their way back. The closer they come to home, the more his heart thumped within his tight chest. Seems every stride forward, 'twas an obstacle ta push him back 'til he remained behind and beyond the beginning. If she nary would consent before the turning, 'twould be mayhap four fortnights before he'd have even a chance. Perhaps 'twould be best ta have Eirik bond her. He shook his head and sighed out loudly. He would, needs must, he would.

Stormbringer came to a skidding halt just outside the entrance to the longhouse and both men dropped from the horse. Leif loosened the saddle then hastily went through the door. Seeing Kristin sitting by the central fire in one of two chairs and a small table between them, with some fabric in her hands nearly caused him to collapse into a heap of relief. Instead, he rushed toward her, swooped her up into his arms, and hugged her tightly with his face buried in her neck. He just held her, whispering below his breath, "Please, please, please."

Sara stared wide-eyed at the pair, a bit startled by the sudden action, as well as at the one standing near the door, who looked uncertain what to do. She then moved toward them and nudged Leif toward his room, closing the door behind them before addressing the newcomer.

"Greetings," she said with a half-smile.

He dipped his head at her. "Milady," he mumbled awkwardly

and averted his eyes.

"I'm Sara," she said as she extended her hand out to him. He took it, but when it looked like he didn't know what to do with it, she brought it back.

"Torvald," he said.

"Well, Torvald, what brings you to us?" she asked and felt as if she was trying to get a rock to talk.

"Milord said he'd grant me sanctuary from my heritor, Milady," he said rather nervously. "'Twas hiding at Jasmin's two days past."

"Ah, I see. Welcome," she smiled as she closed the door behind him and gestured for him to come in. "We're about to sit down for dinner. Please, join us." She then turned to the kitchen and faltered a step seeing Jesse leaning against the doorframe with his arms crossed, watching.

"Well, aren't you intimidating," she chuckled out in a whisper as she passed by him, patting her hand on his chest to soothe him. She retrieved another place setting and then paused in thought. Torvald looks an awful lot like Leif. I wonder if that's what has him so upset. Where are the others? Then of a sudden, her thoughts were interrupted by a vision. A vision of a white iridescence and crimson red. She let out a horrific scream and dropped the dishes she was holding.

Saturday Night

Elise zoomed through the clouds playfully, practicing her flying skills as she went towards the southeast where Sara had said she detected the maligned Heill. She darted and flipped her way from cloud to cloud, hoping they would help camouflage her massive body. She snorted. She still found it surreal that she was an actual dragon. She was having fun zipping along and frolicking with the clouds, but then decided that she should probably get serious.

Approaching the area northeast of the thorp, she glided soundlessly lower to scan the terrain. There were some boulder fields mixed among some plowed fields with a few trees to outline pathways. Just then she thought she should have asked Eirik or Leif how she was to identify the malign Heill. With her dragon vision, she could see creatures both big and small, but she had no idea of how they aligned with the island. Or if they were totally natural even. How was she going to do this? She needed to figure out some way to tell the difference.

Elise focused in on what looked like a cow, but could see a lot of red. She assumed that was a heat signature. Then she noticed it was outlined in green. Green's good, right? Hmm. She peered down at her own body and saw she was outlined in blue. Well, what could that mean? She wished she had paid more attention on her first turning to see what colors Eirik and Leif were. Taking in a deep breath, she looked around for another heat signature.

She found another large animal, but it was shaped just a bit different than the cow, more like a horse. This one also had the red heat signature with the green outline, but some misshapen blotch above it that had a black outline. Black equals negative, right? She circled around to get another glimpse. As she rounded, she felt a sharp piercing pain in her right side and let out a roaring howl. She had to make sure she stayed aloft. She pushed hard with her wings to take her higher, but with each stroke the pain seared into her side. She could do this, she could. She could at least make sure she was going north toward Eirik. But she couldn't keep using her wings, the pain was too much. She glided down to a field, but as she got closer, all she could really do is hold her head up, so she didn't face-plant and somersault again.

Elise came skidding across a field, cutting a deep rut with her body. She laid there a moment, catching her breath. Clearly hearing hoofbeats coming closer to her from her right, she knew she needed to get up. She looked around to her right as she got her legs under her and pulled her wings in tight to her body protectively. She could see a rider still some distance away. She hoped she could get her shit together before they got to her. She thought of turning human, but that would leave her even more vulnerable. She would have to defend herself and then make her way back to the homestead... somehow.

Staying close to the ground, Elise inched her way around to face her attacker, giving muted lamenting sounds of pain with each movement as she huffed her breath out. She could feel the blood ooze from her wound as she moved. However, when she got a good look at the horseman, she growled lowly. It was Nidpigger and he had with him a large longbow capable of shooting an arrow high enough to have reached her, but luckily, she saw no more arrows.

"What a prize," Nidpigger said gleefully as he drew closer. "Your head will elate my fame far and wide, nary just on the island." He grinned at her. "'Twill hang it from my house for all ta see." He dismounted and drew his sword.

Elise raised her head higher and followed his movements, allowing the rumbling growl from deep in her belly to become louder. Opening her mouth, she made a hissing as she pulled in a breath then shot out her lightning, barely missing him, but managed to scare off his horse.

Nidpigger gave a shout of surprise, but his grin grew as he readied himself to fight, sword raised high. He slowly circled to her right side and still a bit nearer. Elise swiftly extended her wing then brought it back, swinging at his head. With a quick duck and roll, he got back to his feet, although he was now closer to her.

She eased slowly to her left with each step he took. She drew in another hissing breath just before she brought her tail to her right, sending him rolling again. She thought perhaps she did him damage with that one, but he was soon on his feet once more, ready to fight. Now he was more to her front, and she shot her lightning at him, but of course, she missed. She needed more practice. Shit!

"Ye'er a pretty thing, but nary very talented, aye?" he let out a laugh then started moving again towards her right.

Elise felt herself weakening with her blood loss. She thought hard what to do next as she kept her eyes on him, finding it increasingly more difficult to do so as her eyes closed to mere slits. She knew this would be her last attempt. Her muscles coiled tight in anticipation as she waited for him to position himself right where she wanted him. When he was close enough, in a flash, she struck out her wing at the same time swinging her tail forward and turning to the left till she faced in the opposite direction with her wounded right away from him. She reeled her massive head to her left.

Nidpigger wasn't there. She looked to her right, not there either. She gave her tail a mighty swipe and sent him rolling from behind her. But now she was done. She had no more energy left to fight him and she couldn't keep her eyes open any longer. Depleted, she lowered her head to the ground, unable to keep it raised, and her breaths came and went in laborious huffs. She returned to human as she lost consciousness.

Having nil qualms about taking advantage of an unwitting lass, Nidpigger rushed toward her while her body still retained heat. He may have lost his prize ta hang above his doorway, but he was about ta get a much more enjoyable one in recompence.

Eirik circled over a field with a deep rut cut into it, and within it laid his Elise, naked and unmoving. He saw a man rapidly approaching her, nay, nary a man, 'twas Nidpigger. He roared terrifyingly in warning as he landed gently over Elise's unmoving form. He snarled and grunted at the man just before he blew out his dragon fire above his head. Nidpigger hastily skittered backward away from them, clumsily getting to his feet, and took off as fast as he could run.

Eirik mournfully roared out as he stood above Elise's listless body. Then lowered his head to her and nudged her with his great muzzle. Nothing. Nil response. He ever so carefully grasped her within his talons and leaped into the air. He would have Nidpigger's head for this, for a certain.

It seemed to take hours for Eirik to arrive at the homestead but was only minutes. He came to a gliding halt, landing lightly just outside the longhouse entrance, giving three short barks before he laid Elise at his feet and returned to human. He dropped to his knees and gathered her up in his arms to take her inside.

Leif came rushing out the door at hearing Eirik's call and quickly assessed the situation. Hurrying toward him was Eirik with a lifeless Elise splayed out in his arms. Sara too rushed out the door, gasped sharply, then returned inside. "Clear a table without delay," Leif hollered behind him as he helped Eirik bring her through the door. They gently laid her on the table nearest the fire and Leif pulled the fur lying in the bower over the top of her, covering not only her nakedness but also the deep gash along her right side.

Eirik grasped her hand and bowed over her as murmuring whispers issued from his mouth as Leif belted a cloth around his hips. Bo came closer with a bowl of water shaking in his hands followed by two bound men, to which Leif scowled. Having the water near, Leif pulled back the fur to expose Elise's side and began cleansing it of the blood and mud caked to it. His heart ached for his brother as he tended to the wound. If he lost her, there would be nil consoling him. He would rage out of control and set the island alight with fire, for a certain.

Sara came closer as she wept and reached a hand out to Elise, placing it gently on her sternum. Jesse engulfed her in his arms and breathed into her ear over her shoulder, his calming words in a slow and soft cadence. "Soothing, swaying, peaceful as a summer's day. Marshal your thoughts, assemble your awareness, and observe your positive force finished." He moved her gently forward and swayed with her slowly, gathering Heill.

Elise inhaled deeply with a gasp, drawing all eyes to her, then let the air out slowly. Her veins thrummed with a glowing red like lava, emblazing her wound brightly before it began to close as all watched in amazement, except Eirik. He was still clinging to her hand and his face was lowered down beside her head. With whispered oaths and prayers, he kissed her lips, cheek, and eyes. Then abruptly, he picked her up in his arms and went to his chamber.

With a heavy sigh, Leif looked about him. He felt Kristin standing beside him, clinging to his arm. Sara and Jesse were embraced to his other side. Bo and Tristan stood just out of the way with the two bound men right behind him and another bound man lying in the next bower over. And Torvald sat at the high table staring wide-eyed at them all. He shook his head. What had happened in his own home while he was so absorbed by his own misdeeds. So focused was he on gaining the forgiveness of Kristin that he allowed much ta happen. He looked first to Bo.

"Who be these men that follow ye like pups?" he asked as a scowl creased his face once more and he felt Kristin slide farther behind him.

"Eirik commanded them to follow me," he said with a slight shrug. "I can't even take a piss," he grumbled.

"What more? Who be they?"

Bo glanced at Kristin then looked at him and tightened his

lips briefly. "We found them in the northeast," he said simply, hoping to not have to explain in Kristin's presence. "Eirik told me to bring them straight to the house. So..." He spread his hands wide.

Leif moved closer to the men. "Who be your heritor?" he asked with still a menacing glower on his face.

"'Tis Nidpigger," they spoke in unison causing a gasp to escape from Kristin. He could feel her tremble then.

Leif growled lowly hearing his name then said, "Where were ye and what was ye task?"

Both men tightened their lips as they stared at Leif and shook their heads.

"'Twas at the stone hut, I'd wager," Torvald said as he came closer. "'Twas likely commanded nary ta say as such."

Leif leaned around them to address Torvald. "Ye have nary been so?"

"I've nary been in his presence for nigh three days. His commands wear thin, if nary reinforced often, especially so with me." He gave Leif a slight smile. "'Twas nary my choice ta be enthralled by he," he explained further then lowered his gaze. "So, I hide from him. Makes the suffering much worse when he catches me. 'Tis better than his tasks," he mumbled the last.

"Stone hut?" Leif asked and glanced at Bo, who shook his head slightly as he looked at Kristin.

"Ne'er mind," Leif said then caught the gaze of the two men. "Go sit in that bower and nary move," he said as he gestured toward the next bed closet, the one that held the third man. They nodded and did as he commanded.

"How long has he been out?" Leif asked Bo quietly, nodding his head in the three men's direction.

"Close to an hour, I guess. He should be awake by now though," Bo responded and looked his direction with a frown.

"Aye," Leif agreed and move toward them. He shook the third man and sat him upright. Once he held his gaze, he said, "Sit here quietly and nary do harm." Receiving a nod from him, Leif was about to turn and ask more questions of Torvald, but...

He stood silently and bit at his lip as Kristin came out from behind him, still clasping his arm, and stared over the three, scrutinizing each. All three dressed plainly, even poorly. Her head dropped to their boots; those too were of poor quality. She surged toward them but was caught around the waist by Leif. He pulled her up into his arms and moved away from the three before he set her back on her feet.

"I know your vengeance, dearling, but nary the now. 'Twill sort it when Eirik can pronounce judgement, aye?" He held her to him and kissed her lightly when she hesitantly nodded.

"She be the maid from the hut," Torvald whispered lowly and backed away.

Jesse looked hard at him then grabbed him by the shirt and swiftly moved him into the kitchen away from the others where he held him against the wall. "How do you know that?" he asked through gritted teeth.

"I... I... I... was there," he stuttered out fearfully.

"You what?" Jesse's eyes went wide in disbelief.

Sara tugged on his arm. "Release him, Jess," she said calmly.

Slowly, ever so slowly, Jesse removed his hand from the boy and stood back with his fists at his side and a frown distorting his face.

"I... I... I nary had a choice. 'Twas commanded ta do so. 'Twould ne'er do such deeds on my own accord. Sickens me ta do his bidding." He shook his head.

"How old are you?" Sara asked as her head tilted and she looked into his eyes.

"Ten and six autumns," he replied and licked his lips.

Sara's brows rose then she glanced back at Jesse. "He's just a kid, Jess." Jesse's demeanor softened with that realization, but he still frowned. "Feel his anguish," she whispered, and he nodded. "You should break your bond with Nidpigger and consent to Leif for your heritor," she said as she faced the boy again.

"'Tis possible ta do so?" Torvald questioned, almost hopeful.

"It is for you, but I'm not sure about any others," she said with a shrug then turned away from him and began setting out the platters for their dinner.

Jesse helped her by slicing up the roast but kept his gaze on the boy. He was conflicted by his innocence and the fact that he was one of the men that kidnapped and molested Kristin. It was hard to reconcile. It had to be much harder for Kristin to have the four of them within the same house. How would they get her past this? He felt Sara's hand on his arm and peered down at her. She smiled up at him and he bent, brushing his lips to hers. He knew she did it to disperse his negativity and was thankful for it, although he didn't need reason to kiss Sara. Not anymore. He had always liked her, admired her from a far as they say, before they came here. She was the reason he chose to come on this trip, although he had to convince his father to agree, but when he told him that it would look good on college applications, he was set. His father had always kept him on a short leash with football practices, working out, or some other activity having to do with sports. Never was he allowed to do what he wanted, aside from cooking, but that was only because he needed a specific diet. Even that didn't put him in the same circle as Sara. Except the first time he'd met her when they were sixteen and in a mandatory Home Economics class. But after that, he'd only see her in passing and thought he wasn't her type because she was always with the intellectual Bo. What would she want with a muscle head like him? Little did he know... He grinned at his thoughts.

"Come, help bring this to the table," Sara said to Torvald, who had stayed in the kitchen with them where he felt safer away from the others, were the thoughts of both Sara and Jesse.

Sara handed off a tray of cheese and bread to Torvald then turned to Jesse. "What has you grinning like a cat with a bird?" she asked looking up at him.

"To be honest? You," he chuckled and laid the knife aside. "You have a way of turning me positively positive," he chuckled again.

"Good, we both need to remain positive for the next several

days and disperse it throughout the house. We have a few tasks to perform and at the top of it will be breaking the bond Torvald has with Nidpigger. We also need to stay positive for Kristin and then we'll deal with the three men lastly," she sighed heavily.

"You know," Jesse began as he pulled her against him. "It may take several more of these to keep positive." He kissed her lightly again then slanted his head to deepen it, but it didn't last as long as he wanted, for he felt her withdrawing. He breathed out, "Dinner, I know." He turned back to the roast as she filled the pitchers with water and mead, however she did smile at him. He winked at her. Sara chuckled as she took the pitchers into the hall, passing by Torvald.

"Why do ye work within the threshold?" he asked as he came closer to the table.

"It doesn't make me gay," Jesse responded with creased brows, now knowing the mindset of men in this era.

"Nay, 'twould nary make me so either," Torvald remarked.

"That's not what I meant. I'm happy to help Sara and the others. I even enjoy it most of the time."

"Aye, ta be around such lasses 'twould make me happy too, but nary the women's work. 'Tis nary hard enough work ta keep my strength for battles. Nay, I require the harder work beyond the threshold." He nodded his head as he leaned against the table.

Jesse arched a brow at him. "Oh, have you battled much?" he asked with doubt dripping from his words and then shoved the platter of meat toward him. "Take that to the high table," he ordered as he stabbed the knife point into the tabletop causing Torvald to jump a bit. Torvald did as he said, rushing off to the hall.

Sara snickered lightly as she gazed up at him, eyes sparkling. "He'll learn the first time he tastes your cooking. Come, let's eat." She then moved to get some extra trenchers for their additional guests.

"What are you doing?" Jesse asked as he came around the table to go to the hall.

"They've got to eat too. I told you we need positive energy in the house. If we don't feed them, it will create negative energy."

"Will it? You don't think it will create negative energy seeing you treat Kristin's attackers with kindness?"

"I have never seen a positive action create a negative one," she argued with a lifted brow.

Jesse nodded. "But you don't have to be the one to serve them, do you?"

She smiled up at him as she tugged him closer then kissed him lightly before she said, "Disperse your negativity." She then turned to go to the hall, and he followed.

Torvald was standing just inside still holding the tray of meat staring wide-eyed at Kristin, who was glowering at him. Jesse took the tray from his hands and set it on the table as Sara urged him to a bench.

"He was the one that..." Kristin accused but couldn't voice it completely.

"He nary had a choice, dearling," Leif soothed. "His heritor commanded him ta deed. 'Twas nary of his own thought nor action." Kristin tightened her lips, remembering someone saying no, then she raised her head to Leif and nodded. "Let's sup," he said lowly.

As they began taking their seats, Leif made Torvald move down to his left, leaving room to his right for Kristin and Tristan. Jesse sat across from him, and Bo was on the opposite end, across from Tristan. They had left room for Eirik and Elise between them. Sara was filling a trencher for the three men and Jesse eyed her.

"Not you," he said lowly.

"Then who?" Sara questioned as she drifted her hand through the air, indicating to the others. He looked over the faces of the others and set his jaw, knowing he wouldn't win this one. She took the trencher to the three men and filled their cups with water before she returned and took her seat beside Jesse. Having that handled, she glanced at the others and saw how they disapproved as Jesse tried to tell her. "I have my reasons," she said quietly and patted the left side of her chest then began filling her plate, as did they all.

Just then they heard Eirik's door open and both Eirik and Elise came out and joined them at the table. Eirik helped ease Elise down to her seat before taking his own. He was quiet.

"How are you feeling?" Sara asked, smiling over at Elise.

"I'm okay. My side still hurts a bit, but I'm okay," she returned Sara's smile.

"I be happy to see you up and about. 'Twas nary certain 'twould be after seeing the injury caused you," Leif said. "'Twas quite worrisome."

Elise turned her gaze toward Leif, but paused on Torvald, then on to Leif, and yet back again.

"His name is Torvald," Sara said quietly. "Leif brought him back from the thorp seeking sanctuary from his heritor," she said much louder.

"Who be his heritor?" Eirik asked then drank deeply from his cup.

"He who shall not be named," Sara said with a quirk of her brow. Several noises of disgust erupted around the table. "From what I understand, it wasn't exactly a consensual bonding and he's only sixteen. I also believe the bond can be broken." She then smiled at Eirik then over to Leif. "I think you should take him on."

Kristin gasped quietly and Leif patted her knee before glancing at Torvald then back to Sara. "What makes you think such can be achieved?" he said with his brows low.

"His bond is tenuous at best. I think it can be broken quite easily, for him anyway," she replied and began eating.

"Tenuous?" Leif asked. "'Tis thin, aye?"

Sara nodded. "Weak and fragile. But he must choose to do it... I think." She looked thoughtful. "And trust," she raised a brow at Torvald.

"How do you know all this, Sara?" Elise asked her in amazement, as well as a good dose of skepticism.

Jesse cleared his throat. "She has a much better

understanding of the Heill and the island than I do, but I can sense when she speaks, it's the truth. It's hard for me to explain, but I trust her," he shrugged a bit then winked at Sara.

"Ye certain ye nary a wee krókóttur ta her, lad?" Eirik asked with a curve to his lips.

"Maybe, if I knew what it meant, but it doesn't change the outcome. She speaks the truth," Jesse smiled at him.

"It means crooked, but I think he means bias," Elise said distractedly with a thoughtful look.

"Eat, heartling. If we can achieve it, then we must. If Leif nary wishes ta take another on, then I shall. Needs must we begin rectifying *his* misdeeds," Eirik said then he drank from his cup to wash the distaste from his mouth.

"No, it really should be Leif," Sara said then rose to take her plate to the kitchen.

Leif looked down at Kristin with a heavy sigh, hoping she'd understand his decision before he nodded his head at Eirik. "'Twill do it should the lad consent."

"'Tis possible then?" Torvald spoke up. "Ta break his hold over me?"

"Yea, as Sara says. Ye must renounce ya bond and accept your new heritor freely and wholly so," Eirik said, studying him closely. Though his eyes were but a bit darker in shade as were his brows and lashes, he had a striking resemblance to Leif. He would question his brother in private.

"I consent," Torvald said happily then looked to Leif. "If ye'll have me."

Leif nodded and continued eating. He knew he would have to reason with Kristin about it, but he could nary leave Torvald in Nidpigger's care any longer. If he had his way nil one would be in the nithing's care ever. Which will be one point he'll raise to her. After.

Once they were finished eating, Eirik sat with Elise in the chairs by the fire drinking mead as they waited for the others to finish with the hearth duties. He could feel her mind working. "What be amiss, heartling?" he asked quietly.

"How old are you and Leif?" she said as she stared into the flames then turned her emerald gaze on him.

"Older than I led you ta believe at first. My apologies for the deception, but needs must at the time," he said then straightened in his chair.

"No, honey, I mean your age, exactly how old are you? Well, Leif, to be more precise."

"Thirty and two winters." He cleared his throat.

"So, it's possible?" she asked with a lifted brow.

He nodded but said no more because the others were finished with their task and joining them near the fire. "Ye ready then?" he asked Leif, received a nod, then looked to Torvald as he stood and moved closer to them.

Leif peered down at Kristin and captured her face in his hands then kissed her tenderly before he withdrew and gave his full attention to Eirik.

"Lad, ye certain this be ye wish?" Eirik asked Torvald and received a nod. "Ye too, aye?" he looked to Leif.

"Yea, Sara told me what must be done," Leif said with his eyes cast down, gesturing somewhat off toward the kitchen.

"Remove your shirt, Torvald," Sara said moving closer to the three of them, and he looked at her now uncertain. "Trust," she simply said. He then looked at Eirik who stood in front of him.

"She means your serk," he clarified.

Torvald nodded and brought his serk over his head, holding it loosely in his hands.

As Leif lined up behind Torvald and closed his eyes, Eirik asked, "Do ye renounce the bond with your heritor Nidpigger?"

"With all that I be," Torvald said as he felt Sara's hands slide over both his chest and back, although the hand on his back felt much rougher. Leif felt Sara grasp his hand and began slowly moving it over Torvald's back.

"Do ye freely and fully accept Leif as your heritor?" Eirik asked as he took a step back away from him.

"I do with all that I be," Torvald said as he heard a breath being drawn in from behind him.

When Sara stopped his hand, Leif drew in the Heill, focusing his will to his intention and felt his mouth heat with it. Then with a sudden urge to do so, he bit into Torvald's left shoulder with an animalistic growl and sank with him to the floor, holding him tightly against him.

Torvald yelled out in pain but didn't struggle against Leif as he held him on his knees and bent over him. He could feel the Heill enter him, setting his veins afire, elating him to heights he'd never felt.

Leif withdrew and released the boy, easing him to the floor, then wiped his hand across his mouth as he straightened. He was uncertain when Sara had told him this must be the way. But when she explained that he was going to have to assert his dominance over the Heill that already resided within Torvald, it made more sense to him. In his youth, his brother had bitten him on more than one occasion when he rebelled against his rules. He hastily rushed Kristin into their chamber when he saw the lad's back and the confused look on her face.

Bo and Tristan moved in then with a bowl of water and a bandage for the bite. Bo looked up at Eirik with a bit of concern at seeing what appeared to be an immature dragon tattooed on his back, to which he nodded.

"Luuu-cey, you have some 'splainin' to do," Elise said with a chuckle from her chair, giving rise to several snickers from those familiar with the phrase.

"'Tis nary our concern, heartling," Eirik mumbled as he helped her up from her chair and directed her to their chamber.

"He's your nephew," she whispered to only him, and he nodded.

"Why did you bite him?" Kristin asked as she was rushed through the door.

When Leif had the door closed behind them and securely locked, he faced her. "Sara had said so. 'Twas the only way ta control his Heill, she said. I grasp her meaning." He clasped her hands and urged her toward the bed. "Tis more," he said on a sigh. "I fear what you might think, once you've heard it." He tightened his lips as he sat with her on the bed. "Perhaps we should ready ta abed first, aye?"

"No… You should tell me now," she said as she scanned over his face. This wasn't going to be good.

"I be nigh certain that Torvald be my offspring," he blurted.

Her eyes widened. "But he's almost as old as I am."

"Yea, 'twas when I was a brattle, nigh his age. 'Twas my first."

"You have more than one?" her brows skyrocketed, and her voice grew a bit shrill.

He chuckled and shook his head. "Nay, I have learned much since then. 'Twas nary aware of him 'til this day. Had I known, nary would he have been enthralled by any other. Seems Jasmin kept him from me for some purpose, I know naught."

"Jasmin? The woman you were kissing today?" she bit her lips together, knowing they had already settled that. But it didn't stop the pain from pricking her heart, nor the tears that threatened to spill.

"Aye, 'twas Eirik that sent me to her to keep me from chasing any other when the need arose. 'Twas for the good of the island, for a certain." He lowered his gaze.

"I suppose that's the way of your people," Kristin said quietly, thoughtfully.

"They be your people too now," he said as he pulled his tunic and serk off and gazed at her.

"Leif," she said and then looked up at him. "I want… I freely and wholeheartedly give myself to you."

He grinned. He wasn't expecting that. He leaned into her and kissed her cheek lightly before pulling her closer and finding her lips, sliding tenderly against them before pressing them open. He tilted his head into hers and whispered, "As my mate?"

She nodded and advanced on him, kissing him with everything she had, forcing him backward on the bed. "I've never wanted anything more," she breathed out.

He rolled her to her back and slid his hand up beneath her bodice as her kisses became frantic. "Sh sh sh, dearling. Slowly, we have 'til daybreak." He then pulled the garment from her and was faced with another. He saw nil clasp, so he pulled it over her head. She could show him another day how it fastens. Having her breasts now exposed, her arm came over them to hide them from him. "Nay... Trust me, sweetling," he whispered as he gently pulled her hand away and placed it around him. He bent his head to the first and tenderly rubbed his lips over it as he exhaled, heating her skin. Then gingerly, he smoothed his tongue over and around her whetted nipple before he drew on it, careful not to scrape his teeth. As her back arched, he drew again then laved it before addressing her other one. He continued to ply her with slow kisses and lavings until he felt she was ready to move forward, indicated by her writhing. He paused as he peered down at her then farther. He brushed his hand down her chest and across her abdomen to where her breeches fastened, with a quick jerk he had them open and pulled them from her hips then off.

He was nigh breathless as his eyes wandered over her and his lips curved into a smile. "Ye are the most beautiful my eyes have seen, sweetling," he breathed out then quickly removed his axe and knife before he sat on the side of the bed to unlace his boots. When he stood again to take off his breeches, she got beneath the furs.

He tossed them on a chest then opened the next one and pulled out a ring. It was similar to the one that Eirik had given Elise, but the emblem was smaller, denoting the secondary echelon. He glanced at her and smiled as he returned to her, cupping the ring in his hand. "I speak true, sweetling, nary a need for ye modesty," he said as he lifted the covers and slid in beside her, hovering slightly over her.

"Leif..." she said and bit her lip.

"Yea," he answered and fingered a strand of her hair back.

"You are my first," she whispered and looked away.

"Aye, I be aware," he smiled softly down at her.

"Can you make it quick, so I won't feel the pain?" she asked timidly and bit at her lip.

"Trust me, sweetling, ye'll nary notice any pain. 'Tis a vow," he breathed as he lowered his mouth to hers and kissed her long and slow. He was going to ensure she would enjoy every moment of it. He would worship her as he would Freya, this time and evermore.

He would place the ring after.

(245-227=18)

Sun and Moon Days

Mates

"Jess," Sara whispered softly in her sleep.

Jesse's eyes came open and he stretched his hand out to push aside the cloth, looking into the darkness of the room, uncertain that he heard anything. They had allowed the central fire to die, just in case Torvald couldn't take the heat. However, they did pull the curtain to their bower closed, as did Bo and Tristan.

"Oh, Jess," Sara enticingly moaned out quietly.

"Shooosh, Sara," he hissed to silent her vocalizing. He shook her slightly. He didn't really want to wake her, but he didn't want her to wake up anyone else either. She rolled to her back.

He slid his hand along her side up to her face where he leaned in to kiss her. "Wake up, babe," he whispered. She draped her arm around him and pulled him closer. Oh, he wanted to take full advantage of the situation, but he knew better. He wouldn't have their first time clouded by a sleep haze and induced by a wet dream, even if it was about him. He grinned. "Come on, Sara, wake up."

"I'm awake, Jess," she whispered.

"Are you sure?" he asked as he still held himself away from her. She nudged him down closer. Jesse then brushed his lips to hers. Making sure she was awake before he deepened the kiss, sliding his tongue into her tantalizing mouth and exploring it thoroughly. He was certain now that she was awake, but if he hadn't been, he knew for sure when she brushed her hand down his back, beneath the waistband of his shorts, and squeezed his ass. He lowered his hand to her breast and massaged it rhythmically with his kisses, bringing another provocative muffled moan from her. *Fuck*, he thought. He sucked in a deep breath and focused his desire as he drew in his Heill.

"Okay, let it go, babe." Now she could be as loud as she wanted. He smiled down at her sparkling eyes and regained her lips as he pushed her shirt up and laid his chest against hers, shifting them to his back. Skin to skin, made his eyes roll back in alluring torment, but not as much as the feel of her writhing against him in this position. Their legs were intertwined with one of his between hers as well as one of hers between his and snugged up against him. And her hands! Her hands went from his chest to his hip to brushing along his phallus, which he was sure was blue by now and straining at his shorts for freedom. "Oh, god, Sara," he breathed out and rolled them to her back to try to control this just a little. "I've waited far too long for this to end quickly. We're gonna try to savor it, sweetheart." He then lifted her shirt above her head and off. Moving down her body, he removed her panties before slowly kissing her from her belly to her breasts where he cupped one and brought it toward his mouth. While suckling it gently, her back arched up and she moaned ever so delightfully. He drew on it harder as he rubbed his hand down her side and across her thigh, finding her folds slick and waiting for him. He started to move in that direction when he heard her.

"Please, Jess," she pleaded. "I want you."

He pushed his shorts off and moved in between her thighs, which she raised up on either side of his hips. He slowly rubbed along her furrow before he lifted her hips higher and set his crown to enter her. Raising on his arms, he paused as she tilted her hips and he pushed into her as she hugged into him with a moaning cry and a spark of blue iridescence radiated from her tattoo.

After taking a couple breaths, he pushed the rest of the way to his hilt. His eyes rolled as a red glow emanated from his own marking. He never dreamed it would feel this good with her, and he dreamed of it often. He dreamed of *her* often.

"Don't stop, Jess," she whispered her plea once again in desperation as she hooked her heels behind his back and pulled him in even tighter to her, intensifying her blue aura.

"There's no stopping now, sweetheart. Just needed a little control." He then withdrew and inserted once again, straight to the hilt, drawing another pleasurable moan from her lips, sending out more sparks. He moved within her time and time again then slowly circled his hips until he found the right spot. He knew when he did by the outcry she made. Bringing a smile to his lips and a throbbing aura setting his entire body alight, he then circled his hips a few more times before he couldn't restrain himself any longer. He shortened his strokes and lowered his head to kiss her with all the passion that filled him, his light pulsating with each of his thrusts. When it seemed she was close, by the mounting whimpers, he circled his hips in quick secession before resuming his faster strokes. He wasn't holding back. Hearing her cry out, and the feel of her ripple around him, within a few more strokes, his moan joined hers, setting them both aglow in a shower of ultraviolet sparkles. "Oh, fuck, Sara," he breathed out as he quickly rolled them to his back and hugged her to him.

"Oh, 'twas quite sweet. Although, I've nary slaked my needs in a cock of hay, what more have ye to sate my tastes?" A voice came from the open doorway of the barn stall they were in, startling them both.

"Fuck!" Jesse yelped then held tight to Sara as he focused his Heill and they were back in her bower. "Oh, thank god," he whispered as he let his breath out in a whoosh.

Sara continued to hold on to him as she slowly caught her breath. "That was close," she whispered then reached to kiss him and giggled. "We should alert the dragons that he trespasses on their territory," she said quietly then looked for her clothes.

"How can you switch gears so fast?" Jesse chuckled as he found his shorts, but the rest of his clothes were across the room.

"Needs must!" she replied as she dressed. When Sara was fully dressed, she stopped long enough to kiss him again then she was off to tell the brothers.

Jesse sat on the edge of the bower and shook his head. He rose to his feet and retrieved his clothes from his duffle bag. He donned them swiftly and grabbed his toothbrush then headed to the kitchen, feeling positively energized.

Sara knocked loudly on Eirik's door, unable to raise Leif beyond his locked one. She waited briefly before pounding on it with her fist. One more time and she'll port in, she promised herself.

"Aye!" Eirik growled as he finally opened the door.

"Nidpigger was in the barn," she said quickly then turned away to try Leif again.

Instead of knocking this time, she drew in a breath and ported just on the other side of his door. She glanced around the darkened room then went to the bed. She shook him awake. "Your foe was in the barn not ten minutes ago," she said quietly, not wishing to wake Kristin. "And I'd reinforce your commands to the others before you go off to find him."

Leif rolled out of bed and rapidly found his breeches. "Why were ye in the barn?" he asked pulling them in place and laced his boots then looked for a serk and tunic. "Ye have been warned ta nary go beyond the threshold alone," he reprimanded.

"Um... that's not important. You should hurry," she said deflecting, lifting her hand to his arm to emphasize her words. She paused as she focused. "You've secured your bond with Kristin," she said more to herself than to him.

"Yea," he grinned briefly as he inhaled.

"You've mated." Again, this was not a question.

"As have ye," he commented, making a great show of sniffing her then pulled his serk over his head. "Aye, she agreed and made her oath last eve ta the mate bonding." His grin broadened. "'Twas most unexpected, truly."

"Indeed. Congratulations, my friend. I didn't think she

would so soon after... Well, good. Keep her happy for the next few days." Sara chuckled having that worry delt with.

"I intend ta. Takes three nights of mating for the life-mate bond," he grinned again then donned his tunic and went to his door. Having to unlock it first, he turned to Sara with an uplifted brow. She pushed him out the door.

"He's going to get away. Hurry!" she said then closed the door behind them. "At least she won't be Nidpigger bait anymore," Sara mumbled. And then, "Three nights? Hmm." She and Jesse made no such oath or agreement, but she was certain they had bonded this morning.

Sara found Jesse in the kitchen slicing up pork fat for bacon and approached him cautiously, a bit uncertain of her own intentions. Did she really want the answers? One answer, she only needed to hear one answer from him, and the others would fall into place. She'd had a crush on Jesse since she was sixteen and now, all of a sudden, she sensed this was too good to be true.

"Heya, babe," he greeted her with a dimple-popping smile that made her melt. She bit her lips together and cast her eyes down. He froze, dropping the knife and cleaning his hands off on a nearby cloth. He braced himself for her words that he was certain would crush him.

"Hey," she returned, glancing briefly up at him.

"Fuck no," he said staring down at her. It had to be Bo that stopped her from pursuing this with him.

"No?"

He came around the table and gripped her by the arms with a scowl pinching his face. "No, you're not fucking doing this," he growled between clenched teeth.

She gasped at his violent action. "Not doing what?" she trembled out, wide-eyed.

Jesse lowered his head and blew out his breath then gently pulled her into his arms. "I'm sorry, I thought... For a moment, I thought you wanted to end this, but after I could focus on you, I knew what caused your uncertainty," he said lowly and kissed the top of her head. "I'm not ever letting you go, now that I

finally have you, babe. I've waited years for this," he breathed
out and hugged her to him.

"You know we bonded this morning, right?" she whispered,
still uncertain of his reaction.

"We sure did," he chuckled.

She leaned back to see his eyes and shook her head slightly.
"No, I mean of the lifelong variety," she said slowly, but quickly
followed with, "But if you don't agree... Leif says that it takes
three nights of mating..." She stopped and looked away as her
eyes glassed over.

"Sara?" Jesse said as he tenderly brought her head back to face
him. "Nothing would please me more," he said and hugged her
into him, elated, then chuckled. "I don't think I've ever seen you
at a loss of confidence before." She slugged him lightly.

"Nor you so determined," she retorted up at him with a smile.

"You know, I thought you were having second thoughts
because of Bo," he said over her head.

"You don't have to be jealous of Bo. Bo and I are just friends,
always have been, always will be, except that one time..." She
gasped as he jerked her away from him and held her by the arms
again but clenched his jaw to keep from speaking. "Jess... You
know now that I wasn't a virgin before and I know that you
certainly weren't either," she grinned up at him, defusing his
anger.

He released her and looked away. "How would you know?"
He couldn't quite keep his lips from curving.

"Practice makes perfect," she chuckled. "And you've practiced
a lot."

He then lifted her into his arms and kissed her thoroughly,
wishing they could have an encore. They blinked out of the
kitchen.

At hearing Jesse shout, Bo had started into the kitchen,
but didn't get two strides in before he got the gist of their
conversation and backed out. He leaned on the wall near the
door with his arms crossed over his chest and waited to see if she

needed him to intervene. Sara was his best friend, and he wasn't about to let Jesse hurt her, physically or emotionally. She was strong, but he knew she had her vulnerabilities too. They had expressed their cringe-worthy grief about their crushes to each other early on, having felt they were too... unattainable, thus making them truly crushes, sealing their friendship. There was one brief moment in their friendship when they tried to make it more, becoming physical, whether out of loneliness, hormones, or the need for human touch, but they both had decided they were better as friends. And they were too, having no secrets between them. Sara knew about Tristan, and he knew about Jesse. He was happy for her, as he hoped she was happy for him for it seemed he wasn't the only one to form a mate-bond last night. The silence in the kitchen brought him out of his thoughts.

Bo rounded the corner and entered the vacant kitchen. After scanning over the room, he hurried to the back door and threw it open. They weren't there. Where could they have gone? With a deep sigh, he went back to their chamber to check on Torvald and to see if Tristan was up yet. As he entered, he saw Tristan pulling her sweater in place and he smiled.

"Good morning," he said quietly as he drew closer to her and brushed his lips lightly to hers. "Have you seen Sara and Jesse? I thought they were in the kitchen, but I must've been mistaken."

Tristan smiled and pointed toward Sara's bower before she grabbed her toiletries and urged him out of the room. "They seem to be busy," she snickered when they closed the door.

"Oh," he said still very confused. He was going to ask Sara about it. But for now, someone needed to get breakfast started.

Eirik and Leif returned to the longhouse after nigh an hour of searching. They were confident that Nidpigger had left once he was discovered, but why would he come at all. Mayhap, 'twas they held his three men, four if Torvald were ta be counted. They both felt he was up to nil good, for a certain. They come to a stop just inside the door.

The house was too quiet. Eirik rushed to his chamber as Leif went to his own. Opening the door, Eirik smiled in relief seeing Elise still slept. He quietly closed the door and turned to see Leif doing the same.

"She still sleeps," Leif said and they both grinned.

"The rogues are gone," Eirik said as they continued to the kitchen.

"Yea, 'twas meant to reinforce their command afore we went looking as Sara had said, but I failed ta do so," Leif admitted.

With one on either side of the doorway, they peeked in only to find Ingrid making sweet cakes. "Good morn, Ingrid," Eirik said as he glanced around the room.

"Good morn, Milord," she replied with a slight smile.

"Hath ye nary help this morn?" Leif asked as he made his way to the back door and looked out.

"The fires set alight, the water set ta boil, an' the pork fat was cut an' cooked afore I come, but nary much more than that. 'Twas items set out fer sweet cakes," she said and gestured to the flat sheet she was cooking them on.

"Ye have nary seen any other within or without?" Eirik asked a bit confused. She shook her head.

Both Leif and Eirik started for the guest chamber when she said, "Methinks all are consumed by the mating bond," she nearly chuckled, but kept to her task. When she glanced their way, her eyes gleamed.

Eirik's brow arched. "Ingrid... Does the mating bond affect those within the house?"

She blushed a deep red as she smiled. "Fer a certain," she giggled.

He nary thought he'd ever seen Ingrid giggle afore. "'Twas nary aware of such," he smiled at her and nodded before he left the kitchen with Leif.

"Must needs ta check Torvald and the others, but nary do I wish ta walk in on such nor disturb," Eirik spoke quietly to Leif.

"Together will make quick work, brother," he grinned as they paused outside the guest chamber.

They opened the door and moved in silent footsteps. Leif went to Torvald's bed closet to be assured of his safety and was relieved to find him asleep, though restless. Eirik paused outside of Tristan's bower as Leif did Sara's. After a few moments, they both retreated, soundlessly closing the door behind them.

"Hmm," Eirik murmured as they made their way to the high table. "Sara did say something about needing to stay happy for a few days. She called it 'positive reinforcement'."

"Yea, she said as such ta me this morn about Kristin." He sat heavily on the bench.

"Sara draws such strong Heill... 'Tis seem Jesse assists her in some way. 'Tis good they bond," Eirik said as he poured them both cups of mead.

"She entered my chamber this morn without unlocking the door. I nary had the chance ta ask her how, as of yet," Leif remarked as he drank deeply from his cup.

"'Twas a simple life nary a fortnight ago," Eirik commented after a few moments, looking into his cup.

Leif looked at him with a lifted brow. "Nary would I give up what I've gained ta return ta that life and methinks nary would ye, brother."

"Nay," his lips creased. "Nary even for the span of a dragon's life. We have family now and evermore." He then sat quietly in thought as they gazed about the silent hall, waiting.

"What be amiss with all the cats in the barn?" Eirik questioned out of the blue.

"Ah, I told Grimal he and the others could come here for sanctuary."

"'Tis a lot of cats," Eirik chuckled.

"Aye, mayhap they'll nary be affected by the mate bonding, 'twould be a lot more," Leif chuckled out and finished his mead.

"Mayhap they'll catch the mice running about," Eirik laughed lightly then looked about the empty hall. "Mayhap we should go do chores 'til the others arise, eh?"

"Mayhap we should tend ta our own mates," Leif said grinning.

As they both began to rise together, Eirik's door opened, and Elise came out smiling in their direction. Eirik smiled at her then swung his head to his left. Nearly at the same time, Jesse and Sara came from the guest chamber, hand in hand, but Sara's hair hung in wet clumps as if she had just bathed and Jesse's hair seemed wet as well.

"Good morn," Eirik eyed them both and arched his brow before he looked back at Elise to gage her reaction.

Elise studied them as she drew closer to the high table then smiled and nodded as if she had just made some decision or approval. Mayhap 'twas the 'positive reinforcement' Sara spoke of. Regardless, she was happy and that was all Eirik wanted for her.

"I'm sorry, but I just couldn't drag myself out of bed this morning," she peered down at Eirik as her eyes glittered as green emeralds.

"Freya wept," Eirik mumbled, sensing her emotions and stood.

Leif grinned as he got to his feet. "Let us get ta the barn afore any issues arise. Come Jesse, we'll make quick work of it and then ye may return ta further ye activities," he chuckled.

Elise shook her head at the retreating men, who seemed to move more rapidly than usual. She looked to Sara for an explanation.

"Today and maybe tomorrow will be different than most," Sara said as she draped her arm over Elise's shoulders. "We have to keep the atmosphere positively charged for Torvald... well, negatively charged, but with a positive effect. I believe it will help remove any staining caused by Nidpigger's influence. And... it should help Kristin too."

"How are we supposed to do that?" Elise asked, feeling somehow her students have surpassed her, by leaps and bounds.

"Sex, Lady Elise. Lots and lots of sex," she giggled.

Elise had several thoughts race through her mind all at once with that statement before she said, "Even Bo?"

Sara chuckled. "Most certainly Bo. You know, he isn't the

innocent naive little boy you make him out to be. Sweet he is, but that boy has moves. I believe he's snared his ladylove and will make it permanent as I have with Jess."

Stunned to silence, Elise's eyes opened wide as she looked at Sara. "Um..."

Sara grinned. "Lady Elise, don't fret. Everyone's happy."

"You don't have to call me that," she said offhandedly, finding it the easiest subject to comment on.

"Oh, but I do. From what I understand, it's either that or your majesty," she snickered. "Your highness? I forget how the titles go. It'll be just easier to call you both Lady."

"Both? You mean Kristin has consented to Leif? As a life-mate?" My god, where has she been when all this had been going on?

"That she has, although they have two more nights of mating to complete the ritual, as do I, I guess," she said the last thoughtfully.

"Is there anything else I missed?" Elise asked feeling a bit overwhelmed by this new information, however there was still that undercurrent of arousal that she felt when she woke up this morning.

"Let me think," Sara said as she thought about not telling her about Nidpigger because she felt it would go against what she was trying to accomplish today, but no secrets. "Nidpigger was here today and took back his men, but I think that's it." She smiled brightly to reassure her.

"Oh," she said and peered around the hall. "I hadn't even noticed," she chuckled and shook her head.

"Okay, you sit here, Milady, while I go help Ingrid with breakfast," Sara said as she guided her to her seat feeling as if she needed some time to process. "How about some tea?" she asked then disappeared into the kitchen.

Soon, both Sara and Ingrid came from the kitchen with the tea. When it was poured, they took seats, Sara beside her and Ingrid across from them looking a bit uncomfortable in her company.

"Lady Elise, I thought Ingrid could join us for tea while we wait for the men to finish the outwork before breakfast. You don't mind, do you?"

"Not at all," Elise said smiling. "I had promised to do so, however I meant to ask before now. Thank you for joining us, Ingrid."

"'Tis my pleasure, Milady," she smiled and glanced up at her before taking a sip of her tea.

"Anything of interest going on at the thorp?" Sara asked and leaned in, as if she would spill some juicy gossip.

"Of interest ta ye?" she asked then peered about the hall as if looking for eavesdroppers.

"Aye," Sara said.

"I nary wish ta speak again' milord," she said then lowered her voice to nearly a whisper. "Sir Leif 'twas seen visitin' Jasmin a day ago." Both ladies nodded in encouragement. "'Twas said the visit nary took long and he left with a lad." Her eyes went wide as she nodded as if she meant more than what she was saying.

Elise sipped at her tea thoughtfully before she said, "Ingrid... The lad's name is Torvald and he's Leif's son."

To that, Ingrid's eyes went wide in surprise. "I ne'er knew he had such."

"Apparently neither did he," Sara muttered and smiled.

Elise elbowed Sara and said, "Torvald asked Leif for sanctuary, and he granted it. Do you have any other news?"

"Nidpigger be on the run from the lords. His foul deeds have finally caught him," she grinned then finished her tea.

"You wouldn't happen to know where he hides, do you?" Elise asked.

"'Tis likely among his thralls." She nodded.

"How many does he have?" Sara asked.

"'Tis the three or four women and four or five men. But if ye have Torvald, 'tis one less. I ne'er thought he was of the same ilk."

"He isn't," Sara said then looked up when she heard the door open.

Ingrid turned to see the lords and a lad coming in and quickly stood to face them with her head lowered. "Milady asked me ta have tea with her, Milord," she said rushing through her words as an explanation for her sitting idly.

"Aye, Ingrid. Anything milady wishes," Eirik said and then smiled up at Elise. "We'll just wash up," he said then entered his chamber.

Leif had already gone into his own, but Jesse came toward Sara with another dimple-popping grin and his eyes glinting. When he reached Sara, he bent to kiss her lightly. "Two shakes, babe," he said and to which she nodded then he swaggered off to their room.

"Glad tidings, milady," Ingrid smiled toward Sara, her face aglow. "He makes for a wonderful mate for ye. Built much as the lords," she gushed with a blush.

Sara and Elise chuckled, then Sara said, "Thank you, Ingrid. Now how about we get the table set for them?" She then stood and they both went into the kitchen leaving Elise alone with her tea.

With the table heavily ladened with food, Elise and Eirik, and Sara and Jesse ate their fill, however, when they finished, instead of taking the remainder back to the kitchen, they left it on the table covered with cloths. The others would want to eat soon enough and there was no reason for them to have to go searching for it. While Sara washed up their trenchers, Elise and Eirik disappeared, most likely into their chamber, so Sara thought.

"Why are you the one always cleaning up after the others?" Jesse said lowly in Sara's ear as he stood behind her, pressing in close with a hand held to her stomach, while she finished.

"Everyone else is indisposed, Jess," she said with a smile. "We'll have our turn."

He lowered his lips to her neck and then slid his nose along her skin 'til he pulled in her earlobe and exhaled hotly. "Don't make me beg, sweetheart, though I would," he chuckled huskily into her ear.

"I'd like to see that," she laughed lightly and grabbed his hand that ventured lower.

"I'd do it for you. Never anyone else have I begged, but you..." He groaned.

"If you keep stimulating yourself as you are, you won't last, lover boy," she said playfully.

"Sounds like a challenge," he said as he pushed even more into her having her trapped between him and the table.

Sara lowered her head and placed her palms on the table as she gathered her wits, then she turned and pulled him out of the kitchen into the hall where she stopped short.

"Oh, hey guys," she greeted Bo and Tristan with a smile. Jesse tugged on her hand.

"Hey," they said in unison and smiled up at them.

"Torvald still sleeps. He's quiet now, but he was restless earlier," Bo said and winked at Sara.

"We're on it," she chuckled and moved with Jesse into the chamber. She had already told Bo her plan for removing any maligned Heill from Torvald and he agreed wholeheartedly... as did Jesse.

Entering the darkened room, Sara checked on Torvald. She knelt beside his bower and drew a freshly wetted cloth over his face and chest, then dribbled some water in his mouth as Jesse undressed. "Help me turn him," she whispered.

Jesse looked down at himself and clenched his jaw before doing what she asked. He bent and eased the boy over onto his stomach and stood back so Sara could continue.

When Sara was finished, she straightened and looked at Jesse with a smile. "Feel like begging yet?"

"You have no idea," he groaned as he grasped the tail of her shirt and pulled it from over her head then descended on her lips hungrily. Adeptly, he unfastened her jeans and pushed the opening wider then downward while he maintained his wild kisses. He wanted to crawl inside her so desperately, but then the unwanted thought of what she had said earlier about being overstimulated came to him. Needing to slow his torrent and catch his breath, he lingeringly kissed her deliberately slow as he unfastened her bra and let it slip from her shoulders. He worked his hands down the inside of her jeans and over her ass, shoving the garment down lower before he cupped the inner most part of her cheek and tightened his hold on her. She let out a soft moan into his mouth. He lifted her slowly and laid her on the bed then eased back, pulling her jeans off, followed by her panties.

As he crawled in over the top of her and settled delightfully between her thighs, he said, "Next time, you'll have less clothes." He grinned as he pulled the curtain closed and then leaned down, pressing his mouth to hers as he entwined their hands with laced fingers, and kissed her with a relaxed and gentle ease.

Although that was far from what his body felt. No, that was in a state of urgency. So was hers, he was certain. With each delicate brush of his crown to her root as he moved with each kiss, he knew, by the mounting moans and gasps she assailed on his ears, urging him on. And he wanted to bring her elation many times over. He just had to hold out.

Ever so slowly, he disengaged their kiss and brushed his cheek to hers, bowing his head to catch his breath. He kissed her lightly down her neck, pushing himself lower till he was even with her breasts and began nuzzling and suckling them, and he felt her wetness where his belly met her apex. She released his hands and enfolded him in her arms, pulling him tighter against her, even as she arched her back, she alternated with her hips, issuing more glorious moans.

He paused his actions and peered up at her, smiling. "Just say the words, babe, and I'll help you," he said as he smoothed his hand down between them and slid his fingers through her folds.

"Oh, Jess," she keened frantically as she writhed beneath him and gripped at him. He curled his fingers upward, leisurely rubbing her internal front wall, but kept his eyes on her face. She was so beautiful like this. He thought her beautiful anyway, but filled with extasy... "Mmm," he vocalized and licked his lips then lowered his mouth to her breast once again as he worked his fingers in alternating quick secession. As he brought her to climax, he watched her chest throb in an iridescent blue glow and was in awe.

He raised himself on his hands and knees to move up her body and position himself before she could come all the way down, but before he could, she lifted her leg around him and turned over. She raised beneath him and rubbed herself against him with sultry breaths of encouragement. Licking his lips, he straightened, and with one hand on her back, he pushed in his crown then drove the rest into her as she pushed back into him. "Sara," he breathed out as he wrapped his arm around her waist to hold her still and allow him to savor this moment. Her channel still undulated, and it felt fucking awesome. So much so, his brand began to glow.

He slid his hands slowly over her back, down her sides and stopped at her hips then he began moving within her. His movements became faster as her extasy became more vocal and with the power of his thrusts and the weight of him on her back, she was nearly pressed into the bed. He glowed like molten lava so strong was this feeling, so painfully sharp. He skimmed a hand around her and pressed into her core as his other hand moved to embrace her across her chest. The intensity of his feelings for her overpowered him to such an extent he didn't want it to end, though his body demanded more. He pulled her higher upright with him with his continued rapid thrusts and held her closely against his chest. He could feel her Heill begin to consume him as his merged with her. He clutched her tighter. And then... and then... Ah...Ah... Ah... The ultraviolet shower rained down on them as they became overwhelmed with a magnitude of euphoria. He bowed his head to her shoulder as he set them back on his haunches and breathed heavily down over her front, holding her within both arms. Still embraced, still engaged, and still tremoring, so intense was their mating.

Sara was the first to recover. She reached her hand up to his head as she hugged his arms to her, turning her head toward his, she brushed her lips to his face. He squeezed her gently and slightly shook his head.

"Uh uh... Not yet," he whispered and kissed her shoulder where his lips rested.

"It's okay," she whispered softly and kissed his cheek again. "It's okay," she repeated and turned slightly to kiss him again. She then waited. He turned his head to her. "It's okay," she said once more before she pushed her lips into his, and as he allowed her to move, she lifted off and faced him, continuing her comforting kisses. When she felt he had gathered himself, she drew back and smiled.

He held her head between his palms as he grazed his thumbs beneath her eyes and over her cheeks to remove her tears then kissed her lightly. His lips pulled back as if he was going to speak, but he shook his head instead, not finding the words that could possibly express what he was feeling. The enormity of it. The profoundness. The...

"That was..." she paused looking for the right word. "Incredibly indefinable," she finished in whispered tones.

"Humbling," he said lowly at the same time she spoke to supply a word and then moved up beside her and stretched out his form, closing his eyes.

"Humbling?" she asked lying next to him. He could hear the smile in her voice.

"Uh uh... Don't do that," he muttered.

"Do what?" She leaned over and softly kissed his chest. He looked down at her.

"Don't make light of it, Sara. Please," he said as he slid his fingers into her hair to hold it back where he could see her face. Oddly enough, he could see her face.

She tilted her face up to his. "Honey, I'm just happy. Okay? I can feel you here," she patted his heart. "You, my love, are a very passionate man." She grinned, and he grazed his thumb over her cheek.

"One that has loved you since he was sixteen," he said and lifted his brows briefly.

She gasped in surprise then said, "And I, you," she chuckled. "Had we only known, huh?" He nodded. "Now show me your panty-melting dimpled smile."

To that he grinned, a dimple-popping grin just before he reached to kiss her then laid back and squeezed his arm around her.

"We should check on Torvald," she said.

"Alright," he agreed on a sigh. "But you aren't getting dressed."

"How about just shorts and a t-shirt?"

"Fine, but nothing else," he chuckled and sat up, then opened the curtain.

Before they dressed, they washed up in cold water and then tended to Torvald, who was back to his restless state. Sara smiled at that as she skimmed the cloth over his back even though it appeared his fever had broken and noticed his tattoo had enlarged a bit with more definition. Satisfied, she rose to her feet.

"Hungry?" Jesse asked. "I'm starving." he clasped her hand and pulled her toward the door. When he opened it, he had to shield his eyes from the light. "Fuck no," he said then went to his bag and dug out his sunglasses. Placing them on his face, he grabbed Sara's hand and went through the door.

Odin's Day

Reverse

To Sara and Jesse's surprise, nearly everyone was in the hall. The table had fresh food even though it was only midday, by Sara's reckoning. She smiled as they greeted everyone and took their usual seats.

"How's Torvald?" Bo said grinning at Sara.

"Restless as ever," she winked. "His fever broke, he should be good for a while." She smiled, couldn't help it.

"I should hope so," Tristan murmured and then her cheeks pinked.

"Remove those, when you're at the table," Elise said pointing to Jesse's sunglasses, uncertain how to deal with the shift of innocence, to her anyway. These were her kids, her responsibility. Now, all the sudden, they were adults, doing adult things. Eirik put his hand on her knee and smiled when she looked up at him. She sighed out her breath.

Jesse started to take them off then pushed them back into place and shook his head. "Not today. It's too bright in here," he said then began filling his plate.

"Really?" Sara asked in alarm and turned toward him. "Close your eyes," she said as she removed them and then, "Try to open them." When Jesse opened his eyes, he could only keep them open for a few seconds at a time. She held one of his lids open so she could see his eye then released it and placed a gentle kiss to one and then the other as she put his glasses in his hand. "It looks like flash burn, like what welders get sometimes. Keep them on, Jess."

"How'd he get flash burns in your room?" Elise almost chuckled at the ridiculousness. "Never mind, I don't want to know."

"I do," Bo said smiling then began to chuckle. "I've heard of other things causing blindness, but never when two people are involved." He laughed.

"Bo!" Elise admonished and then laughed and the other snickered, well those that understood anyway, even Jesse.

"No, really, I'd like to know. You know, forewarned is forearmed and all," he snickered again. "I'd also like to know your secret. Two days, Sara? Talk about prolonging the experience," he said smiling.

To that both Sara and Jesse looked at him, stunned to silence at first, then Sara said, "Where's Kristin?"

"She'll be rising from her torpor at any moment today," Leif grinned and then, as if suddenly reminded, said, "'Twould like ta know how ye enter locked doors."

"Or bathe without going to the tarn," Eirik said.

"It's been two days?" Jesse said then a slow grin crept over his face. "Must be how I got the flash burn then," he mumbled.

"'Twould be grinning too," Eirik said. "'Tis that stamina ye spoke of?" he asked Elise.

"No doubt, if not excessive," she chuckled and shook her head.

"Well," Sara began. "We didn't get the shapeshifting ability that the rest of you have, as you know. However, we can focus our Heill and teleport, among other things," she said then looked at them all innocently, as if that explained everything.

"It's more than that, Sara. You cleaned the kitchen in a blink of an eye," Jesse said quietly to her as he grasped her hand. "Yeah, I know what I did too."

"That would explain most of it," Bo said. "But not the flash burn." Leave it to Bo to call bullshit on her.

"And you helped heal Elise," Tristan added.

"Okay, let's just call it magic then," she chuckled. "When Jess and I both focus, we can do some things," she shrugged. "As for the flash burn, well, together we make ultraviolet and with prolonged exposure, which was an accident, by the way, can cause flash burns."

"Yea, the Heill about ye both has a different glow," Eirik confirmed.

"Bo, I was wondering if you knew how to change positive ions to negative ones?" Sara asked, seemingly off topic.

Bo chuckled at her deflecting. "Well, that's a complicated subject. At first blush, I'd say you were already doing it. Sunshine, waterfalls, strong winds, even lightning from storms, can produce a negative charge, including your ultraviolet light."

"Lightning?" Elise said with a raised brow.

"What be lightning?" Leif asked

"Skyfire," she said still looking at Bo for an answer.

"Yes, most lightning is negatively charged and is drawn to the pockets or pools of positive ions in the ground, but there's also positive lightning that's far more dangerous for it's more intense with a higher voltage, like a billion volts. And can strike from up to ten miles away, if not farther."

"Bragi wept," Eirik sighed out his breath. "I nary nigh grasp what you say. Nil of it, truth be told, but the dangers of which ye speak. That, I do grasp. And mayhap Sara's corona be a danger as well for it nigh blinds her own mate."

"How do you feel following a storm?" Bo asked Eirik.

"Invigored," he smiled. "'Tis the same when in flight or bathing in the bathhouse," he nodded.

"Yes, the steam in the bath house would do it."

"What he's saying is that we may be able to cleanse the island of the tainted Heill, Eirik, with our ultraviolet. That's why we, all of us, feel good right now." Sara grinned.

"'Twould wager the swiving had more ta do with that," Leif muttered, grinning.

"But first, we have to deal with Nidpigger. We need to find him and his cohorts and bring them back here."

"Ingrid said he's probably hiding somewhere with his thralls, maybe eight to ten of them," Elise said unclear with the count.

"I have an idea that will take care of them without needing any kind of proof AND cleanse the island at the same time."

Both Eirik and Leif nodded, but Eirik said, "Can ye hunt them as ye did before?"

"I think so," she smiled and turned to Jesse and winked. "Sway with me?"

As Jesse and Sara searched for Nidpigger and his rogues, the others busied themselves with cleaning up. This went easier without having to go to the pond for the water, but Bo had yet to start a hot water heater. Personally, Elise thought he should have been working on a bathroom, in the modern sense of the word, but eventually, he would work that out too. Elise leaned against the doorway and watched Jesse and Sara as they swayed together within each other's arms. This was different than what she'd seen them do before, this looked more like slow dancing. When Jesse slid his hands to either side of Sara's head and bent his forehead to hers, it was confirmed. They were dancing, as two that had deep feelings, as lovers. She smiled and started to turn away when they separated.

"Did you find them?" Elise asked when they looked her way.

"I think they're at the north bay," Sara said and smiled, lacing her hand with Jesse's.

"Okay, I'll let Eirik know," she smiled awkwardly.

"They just need to bring them back here," Sara said. "Try to make sure they don't kill them," she grinned, and Elise nodded.

With Jesse and Sara guarding Torvald, the others made their way north, three dragons and a very frightened, claws extended, panther riding the back of a gryphon followed by a raven. If it weren't for the seriousness of the situation, it would have been comical. They circled the harbor until they homed in on the tainted Heill in a building on the edge of the harbor, then they landed nearby. Both Eirik and Leif shifted and dressed quickly, leaving the others in their animal forms for their protection.

Kristin flew to the top of the building and looked for an opening as Tristan slunk around the side to see if there were any exits and Bo to the other, meeting at the back. Elise stayed in the front, watching as Eirik and Leif moved toward the entrance. Just as they were about to open the door, it burst open and several people came rushing out, men and women alike.

Elise opened her wings to help corral them and even swung her tail forward knocking a man back while she grabbed another one in her clawed hand. Tristan had two women trapped up against the wall and Bo had pounced on another man. Kristin flapped and squawked at the head of another man, and she was sure there was some pecking involved too. Eirik and Leif, swords in hand, faced Nidpigger as anger rolled off them. She could feel Eirik's rage and intent. She fired off a streak of lightning above their heads in warning. They were to bring them back, not kill them.

Eirik ducked his head briefly then turned to look at her with a lifted brow. She gave him a snort. He turned back to face Nidpigger. "Ye be coming with us. 'Tis time we put ye deeds ta rest."

"What proof have ye of any wrongdoing?" Nidpigger tried to argue.

"Me and my mate charge ye." Leif growled out.

"My mate... my clan charges ye," Eirik bellowed. "I have every right ta take ye head where we stand."

Nidpigger shook his head and started to argue again, but...

Elise lowered her head level to Nidpigger's. Emitting a low rolling growl from deep within her throat and curling her lips away from her teeth, she eyed him most ominously. He looked at her with wide fearful eyes, but when he began to quake, she snorted hot air at him.

When she backed away, she saw Tristan had released the two women and held a man, the one who Kristin had been picking on, by the throat on the ground. Bo had one, and the one she held made all of them.

Eirik made certain that none of them carried weapons while

Leif went to transform, bringing back the pack with him. He dropped it on the ground and grasped Nidpigger in his claws, so Eirik could change. Then when each held two men, they all alighted into the sky, Tristan gripping for dear life onto Bo's back once again, and Kristin following behind.

Arriving back at the homestead, they came to a gliding halt in front of the house. Torvald came out to greet them, smiling. "Ye caught the bastard, eh?" he said and took the pack from Elise's clawed hand. She went off toward the barn with Bo while Tristan and Kristin went through the door. He pulled out a sword and aimed it at Nidpigger as Eirik sat him and the other man on the ground at his feet before he transformed.

"Nil doubts," Eirik grinned as he pulled his breeches on and began lacing up his boots. When he was dressed, he pulled out the second sword to allow Leif to do the same.

"Sara says must needs ta take them to the bathhouse," Torvald said with a shrug, telling him he nary knew why.

As Sara and Jesse entered the now warm bathhouse, she said, "This will make it final, Jess, permanent. Are you sure?" She turned and lit the candles on one side of the bath as he did on the other.

"Are you? You're the one that keeps questioning this, Sara. I'm all in, babe." He smiled over at her and began to undress.

She nodded, "Me, too." Then she removed the robe she had borrowed from Elise and stepped into the heated water, looking up at Jesse.

He came towards her, entering the water, and said, "With all that I am, sweetheart, with all that I am." Then lowered his head to kiss her. He could easily spend the rest of his days with her.

"We must go slow to feed the island as much as we can, Jess, so no rushing," she said lowly as he kissed down her neck.

"Shhh," Jesse hissed. "Allow the sweet Heill to fill you and focus on us, what you feel," he whispered as he sensually worshipped her with sultry caresses and loving kisses. He had so much love for her, and he meant to show her within each touch and kiss he gave her. Every move he made was deliberate, even when he raised her out of the water to tenderly suckle her breasts as he entered her.

In turn, he also felt the love she had for him, from her soft caresses to her gentle kisses, and she glowed. A glow so brilliant it blurred anything beyond her, till there was only her. Nothing around them, not even the water within which they stood, nor gravity to keep them grounded. Just the two of them existed. And as their auras merged, precariously on the edge of elation, she cried out with her head tossed back.

Something was wrong! Something was wrong with Sara, he realized as he felt the warm liquid pour over his arm that he held to her back.

"No, Sara, no no no," he uttered. "Stay with me, please, please, please. I can't lose you now. We haven't had enough time," he cried out as he lowered his head to her chest and held her.

As Eirik frog-marched Nidpigger into the bathhouse, he hesitated then moved to the side to allow the others in. Ever so slowly, they all surrounded the bath, unable to take their gaze away from the two illuminating figures within the pool, wrapped in an intimate embrace and floating above the water as if they were weightless.

Then all hell broke loose. In what seemed simultaneous accuracy, a dagger zinged through the air toward the couple in the pool, who pulsed brighter with an iridescent glitter, the four men shrank down into cats, and Elise, Kristin, Tristan, and Bo vanished.

"Sara!" Elise woke up screaming as her eyes darted wildly around her.

"Sh sh sh," someone was saying and then said something else she didn't quite get.

"What?" she asked with a myriad of emotion in her eyes as they looked up into the eyes of a stranger.

"You're okay now, miss," the man said with a heavy accent.

"Where?" she swallowed hard and started shaking violently with shivers. "Wha wha wha Where?"

The man held a bottle of water to her lips and said, "Drink. You're aboard a Kystvakten ship... uh... coast guard," he smiled down to her. He pulled the warming blanket up around her.

"Wha wha where's," she gritted her teeth and groaned out her frustration.

"The others are in a warming cabin. They're safe. All are safe now," he tried to reassure her.

"Alllll?" she drew out the word unintentionally with her shivers.

He nodded and then tightened his lips. "All the passengers but the two we couldn't find," he glanced away.

"I... I wha wha want to ssseee them," she stuttered out and began to sit up.

"No, no, you mustn't move. I'll have them come to you." He then turned to another man and spoke to him before he turned back to her with a smile.

"How long?" she asked.

He bit his lips together before he answered. "Nearly two weeks since your plane went down. We thought this was a recovery but overjoyed that it's a rescue." He continued to smile then glanced behind him before he whispered, "And your baby is doing well, too."

"What?" she chuckled, perhaps out of hysteria.

"I'm sorry, I assumed you knew, though I can see how you might not. It's standard practice to test incapacitated women so we don't do harm."

"No, it's okay, thank you," she said as her eyes glassed with unshed tears.

"It's truly a miracle, really," he smiled.

"I'll say," she chuckled wryly and lowered her eyes.

Bo came through the door and wordlessly engulfed her in his arms then the girls flanked him in a group hug. "We were so worried about you," Bo whispered but his words were muffled.

"Sara and Jesse," she whispered in return, and they tightened their hold.

After a few moments of silent hugging, Bo backed off but left his arm around Tristan. "They're taking us to Oslo and then we can find passage back to the US," he said as he wiped his cheek on his shoulder.

Elise shook her head. "Not yet, I don't want to go back yet."

"Good, because we don't either," Kristin said and grabbed her hand up in hers, clicking her nail against the ring she still wore.

Elise's eyes went from her to her own hand and then to Kristin's left. They still had the rings! But what hope did they have of finding the island again? They never heard them speak of any towns on the mainland. They had no reference points really. And the brothers would be long dead by now, then a thought occurred to her. She flipped her hand over and pressed it to Kristin's belly as she raised her eyes to her. With Kristin's nod, she then looked to Tristan and Bo, they too nodded and smiled.

"Then when we get to Oslo, we'll find a place to stay and start looking," Elise said squeezing their hands as she smiled.

Oddly enough, it took them just over seven months to find the right island. Being in the middle of winter made it more difficult but not impossible for travel, even with all three women profoundly pregnant. Bo wanted to protest for their safety, but he too wanted to see the island, moreover, he wanted his baby born there. They were going to name her Sara Jessica, for obvious reasons and Elise and Kristin were both having boys. They hadn't decided on their names yet, to his knowledge. These last seven months had been an emotional rollercoaster for all of them. Between the disappointments about not finding the island and the joy of marital bliss, having this baby, and the overall hormonal emotions of three pregnant women, most days had him chasing his tail. Today, they were going to the island.

The ferry ride was slow going, but they all watched with prickling anticipation in the dim lighting of the fading sunlight as the island grew closer.   Bo stretched his arms out to accommodate all three as each of them held hands with the one next to them. He was certain they were a sight and only imagined what others may think, but he didn't care. This was his family. They had made accommodations at an inn at the village, it was more of a B&B, which was perfect for them. However, they all wanted to see the homestead first.

With tension high, they waited patiently for the ferry to dock, but Kristin began bouncing on her toes making it impossible for him to keep his arm in place.

"Let's get our things," he said as he dropped his arms and went to where they stowed their cases. With the help of a porter, they loaded their luggage on a trolly, and Bo chuckled with a sense of near dejavu as he pushed it down the ramp following the three women with interlocked arms.

As they carefully moved down the street, it was difficult for Elise to recognize anything, with the wintery weather and more modern buildings lit by amber streetlamps, though not completely so. She felt her eyes prick with disappointment. She had been hoping that it had retained its quaint village ambiance. The porter stopped them in front of a building and opened the door for them to enter. It was their inn.

When Elise came through the door, she glanced around, the room was somewhat familiar to her. It almost looked like Ingrid's living room, but of course different. Then they were greeted by a young woman with dark hair, and she smiled as she introduced herself as Isa.

After they checked in and put their luggage in their rooms, Elise made her way back to the lobby/living room once again and settled into one of the comfortable sitting chairs near the fire.

"Lady Elise, may I get you a warm beverage?" the woman, Isa, asked. "Perhaps some tea?"

"That would be lovely, thank you," Elise said with an uplifted brow.

When she brought it in, Elise asked, "Why did you call me Lady Elise?"

The woman glanced at her briefly then retrieved a postcard and handed it to her. "'Tis the Lady Elise," she said.

Elise peered at the picture and gasped, it was of a stone carving of a woman breaking through the heart of a dragon. The woman looked very much like her, but the dragon was certainly Eirik. Then she gave her several more. The next resembled the first, except the dragon was Leif and the woman was Kristin. Then, one of a gryphon lying alongside a panther. She couldn't bear to see any more of them.

"Where are these?" Elise asked.

"They're up over the west ridge in the mythical gardens and shrine," she replied. "They're very old. Legend says the dragon lords of the island, a thousand years ago, fell in love with two women and became life-mates with them. For a dragon, much like a gryphon, will only love once in their lifetime. When they lost their mates in a fight against some evil thing that threatened the island, they went feral and mad with anger at the injustice and broken hearts. In their grief and love, they began sculpting these statues to keep their memories alive. No one knows what happened to them after they finished the gardens. The estate has been maintained by a steward since then. They say their awaiting the rightful heir to arrive."

Elise sniffled and wiped at her eyes, when she saw the others had joined them and Kristin grasped her hand. She, too, had tears in her eyes, she must have heard the story as well. She handed her the postcards and then look to Bo. "I want to go," she said tearfully unable to stop.

"See, I knew this was going to be too hard on you, on you both," he said with frustration as he bent at her knee and put his hand on their joined ones.

"No, I want to go to the gardens, not leave."

"Is there a vehicle for hire?" Bo asked looking at the woman.

"Only sleighs this time of year. Would you like me to make the arrangements?"

"Yes, please. For tomorrow morning, if at all possible," Bo said with a mix of emotion. When she left to do just that, he turned to Elise and Kristin and then reached also for Tristan's hand. "You three have to promise me no more tears, please. This is supposed to be a joyous time for all of us, okay? We knew it would be bittersweet, but more sweet than bitter, right?"

"Is ten all right with you, lord... um... Mister Ornirdreki?" the woman asked from the doorway to another room. "Any earlier than that and it would still be dark, not much to see."

"Yes, that's fine," he said over his shoulder then looked to the three ladies in front of him. "Tomorrow morning, okay?" They all three nodded.

The next morning, they all rushed to get ready, Elise especially so, although she did slow down descending the stairs, but Kristin was right on her heels. They entered the dining room together.

"Good morn, Lady Elise and Lady Kristin," an older woman greeted them kindly.

"Good morning," they said at once and then laughed lightly at the titles as they took seats at the table to eat a quick breakfast before they left.

"We have a traditional breakfast in this house that we hope you all will enjoy," she said as she poured their tea. "Although we don't get many Americans, we've heard it'll be familiar." Then without haste, she left to get their food.

She soon returned with a mound of pancakes and fried pork fat and placed them on the table.

"Sweet cakes?" Kristin asked and grinned at Elise.

"Aye, 'tis been a family tradition for many generations," the woman beamed proudly.

"I wonder for how many generations," Kristin said under her breath.

Elise just stared at the pancakes with a tear sliding down her cheek before she caught it with her napkin and looked at Kristin. "Don't tell Bo," she whispered. Kristin grinned then raised her eyes to over Elise's head.

"Don't tell Bo what?" Bo said as he came in with Tristan and pulled out her chair before he sat himself.

"Nothing," they said in unison, but when he saw what they were eating for breakfast, he knew. With a heavy sigh, he filled his plate. This was going to be a heart wrenching day; he just knew it.

After they finished eating and securely bundled up in the sleigh drawn by two black Friesians, they were finally on their way... home. It would always be home to them even if they couldn't live there. Kristin and Elise sat facing forward and Bo, with his arm stretched around Tristan, sat backward, facing them. Elise watched with every footstep the horses made that revealed just a little more of the road ahead. She clutched at Kristin's hand beneath the fur lined blanket over their laps in anticipation.

As they topped the rise and the countryside was laid out before them, she gasped, causing Tristan and Bo to turn and look. Their little homestead was no longer little. There was now a large stone building that resided by the pond with steam drifting out of it and stone statues of all shapes and sizes were scattered over the grounds with cleared walkways to guide one through to each. It all led up to a small castle, put plainly, and barn. The dawning sun casted rays on at least four life sized dragons, two were in the postcards, one she didn't recognize, and the last one was of her. Her eyes darted to Bo when she felt them burn, but she quickly looked away before he could see. They stopped just outside the torchlit shrine and Bo and the driver helped them down. She could easily see the gryphon from where she stood and the panther that laid beside it, but also there were a plethora of cat statuettes and so many ravens in different poses. She glanced at Kristin to see if she saw them yet, and by the tears on her face, she had. She pulled her in to a hug.

"It's not fair," Kristin whispered.

"I know, honey, I know." She sniffled and dried her own eyes as she pulled away from her. "Let's go see the old bathhouse, maybe that'll cheer us up, huh?"

Kristin nodded and they turned that direction. When they

entered, steam billowed out and it was so warm inside they quickly shed their coats. The interior of the shrine was intricately carved with scrolls, leaves, and flowers, some she identified as heather, and the scent of lavender permeated the room. The ceiling was mostly stained glass with dragon, panther, gryphon, and raven motifs. Everywhere she looked some representation of them was there. Then she looked in the bathhouse and screamed out as she nearly fell to her knees. They were still there!

Someone caught her and held her upright as she slowly moved closer to the small pool. She heard other gasps and shouts but paid them no attention. It was as if they were suspended in time. Frozen statues, like the many that adorned the grounds. Jesse forever embraced Sara with his perpetual love as she did him. It looked as if they were floating just above the water but was just close enough to the waterfall that it was hard to tell. Jesse tilted back, perfectly balanced as he embraced Sara with one arm around her waist just above her hips at the small of her back and the other along the length of her back up to her head, immersed in her hair, and his head bowed to her chest. Sara sat astride Jesse with her hands on his shoulders and her head thrown back in extasy, or was it? As she edged down the side, she could see the dagger in her back and the blood that flowed over Jesse's arm. She screamed out again and turned into the person that assisted her, burying her face as she cried.

When her tears had dwindled to mere sniffles, the man who held her against him, said, "They call it 'Eternal Lovers,' but I just call them Sara and Jess."

"How do you know their names?" she asked then raised her head to see the man that seem to have less reverence for the two than obviously whoever built all this for them.

She about lost her legs again, coming eye to startling blue eye, with the dark headed man, who caught her once again. This had to be a descendant of Eirik's. That would mean the legend wasn't exactly true, was it? He had found a new love and had children to continue his family line. She put her hand to her stomach and straightened as she brushed his arms away from her. Stiffening her lips, she turned to leave. With blurry vision from the tears yet to fall, she quickly found her coat and went outside unable to take anymore heartache. She had enough. She should have listened to Bo. She slipped and slid her way toward the sleigh until she landed on her knees bent over in pain. Pain in her heart. Pain that stole her breath and made her nauseous. The same pain she felt since waking up on that ship, except this was sharper. She rocked with her grief.

Bo's breath caught in his throat at seeing Sara and Jesse just as they had left them. He couldn't move from where he stood. He felt Tristan rubbing her hand over his back, but the significance didn't register on him, nor the two people that rushed by him. His lip quivered as he moved closer by the inch. He knew that whatever they did that day, not only fixed the island, but also sent them back to their own time... without them. Blessing or a curse, it was done.

As he stood on the edge of the pool, he tilted his head slightly. Now he could see the dagger protruding from her back. This was why they suspended animation. He studied them longer and circled the pool. He inhaled deeply, hoping a bit of luck drew in with his breath and reached out, wrapped his fingers around the knife, and pulled.

As the dagger came free, the two dropped into the water. Bo jumped in as well and pulled Sara to the surface and out of the pool with Jesse's help. He then rolled her to her stomach and pressed his hand over her wound.

"Hold on, Sara," Bo said and then looked at Jesse. "Put your hand here," he said as he moved his hand over her wound and then went out the door quickly, needing more space.

Bo started undressing as fast as he could, and then, with a prayer, he transformed into his gryphon. He brought a wing forward and grasped a hold, jerking several times until a feather came loose in his beak then went back to human again. Without stopping to dress, he ran back in the bathhouse. He dropped to his knees and pressed the feather over her wound along with Jesse's hand.

"Use your magic, Jesse, please," Bo begged him. And then, "If you don't, you're going to lose her," he said scowling down at him.

Jesse focused and inhaled, drawing in the Heill, then fed it into Sara with everything he had in him. Wishing. Hoping. Seeing her alive and happy, loving him as he did her. His hand heated and her wound glowed brightly before it began to close

"Oh, thank god," Bo said on a whooshy exhale. Then he hugged Jesse. "You did it!"

He got up and began dressing when Tristan brought him his clothes, then sat happily on the bench with her. He hugged her into him and kissed her head.

Elise felt herself being lifted out of the snow and carried, but she didn't care as long as they were taking her away from here. It was too much pain. She was uncertain what hope she had when they found the island, but this wasn't it. Maybe it was to be sent back to the past, she didn't know. Not this.

When she realized he wasn't taking her to the sleigh, she realized it wasn't Bo doing the carrying either. "Bo!" she yelled and looked around for him.

"Bo's busy, I'll have to due," the man groused and then entered the building and took her up the steps to a room before he finally released her on a bed and stood back a bit. "Elise," he whispered.

Her eyes darted up to his and she shook her head as tears dripped from her chin. "How?"

"Are you all right? Are you in pain?" he asked as he picked up her hand and studied her ring. "You wear the insignia of the clan."

She pulled her hand free from his and pushed herself backward toward the head of the bed and away from him. "Who are you?" she asked with a quavering voice.

"I'm Thorvald Torvaldson, the steward of the estate." He sighed and sat on the foot of the bed. He held his hand out to her, displaying his own ring, though with a significantly smaller insignia. "I think I've been waiting for you. I know those at the fountain because of the stories I've been told since I was old enough to understand and repeat them. You're Lady Elise. Uncle Eirik got you spot on," he smiled up at her. "Hey, can I get you some tea or something? You look like you've had a hell of a day," he said as he stood.

"Wait," she said. "Does that mean that you're Torvald's son? Not a descendant of Eirik's?"

"Uncle Eirik had no children," he said then bit his lips together as his eyes dropped to her belly then back to her eyes. "I'll get you that tea," he said and left the room.

He had found no one else and had no children, she thought as she grazed her hand over her corpulent belly. Her heart ached for him. He was alone up till the day he died. Her eyes burned at the thought. As she will be. She brushed her tears away when Thorvald came back in carrying a tray of tea. He sat it down on a table near the bed and poured her a cup. Instead of handing it to her, he stood before her, deep in thought.

Coming to some decision, he turned to her. "If you're feeling up to it, I'd like to show you something." He smiled and held his hand out to her.

Elise scooted to the edge of the bed, and he helped her off and then they walked back the way he had brought her. As they went down the steps, he held her hand with his arm around her to make sure she didn't fall. "I was told of a room here that has a lock with no key," he said as he guided her around the stairs to a door below them, hidden by a heavy drape. "If you have that key, Lady Elise, it will change your life," he gave her a crooked smile, nearly boyish.

"I have a key that used to open a lock, but that building doesn't exist anymore," she said putting a hand to her back and inhaled slowly.

"Do you have it with you?" he asked drawing the drape aside, revealing the door. She nodded as she breathed out and pulled it out from around her neck. He raised a brow at her. "Are you okay?"

"Braxton Hicks all week. I'm okay though," she smiled feebly up at him. She pushed the key into the lock, and she heard it snick when she turned it. "It's the same door?" she chuckled.

"More likely the same lock," he said and shouldered the door open. "I'll get a light," he said as he disappeared somewhere behind her.

Elise looked in while she waited, but all she saw were more stairs... and cobwebs. Then slowly the walls began to illuminate, and she stepped in, remembering to get the key from the lock. Thorvald came in behind her and they descended the steps together. When they got to the bottom, he found a torch and lit it, but it only shone on the immediate area, however it was enough to let her know where she was.

"That plate used to be polished to reflect the light," Elise said, but she wasn't about to touch it.

"You've been down here before?" he asked, a little in awe.

"Maybe not here exactly, but I've been in the treasure room in the longhouse," she chuckled and made her way forward as he shined the light around the room quickly, casting it upon the many treasures therein. In the flashing light, she approached a darkened shape. She ran her hands along it, not recognizing the feel of it until she did. She could have died. "Thorvald! Come over here with the light," she said as she moved her hands gingerly over each bump and spike and horn. When he came closer and shined the beam of light in her direction, she could see it was a dragon's head, but the color was off. "Look around for the other one. I think this is Leif," she cried out, ecstatic that she could feel the shallow heated breaths coming from him.

"Father should be down here too. They must have gone into a torpor," he said as he searched excitedly.

"How do we wake them?" she asked a bit awestruck as she traced her hand over his face.

"I don't know," he answered from a distance away.

"Leif," she said as she pushed on his head. "Kristen's here. She's come back for you. Please wake up!" she shouted the last.

She gasped when his big eye opened and focused on her, then suddenly he was standing before her and pulled her into his arms. She yelped at the firmness of his grip. "She's at the bathhouse," she squeaked out, and he ran out, swallowed by the darkness. "Where's Eirik?" she hollered after him but got no answer.

Then she heard it, the low rumbling purr so familiar to her. She followed the sound deeper into the room and into the dark. She couldn't see anything, and she had no idea where Thorvald went, but she couldn't stop. Not now. She pressed her hand to her back and kept moving. "Ah," she groaned. Taking a deep breath through her nose and exhaled it out her mouth slowly as she drew closer to the sound. She was so close. "Eirik!" she shouted. "Eirik! Please..." she cried in desperation. Taking in a couple breaths, she went farther in, blindly. "Eirik!" she shouted once again before she fell to her knees and rolled over on her back beneath the heated exhalations of a sleeping dragon. "Hear me," she pleaded tearfully, "Feel me," she panted.

Eirik groaned in his sleep. He was dreaming again of Elise. He sighed heavily at the bittersweetness. His nose twitched at the familiar scent, he snorted, his senses enlivened by it. As his mind became more alert, he felt his essence-flame ignite and he then transformed. "Heartling?" he whispered in disbelief as he gathered her in his arms, feeling her pain.

"I think my water just broke."

Being awakened by Elise, Leif hugged her tightly, elated to see her, but as her words sank in, he grabbed his clothes and ran to the stairs, dressing on the way. By the time he exited the house, he had his breeches and boots on, although not tied nor laced, and was pulling his serk on over his head as he ran to the bathhouse. He arrived just in time to see Jesse and Bo heal Sara and he scanned the room for Kristin. His eyes fell upon her at the same time she flung herself at him. Catching her, he lifted her into his arms and buried his head in her neck. He had nil words to express his overwhelming feelings.

Just then Kristin cried out, and as if in echo, Tristan exclaimed also. "It's time," she said on a heavy breath.

"Nary do I grasp what ye say, heartling," Eirik said as he kissed at her, overjoyed to have her back. She healed his flame and made it grow beyond the raven's wing.

"We're having a baby… now," she grunted the last word.

"Ah, nary here," he said as he lifted her in his arms and made his way to the stairs. He carried her through the room, up the stairs, and to the very same chamber Thorvald had brought her to, before laying her on the bed, yelling for Thorvald the entire way.

"Yes, Milord," Thorvald panted out as he entered the doorway, but glanced behind him.

"Get a healer. She gives birth," Eirik said looking at Elise with all sorts of wonder and awe.

"I've sent the driver to fetch him. Lady Kristin and Tristan are also in labor," he chuckled hysterically. "Ye wish a lifetime for an heir, and when least expected, ye get a day like today," he laughed.

Printed in Great Britain
by Amazon